THE STUFF OF MAYHEM

THE STUFF OF MAYHEM

AN OLD STUFF MYSTERY

KATHLEEN MARPLE KALB

For my Sibs, at Sisters in Crime National, NY/SinC, and SinC CT, with deep gratitude for their support and companionship every step of the way. No one gets here alone.

Praise for The Stuff of Mayhem

"A Fun, History-laden Whodunit That Will Blow You Away!

"If you're looking for a cozy mystery that will keep you on the edge of your seat, look no further than The Stuff of Mayhem. Book Two in the Old Stuff Mystery series is a real blast, and I mean that quite literally! The explosive death of Rowland Stark sets off a chain of events that will have you turning pages faster than a cannonball.

"Historian Christian Shaw and Assistant State's Attorney Joe Poli team up to unravel secrets in the charming New England town of Unity. Their investigation is full of twists, and antique artifacts add to the intrigue. Fans of modern mysteries with a historical twist will undoubtedly enjoy this fun, fresh cozy and be left eager for the next installment!" —Sarah E. Burr, award-winning author of the Trending Topic Mysteries and other cozies

"Christian Shaw returns in *The Stuff of Mayhem,* and this second outing is every bit as good as the first.

"Kathleen Maple Kalb excels in drawing modern small town life, filled with characters who feel authentic, while combining realistic problems and issues with warmth and optimism. It's impossible not to feel invested in Christian, her son Henry, and her friends. This series also combines two of my favourite things—history and mystery! Christian's position in the local historical society leads to intriguing situations. In The Stuff of Mayhem, a historical reenactment on July 4th backfires spectacularly when a local is killed, but that's just the start of the chaos. Against a backdrop of seemingly ordinary life, the mystery unfurls at a satisfying rate. Christian is helped by the lovely lawyer, Joe, and her perceptive son Henry, who is—like my own child—a type-1 diabetic. It's great to see this condition represented and, most importantly, handled so accurately.

"If you like small town life, well-crafted mysteries and great characters, *The Stuff of Mayhem* should be your next read!"—Nina Hayes, author of The Old Bat Chronicles, and the Ellie & Lexi Mystery Series

Praise for the Old Stuff Series:

"…pretty much top of the heap. Her voice, pacing and storytelling ability are just terrific. I can't recommend her books more highly."—Aunt Agatha's Mysteries (Robin Agnew)

"*The Stuff of Murder* is for you if you like cozy mysteries, charming characters, and everyday old stuff."—T.G. Wolff's Toe Tag Podcast

"*The Stuff of Murder* checks all the boxes of a great, modern murder mystery. A strong lead with a diverse supporting cast, Kalb's latest is a charming read for mystery fans."—Sarah E. Burr, award-winning author of the Trending Topic Mysteries and other cozies

"This is a thoroughly enjoyable modern murder mystery with a likeable, diverse cast of characters and a town that has a charming sense of community. An additional plus for me was the addition of a young character with Type 1 diabetes, and as the parent of a 9 yr old with the same, the descriptions of diagnosis and general life with T1D were accurate, positive and at one point, brought tears to my eyes."—Geraldine Byrne, author of the Irish Music Shop and Caroline Jordan Mystery Series

Chapter One: And Then It Went Boom

Nothing says Happy Independence Day like blowing stuff up.

The problem is when somebody gets blown up with it.

That's how a festive Fourth of July in Unity ended in our little town's latest bizarre murder, not to mention ruining a perfectly good picnic.

It had been a pretty terrific day until then.

Unity, like many small New England communities, does a nice old-fashioned splash for the Fourth. Ours starts with the firing of a Revolutionary War cannon on the Green and ends with fireworks at the Little League field. In between, it's classic potluck picnics in backyards across town, with the extra flavor of New Haven County Italian heritage.

The rest of the country has potato salad and hot dogs. We have caprese and sausage-and-peppers. And we like it that way.

The dads I should have had, my mentor Garrett and his husband Ed Kenney, host the picnic every year at their wonderful old saltbox house a block or so from the Green. Garrett makes salad with his heirloom tomatoes; Ed makes a grill-full of sausage and peppers—the one thing he can cook—and everyone else brings the rest of the feast.

My contribution is always a batch of my grandmother's Scottish shortbread and her lemon meringue pie. I'm an uneven baker at best, but this is a special day, and Garrett and Ed are special to me.

Our good friend Tiffany Medina had dropped off the chips and her mother's salsa, as well as her own famous chocolate chunk cookies, earlier in the day. As the EMT captain, she was on duty until the cannon had safely fired. Famous last words, there.

My other good pal, Rabbi Dina Aaron, and her eye-surgeon husband Ben, usually brought knishes, coleslaw, and half-sharp pickles from Metz's Deli, adding to the multi-cultural flair of the festivities.

This year, the picnic would also include cannoli from Libby's Bakery, and Cannoli, the dog, to keep Garrett and Ed's big red mutt, Norm, company.

And I had Cannoli's owner, one Joe Poli, to keep me company.

Joe, an Assistant State's Attorney, smart as all-get-out, fond of quoting John Donne, and not incidentally gorgeous in a tall, blond, dark-eyed Northern Italian way, had been around for the last several weeks. We had a wonderful, more than slightly old-school, slow-burn courtship going.

There hadn't been time for a lot of boy-girl dates, but Joe stopped at my office at the Historical Society for coffee more mornings than not, sometimes jogged over to my house for late-evening conversations, and took my eight-year-old son Henry and me out for bowling or mini golf on Sunday afternoons. A very good start for a widow who'd thought she'd never love again and a guy whose divorce had been bruising enough to convince him he might not want to.

While all my friends knew about Joe, and Garrett and Ed had thoroughly vetted him (very thoroughly indeed—Ed is a retired state trooper!) the Fourth was our first town event as a couple. Unity may be a New Haven bedroom community, but it's still a little New England town, and everyone is very well aware of everyone else's business. So when Joe and I walked onto the Green holding hands, it was an announcement.

Ed, Dina, and Ben were already in place near the front of the crowd, which was loose enough that we easily threaded our way over to them.

Just people, though; Ed, like Joe, had left the dog at home, as any responsible pet owner would. Cannon fire is not a dog thing.

"Well, you're looking happy, kids," Ed observed, giving Joe just a tiny bit of the hard look. He wasn't a hundred percent convinced Joe is the right guy for me, since he knows all too well about how prosecutors' private lives suffer during big cases.

But he was slowly coming around.

"What's not to be happy?" Joe asked as he shook hands with Ed. "An actual day off with some of my favorite folks, and this one providing commentary on the re-enactment."

He nodded to me with a grin. The admiration wasn't for Ed's benefit; Joe's genuinely impressed by my academic achievements—he got through Yale Law on a scholarship, so he knows how hard I worked for that PhD.

Today, though, I wasn't using my primary area of expertise, but the knowledge of old armaments I'd picked up on a summer internship in Colonial Williamsburg. I had no intention of telling Joe the reason I knew so much was I'd had a huge crush on the armorer and followed him around like a lovesick baby duck. It was even more embarrassing because the guy never looked twice at me.

"I won't be the only one commenting," I reminded Joe, nodding to the re-enactors setting up on the Green. Though Garrett was a Lincoln scholar, he belonged to Unity's Revolutionary fife-and-drum corps, and a few times a year, he whipped out the greatcoat and knee breeches.

"Plenty of drama as usual," Ed said with a shake of his head. "I'm always amazed at what little divas those boys are."

"Of course they are," Dina said. "Men in costumes showing off for a crowd, why wouldn't they be?"

Everyone laughed, and Joe and I finished the round of greeting hugs and handshakes. Joe fits very well into my world, without much effort.

"Hey, Ma, can Ava and I get a little closer?" Henry asked, popping up in front of me, with Tiffany's daughter. She was waiting for her mom with us because her New Haven firefighter dad, Jorge, had gotten stuck with the day shift.

"Let's not," I said. It wasn't that I was expecting trouble, but I was always extra cautious when we had Ava with us. "Why don't you two just stay here? You can make funny faces at Uncle Garrett when the fifes walk by."

"Let's go up on the *shul* stairs," Ben suggested. "The view's a lot better."

"Oh, all right." Henry and Ava grumbled a little but moved in the right direction.

At the top of the stairs, Henry waved at Garrett, who responded with a little twitch of a smile, but nothing more.

"What's with the gold thing on his shoulder, Uncle Ed?" Henry pointed to the extra loop of braid on one epaulet. "He didn't have that last year."

"He got promoted, buddy." Ed, who had retired from the State Police as a detective sergeant, chuckled. "Uncle Garrett is the proud leader of the Second Fifes."

Ben gave me a puzzled look, and Dina whispered in his ear.

She was probably reminding him about Henry's photographic memory, which can sometimes be a bit disconcerting.

Ed elbowed me. "You'd think Garrett had been made Admiral of the Fleet the way he's been preening."

"I don't doubt it," I laughed. Garrett describes the Fife-and-Drum Corps as his one "Dead White Guy Activity," and like all re-enactors, takes it very seriously. Unlike most, though, he leaves the drama with the uniform.

"All men preen," Dina observed. "It's just a matter of degree."

Our three fellas—none of whom could be described as scruffy—looked a tiny bit wounded. Dina cut her eyes to me and leaned over to whisper something to Ben. He turned to her with a smile.

They've been married for well over twenty years, but it's clear they still appreciate each other. Nice.

Joe caught it, too, and then glanced over at me.

He was thinking the same thing. And maybe something else. Maybe it might be cool to be like them someday.

It would.

The sun was shining, a breeze ruffled the trees, and it was a picture postcard day in our cute little town. Later I would wonder if I was enjoying the moment too much.

At the time, I was honestly just glad for a day off from the craziness in my life.

Starting with the usual summer fun at the Historical Society. We get a few day camp field trips, but it's not a big visitor season. So, we catch up on paperwork and documentation, which is even less delightful than it sounds.

The whole reason I'm running the Historical Society is my love for old stuff. Technically, I'm a duly accredited authority on eighteenth- and nineteenth-century household goods, but since I'm no longer trying (vainly) to please a tenure committee, "old stuff" will do just fine.

The hands-on part of the job is a thrill. The paperwork, not so much.

My latest client was also giving me *agita*. Trust the New Haven Italians to find a nicer way to say heartburn! Usually, I consult with movie or TV crews on period pieces, working to make sure the details of costumes, props, and sets are accurate. It's mostly done by email and Zoom and brings in stupid money, so it's a great side hustle.

Once in a great while, I actually go on-set, as I had when Filmagic came to town a few months ago for a *Scarlet Letter* reboot that ended in murder and other disasters. I hadn't been eager to take on a big project after that, but a local writer who was developing a reality show reached out to me.

Jensen Brockway, despite a Yale Masters' in drama and a thriller or two in print, had decided she wasn't getting anywhere with books and decided to really sell out. Now, she was picking my brain on a regular basis for a reality show called *Regency Love*. As far as I could tell, it was basically intended to be one of those dating house shows, only with costumes circa 1800.

She was paying my usual hourly rate, so I didn't have much room to complain, but it was getting wearing, pun intended.

The fact that tiny blonde Jensen made me, six feet tall with flaming red hair, feel like a larger, less-evolved species only added to the admittedly irrational irritation.

Things hadn't been a lot of fun at Joe's office, either. He'd just finished a routine and terribly sad murder trial, ending in a conviction that didn't feel like a win for anyone.

Toward the end, he'd taken to late-night jogs, winding up at my house after Henry went to bed. I'd pour him a glass of chianti and just listen.

After everything, the holiday felt like a gift—and a break.

"Look, Ma, they're getting ready!" Henry pointed. He and Ava, a cute, matched pair in their poison green tees from last week's Builders' (as in Lego) Day Camp program, moved to a corner of the portico for the best view.

A few other friends and congregants from the temple, originally Unity's

Congregational Church, had joined us on the steps because the view really was great.

Down on the Green, the Fife and Drum Corps—including the Second Fifes, ably led by Garrett—marched a short distance away from the cannon and then started playing "Yankee Doodle."

There was a pitched battle every year over whether they should play the "Star Spangled Banner," since it wasn't to period, and every year, the outcome was different. I don't need to tell you the leader of the Second Fifes was squarely in the "Yankee Doodle" camp.

"Oh, that jerk." Ed shook his head as a round-faced guy with a self-satisfied smile and a gut ruining the line of his cross belts marched toward the cannon. "Rowland Stark, pillar of the community—just ask him."

"Rowland Stark?" Joe asked. "Creep."

Neither the word nor the tone was his usual, and I turned sharply to him.

"My old firm dropped him after he tried to drag us into something unethical."

"Oh," I said. "I just know his wife, Linley."

"Yeah?" Joe asked.

"Longtime volunteer and donor at the Society." I nodded to a carefully slim, very blond woman in a blue gingham shift with a hair band, driving mocs, and status bag, all in a perfectly matched azure suede. There was never a moment when she didn't make sure I knew I was supposed to be grateful for her time and money. Fortunately, she wasn't around too often. "You know the type."

Shared nods.

"Probably harmless, though," Dina said. She always tries to see the best in everyone.

"Better than the husband, I'm sure." Joe's mouth twisted in disgust. "I had more than enough of those business guys playing the edges. We don't get that at the prosecutor's office."

"Unless you're putting 'em away." Ed gave him a dry and respectful smile, and Joe nodded.

Ed also pretended not to notice as Joe reached for my hand and laced fingers, something he'd taken to doing during those late-night conversations of ours. It wasn't a romantic gesture, but something more.

A reason we might just end up like Dina and Ben if we were lucky.

Irony alert: that's what I was thinking about when everything blew up.

Chapter Two: In the Blast Zone

For an explosion in the middle of a crowded Town Green, it wasn't nearly as bad as it could have been. All the safety precautions worked, more or less.

It took a while to figure that out, though.

Just about everyone knew immediately the sound was different than a cannon—and so were the shouts of horror from the blast zone.

People started running.

I grabbed Henry and Ava. Dina turned to the *shul* door, opening a safe place. We shepherded them in, assuring them everything was okay with the determined hope parents always offer at terrifying moments. Both kids seemed calm, though I knew it might not last.

Back in the doorway, Joe was nodding as Ben patted his arm.

"He's going to help," Dina said. "He worked at a Tel Aviv ER while I studied for a couple of years."

"I need to get down there, too," Joe said. "I don't know yet if it's a criminal matter, but…"

"You can't afford not to," I nodded. He gave me a quick kiss on the cheek and ran out.

Dina's eyebrow flicked. We'd be talking about that later over coffee…I hoped.

"Can you watch the kids?" I asked. "I've got a first aid certification, and I might be able to pitch in somehow."

"Be careful, Christian." She nodded to me and put on a smile as she turned to Henry and Ava and reached for her phone. "So, kids, maybe you can explain this new game that my twins are into this month…"

Outside, it was mayhem.

There were still people straggling away on the side streets, but none of them looked physically hurt, just stunned.

The Green was a different story.

The participants in the event, some in uniform, and others in summer clothes, were staggering around, in varying degrees of shock. Nobody seemed especially bloody, though, which was a surprise, considering.

Closest to the cannon, there were three or four re-enactors on the ground. They *were* covered in blood, with paramedics working on them. It only took me a couple of seconds to get there, to Tiffany, who was checking on an older guy in the uniform of the cannon crew.

I didn't want to interrupt, but she needed to know one thing.

"He's shocky, Christian. I can't talk to you—"

"Ava is safe inside the temple."

Her face relaxed into a smile. "Thank you."

"You'd do it for me."

"Christian! Get the hell out of here!"

Ed.

He was maybe ten yards away, with Garrett. "I'm trying to convince this dunce to get inside until we can get him checked out. I don't need you—"

"We all have First Aid certifications," I reminded him. "We can help."

Ed growled.

"Hey! Ed!" Tony DiBiasi, a fellow retired Statie, now Unity's acting Police Chief and a third of the whole department, waved from his spot in a knot of upset select board members. "Any chance I can draft you to do crowd control?"

"Sure thing." Ed turned to Garrett and me. "Stay out of trouble."

Garrett and I nodded.

Non-verbal gestures don't count as lying.

From there, the next several hours were pretty much a whirlwind. Ed, with the help of a couple of other retired cops from his Monday morning diner coffee group, quickly herded the unhurt to the far end of the Green and the much smaller number of wounded toward the paramedics. Tiffany sent the first ambulance away with her patient and a spectator who seemed to be having a heart attack and then joined her minions in assessing the rest of the cannon crew while they waited for Mutual Aid crews from surrounding towns.

The wife of one of the First Fifes was the Red Cross instructor, and she quickly set up an aid station, putting Ben and two other local docs in charge of visible injuries and sending Garrett, me, and other volunteers out into the crowd to make sure everyone else was okay. Ben, with his experience in Tel Aviv, told us to pay particular attention to anyone who'd been close, even if they looked all right, so we didn't miss anything.

At one point, as I dragged a pale and peaked, but feisty, eighty-five-year-old over to Ben for a second look, I glanced up to see Joe and one of the remaining Unity officers standing by the cannon. There was a tarp on the ground beside it.

Meaning at least one fatality.

Ed's old pals from State Police Major Crimes were there within the hour, with the Medical Examiner's van, but it still took a long time to get everything settled. It was hours later when we civilians were finally asked for our contact info and set free.

Ed was with DiBiasi and the lead Major Crimes detective, so Garrett gave him a wave and followed Ben and me back toward the temple.

"Helluva thing," Garrett said.

"Haven't seen anything like that in a long time," Ben agreed, taking another look at Garrett. "You sure you're okay?"

"Of course." He shook his head. "Worry about someone who needs it."

"It's just—the human body reacts really weirdly to explosions. Concussion waves are nasty stuff." Ben's brown eyes were weary. "I'm telling you, and I'll tell Ed the same—you just be extra aware of how you're feeling for the next few days, okay?"

"Okay, doc." Garrett patted his arm. "This wasn't Tel Aviv, you know."

"I know." Ben sighed, looking to me. "You know, both of you did great today."

"Thanks." I shrugged. "We took the First Aid course just in case…but this wasn't the just in case we meant."

"No way." Garrett sighed.

"Henry." Ben nodded and patted my arm. "Don't worry. I'm sure Dina kept an eye on his numbers."

"I'm sure she did." No doubt in my mind. It's probably a good time to let you know Henry has Type-1 Diabetes, and while it doesn't rule his life, we do have to watch out for him.

He was diagnosed more than a year ago, after some very scary symptoms, including the classic thirst, weight loss, and tiredness—and a lot of "Ma, I just don't feel right."

I'd been terrified. Losing him is the one thing I couldn't survive. So when it turned out to be a serious, but manageable condition, it was almost a relief.

These days, it's just our lives.

Which doesn't mean I'm always cool about it.

The old rectory, which is now temple offices on the first floor and Ben and Dina's home on the upper two, is every bit as historic and elegant as the *shul* itself, complete with gracious lawn and garden. Green-thumbed members handle the gardening. Ben handles the mowing because it's relaxing. He's right—I mow my own lawn too!

Dina met us at the gate with a giant bubble wand in her hand and glitter in her hair.

"Well, aren't you all a sight for sore eyes."

"Ma!" Henry came up and tackle-hugged me. I gave him a good hard squeeze in return, the knot of anxiety in my gut unwinding at the sight of my safe, healthy boy.

"Glad you guys are here," Dina said. "I've got to get over to Amy Taylor's."

The three of us must have given her an alarmed glance.

"No, no," Dina said. "She's studying for her Bat Mitzvah, and I don't want to let her down."

"Bat Mitzvah?" Ed asked.

Amy's one of the cool grandmas—maybe great-grandmas—who have breakfast at the same diner where Ed meets his retired cop buddies on

Mondays.

Dina nodded. "I know it sounds weird, but girls didn't always get them when she was growing up in the Netherlands in the 1930s, and then…"

"Things got ugly." Garrett met her gaze.

"Really ugly." Dina didn't elaborate.

No need. We all knew the outline, if not the specifics.

"So she's going to be a Bat Mitzvah at 90-something?" I asked. "Pretty cool."

"Extremely cool." The rabbi couldn't stop a grin. "And we've been studying Torah together three nights a week. We didn't want to miss because of the holiday."

"You don't have to," Ben said. "I'll watch the stragglers till the parents get over here."

"You?" Dina asked.

"Me." He took the bubble wand. "I got this."

"If you say so." She got on tiptoe and kissed his cheek.

"Later, honey." Ben gave Dina one of those little half-hugs that says everything about a long-standing couple. "Give her my best."

"I think she may be helping me more tonight."

"No truer words." Garrett patted Dina's arm. "Let's reconvene in the backyard on another night."

I took Henry's hand, and he didn't resist. I knew what it meant. "Sounds good to me."

Chapter Three: Long Way Home

Henry's blood sugar was just edging toward low, so I walked him across the little side street to my office at the Historical Society for a quick snack from the stash I keep there. A few carefully calibrated carbs later, it was safe to walk home, with a stop by Garrett and Ed's.

They were sitting in the backyard, which had the sad, deserted look of a party that never happened, with good cause. Both looked tired, worn, and every second of their age—which never happens.

Garrett had changed out of his uniform into a navy polo and khakis and started nursing a Scotch. Ed had one, too. The drink alone said it was serious; they both enjoy a good glass of wine but rarely go for the hard stuff.

Scotch, as I knew from my marriage to a reporter, was for processing serious things. Frank, who'd done a lot of breaking news coverage back when New Haven still had a real paper, only drank Scotch after a terrible story. The night he died, I kissed him goodbye as he blasted out to cover a multiple-fatal fire and checked the liquor cabinet on my way back to bed.

He never drank that Scotch because he hit a patch of ice and spun into a pole. The only one I've ever had was the inch Garrett poured for me at the end of the next day.

"Hey, Uncle Garrett! Uncle Ed!" Henry blasted through the gate as I opened it. He was just the ball of good energy they needed…and Norm was just what Henry needed.

Norm, their giant red dog, is the sweetest and most loving creature ever invented. Part Irish setter, part retriever, and part Clifford, he isn't the brightest animal you'll ever meet, but he adores his people. And Henry is very definitely one of his people.

"Norm!" Henry yelled. He knows the name is a *Cheers* reference—we watch a lot of vintage TV because the writing is good and the content reasonably safe—and loves it.

The dog loped over to Henry and gave him a thorough licking, for which we would pay dearly when we got home to our cat, Cookie.

Garrett moved to stand.

"No, no—don't get up. We're just dropping by for a bit on the way home," I said quickly.

"Want a drink?" Ed asked.

"Better not." I shook my head. "Probably have a little wine once Henry's asleep. How are you two?"

"Had better days." Garrett took a quick glance to make sure Henry was busy with Norm. "I got a look at Rowland Stark after."

"Ugh," I said.

"Yeah." He sipped a bit more Scotch. "Never liked the guy, but he didn't deserve that."

"Nope." Ed drank some of his, too. It will not surprise you that the retired state trooper is the strong, silent type.

"I'm sorry you had such a hard day," I said, sitting down on the chair between them.

"I'm sorry you did." Garrett patted my arm.

"I just got to dust off my first aid skills. What I don't understand is how this happened."

"I don't either," Garrett said. "Those guys train every few months."

"And amateurs never, ever screw up." Ed scowled. He was not a fan of the whole re-enactment thing. As far as he was concerned, it was grown men playing dress-up for no good reason. He tolerated the fife and drum corps for Garrett's sake, but he firmly believed only trained professionals should handle weapons. Any weapons.

"I'm not saying that," Garrett replied patiently, as they edged on their annual wrangle over the issue. "What I am saying is they have been doing this for a long time, and they're extremely careful."

"Any changes in the cannon crew?" I asked.

"I don't think so. I know Rowland was doing the same thing he did last year, and the crew was all the same guys. Beyond that, someone would need to check with the group."

"They'll probably want to look at where they got the ammunition, too," Ed said. "They could have done everything right, but if the stuff they put in the cannon was bad…"

I nodded. "There are only a few people who sell those things, and groups generally order very specific items for their equipment."

"That's true," Garrett agreed. "I'm not sure who they used. Someone will need to take a look."

"Wonder who?" Ed asked, eyes on me.

"I know Joe took charge at the scene, because he was there," I said. "Whether he'll stay on it, who knows? Probably depends on whether there's a suspicion of criminality, and whether Major Crimes has the time."

"Major Crimes never has the time," said Ed, who had been on the State Police Major Crimes squad near the end of his career. "But this thing was a big mess. Everyone will be involved until it's nailed down."

"And probably after the lawsuits start," Garrett added. "It's Connecticut. I bet everyone who was within half a mile will sue."

"But who will they sue?" I asked. "I bet the cannon crew had to sign a waiver protecting the town."

"Maybe." Garrett shrugged. "That's for the lawyers."

"And for later," Ed said. "Going to be a mess that keeps on giving."

"About the only good thing is the kids didn't see much." I took a breath.

"Definitely," Ed agreed. He looked over to Norm and Henry and smiled. "Not the worst way to end up after this day."

"Not at all."

The three of us were silent for a while, the only sound Henry's infectious little-boy giggle. Usually, when we heard it, we laughed too. This time, we just exchanged small, rueful smiles.

"The really good news is we're all home and safe," Ed pointed out finally.

"Absolutely."

"I can definitely drink to that," Garrett agreed.

"We all just need a good night's sleep," I said. The light was just starting to fade, and so were my honorary dads. I stood and nodded to Henry. "This guy needs dinner, and he has camp tomorrow, so he'd better get some rest."

"You too," Garrett said. "Have a nice glass of wine and try to sleep."

"Exactly my plan."

Hugs for the humans and a little more patting for Norm, and we were on our way. Hard not to be insanely grateful to walk home tonight.

Chapter Four: Not Tonight, Dear

It's only a couple of blocks from Garrett and Ed's house in the historic district to the converted carriage house where Henry and I live. It's trim and snug, with an open living room in front, a galley kitchen tucked off to one side, and two small bedrooms with a bath between them in the back.

The best thing about the place is the large bay window, which was currently occupied by Cookie, our big, fluffy tuxedo cat. He (yes, he—Henry named him when they were both tiny!) thinks of himself as the lion protector of the home, but he's really just a sweet fuzzball.

Cookie jumped down to meet us at the door and demand tribute. As soon as he got a whiff of Norm on Henry, he snorted and started rubbing his head against his boy's leg to properly re-scent him.

The next few hours were soothing normalcy. Feeding Cookie. Making a quick dinner for Henry—teriyaki chicken and veggies over brown rice was at least nutritious and filling. (Of course, Cookie got a taste of the chicken!) Changing out of my pretty floral dress into yoga pants and an old sweater. Checking Henry's meter and numbers and making sure he was okay for the night, then getting him into his jamas, teeth brushed, and picking out a book.

Routine is incredibly comforting at bad times.

We'd learned that the hard way a couple years ago.

This wasn't nearly as bad a time for us. But it was for some folks in our town. And echoes carry.

"Did a lot of people die, Ma?" Henry asked as he got into bed.

"I only know of one who did." I never lie to Henry, but I will sometimes leave out details that might frighten or upset him.

"Got blown up, right?"

"I think so."

"Ick."

"Very ick."

He thought for a moment. "Do you think he knew what happened to him?"

"Probably not."

"Good." Henry nodded.

I waited. Sometimes, the smartest thing you can do as a parent is wait and see, instead of offering more.

Since his father had died in a car crash, spinning across ice into a pole, and we had all taken some consolation in the idea that Frank didn't suffer because it happened so fast, there was a very real possibility Henry was thinking about it, too. But I didn't want to make him talk unless he wanted to. Better to let him process.

This time, I called it right. Henry patted the bed and called to Cookie, who hopped up, happy for the chance to spend some time with his boy. And to remind the big human who really counts around here.

Fine by me. The big people were ready for a break, too.

I gave Cookie a scratch, and Henry a hug, sneaking in a quick look at his meter. I was pulling back when the doorbell rang.

There was only one good possibility. And a fair number of bad ones.

Nothing bad tonight.

Joe stood on my doorstep, looking more tired than I'd ever seen him.

"Got a few minutes to talk?" he asked.

"All the time you need." I waved him through the door. "I'm just tucking Henry in. Want to come say goodnight?"

"Yeah." Small smile. "I'd really like that."

Henry, who had moved on to memorizing the moons of Jupiter, looked up and grinned when Joe knocked on the open door. "Hey, AlysDad."

Henry had settled on that name because Joe's daughter Aly was his

Welcome Buddy at school a couple years ago, and of course, Henry remembered her. It was perfect for now, and we could worry about later if there was a later.

I was pretty sure there was going to be a later, even if the idea of starting over scared me at times.

"Hey, pal," Joe said, holding his hand out to shake, the way they always greeted each other. A thing among men. "Came over to talk to your mom a little. Thought I'd say goodnight."

"Cool." He shook. "Don't let Ma eat all my chocolate squares."

Shared chuckle. Henry knows I sometimes sneak one of the dark chocolate squares that we've learned are a safe and satisfying treat for him.

"I'll watch out for them."

"Good." Henry picked up the book. "Night."

"Night."

I pulled the door almost closed, and Joe followed me into the living room.

"Coffee or wine?" I asked.

"Oh, wine. Definitely wine."

"That bad, huh?" I asked as I poured from the bottle I'd opened a few nights before. Thank goodness for vacuum sealers.

"Yeah." He took the glass. "Stark was the only one who died, and there were just a few blast injuries. But six cardiac events, two serious, ten panic attacks, and a bunch of minor injuries from the stampede. It could have been even worse."

I picked up my glass and walked to the couch. "Horrible,"

"Yep." He sat, not as close as he usually did, took a sip, and stretched. "Going to be a massive mess whatever this is."

"Whatever this is?"

"We're still going on the assumption that it was an accident. The surviving cannon guys have no idea what happened…which is at least partly trauma." He took another sip and looked at me. "It's also apparently the way they worked. Stark was the guy with the stick, and he was in charge of setting it off."

"Linstock."

"What?"

"The stick is called a linstock." I sat and put down my glass. "Do you want a little primer on cannon firing?"

Eyebrow flick and smile. "You knew I was going to ask."

"Of course I did."

He moved to set his glass on the side table.

"It's okay. Keep drinking."

"After today…"

"Yeah." I nodded. "A cannon requires anywhere from four to ten men—and they're usually men—to fire. Basically, each guy handles one part of the firing process. Loading, ramming, priming, etcetera."

"Makes sense."

"Stark was in charge of the final piece, the slow fuse. It's essentially a wick that's put down into the hole to fire the cannon."

"Do they use real gunpowder?"

"Yes. Various re-enacting groups use the kind they prefer, and because these cannons date from before the Industrial Revolution, each one is a little different. There are some basic safety things that are consistent, but a lot of it is knowing your equipment."

"So to speak." Joe's eyes sparkled a bit.

"Good equipment is important," I replied.

"I've never heard any complaints."

"Good to know. Back to the big guns?" I kept my tone as innocent as I could.

It was almost a spit-take. "Oooh, nice."

"Sorry. I know it's inappropriate, but I couldn't resist."

"Sometimes inappropriate is good." He gave me a wicked chuckle. "When you lose your sense of humor, you're dead."

"True." I sat up a little straighter and pulled my face into serious lines. "That said, I probably should stick to the armaments for now."

"Locked and loaded for you, babe." Joe raised his glass. "But, yeah. I really need to understand what was happening today, and you studied this."

"Yeah." Actually, I studied the guy who was in charge of it, but close enough.

"I think you'll want to talk to each member of the team and find out exactly what they did. The mishap happened when Stark went to fire the cannon with the linstock, but that doesn't mean it was the problem. Doesn't mean it wasn't, either."

"Oh?"

"Well, each step builds on the next. So you really need to know what happened along the way."

"Makes sense."

"Thing is, there's a lot that can go wrong, but we're also dealing with people who do this, three or four times a year, every year, without incident. So that should narrow the field."

"Right."

"We know when it happened, and who it happened with, which will also help."

"Well, we know the blast was the cause of death," Joe said. "Any thoughts on the manner?"

"You mean accident or homicide?" I shook my head. "I had one summer internship. I'm not an armorer. I think you're going to need to at least call a real one."

Joe nodded.

"Is there video?"

"Yes. Some from the crowd and an official town feed. I'll start looking it over in the morning."

"That'll help."

He put the half-finished glass down. Stared off into space for a moment.

"You want to start looking it over tonight."

"Yeah. Do you mind if I—"

"Not at all. Have you eaten?" I asked. "I cooked way too much teriyaki chicken and veggies tonight, and I'd be happy to send you home with a decent meal."

"Aw, that's nice. Yeah. I don't remember the last time I ate, and I shouldn't have had the wine on an empty stomach."

"Only half a glass," I reminded him, heading for the kitchen. "And I'll make you a coffee to go, too."

"You don't have to…"

"I'm glad to," I said. "As long as you don't expect anything at your mom's level."

"No way." Joe laughed. "I'm not that good either."

"Okay." I took containers out of the fridge. His mother, Lidia, is a legendary cook. She picks up her granddaughters at Henry's school, and often regales the pickup crowd with tales of her latest feast. (Yes, I knew his mom before I knew him. Small-town life.)

I popped a plastic lid. "I guess I'm probably safe since this isn't Italian."

"*Dottore*, you're amazing."

I smiled up at him as I put together a smaller container of food, trying to make it look like a decent meal and not the leftovers it was. "Easy enough."

"But really nice."

"Okay." I pulled the Buzz Machine coffee maker out from its spot under the cabinet. "It's not as good as properly brewed, but…"

He nodded. "It'll do."

"I'll owe you a good dark roast in the morning."

"Sounds good." His gaze held. "At the Society, of course."

"Of course."

I rummaged out a travel mug, a brightly colored "TYPE NONE" one from my last Juvenile Diabetes fundraiser, set it under the coffee maker, and fired it.

Joe watched it for a moment.

Then me.

"I'm glad you came over," I said.

"Yeah." He took a breath. "Look, I—"

I'm not sure which of us made the move, but it didn't matter. It was absolutely consensual, mutual, and whatever other criteria we have to meet these days for two ethical adults to give in to sheer lust.

This was nothing like our usual goodnight kisses, which were always delicious, but ever-so-slightly cautious, as if we both knew what was bubbling under the surface and were afraid to let it out. No such qualms this time.

After this day, neither of us had the energy for control or inhibition, and all that mattered was how good it felt. Just sheer pleasure after all the fear and stress.

I'd wondered, on nights when I'd had too much caffeine and not enough chianti, what would happen if he ever really brought it like he meant it.

Damn.

Joe pulled me close, his arms tightening around me as I responded to him.

His lips moved down my jawline to a sensitive spot near my ear I hadn't known I had, and I heard him whispering in that silky voice of his. For an instant, I thought he was calling me by the wrong name—Cara—but then I realized he was speaking Italian.

"Cara mia..."

Neither my Church Latin nor my conversation-class French were much use here. Not that I needed a translation.

No question where this was going, and no question we were both on board for the party...until his phone rang.

"Oh, hell." He pulled back, took a breath.

So did I.

The phone rang again.

"Um—I have to take this. M. E.'s office. Dr. Alexandre doesn't like to wait."

"Not a problem."

It was only two or three sentences, and clearly didn't settle much of anything.

Joe's face was tight and grim as he hit End.

For what seemed like an hour, we stood there staring at each other. How do you get back to the moment after parsing the details of blood and guts?

You don't.

"I'm sorry, *Dottore,*" he said finally.

"I'm not feeling it either now."

"Yeah." He put his hands on my arms, but didn't pull me in, holding my gaze with a new warmth. "See, I don't want to associate something I hope we'll be doing on a regular basis for the rest of our lives with violent death."

"Um, yeah. Um, no." I blinked. "Um, the rest of our lives?"

"Well, it's big and serious for me…"

"Same for me."

"Good." A smile like a sunrise.

I returned the smile, warmed straight through. Maybe a little scared, too, though. "I also don't want to associate any milestones with this."

"Right." Joe rested his hand on my arm, gently working his fingers into the cotton of the sweater, the warmth of his skin soaking into mine. "So let's just leave this at a nice, friendly goodnight hug, and take it up after dinner at Due Fiori once this is sorted out."

"I like it. I'm sure Garrett and Ed will kid-sit."

"Well, if I grovel to Ed. He's still not sure about me, you know."

Another shared smile.

"He's protective and worried you'll neglect me—or Henry—in the middle of a case."

"It's a fair question. So maybe this is my chance to show him I can do both…"

"You do what you have to do," I said. "Remember. I was a reporter's wife. I know about this stuff."

"Okay." He kissed my cheek. "I'm glad you get this."

"You're worth it." I grinned. "I didn't know you were bilingual."

He blushed. Adorably. "Kind of."

"I like it."

"Yeah?"

"Yeah. Once I figured out that you weren't calling me Cara, it was really hot."

"Good." Joe held my gaze, clearly debating whether to say more. Then, deciding against it, he just pulled me in for a light hug. "Get some sleep."

"Probably not." I rested my head on his shoulder, and he wrapped his arms around me. This wasn't hot. It was reassuring in a way I hadn't known I missed. The sense of belonging, of having each other's backs, of pulling together in the face of a difficult world you only get with a partner.

"Me either." He rested his head on mine, and I knew he was feeling it, too.

"I like having you around, *cara*."

"I like having you around."

A very good way to end a bad day.

Chapter 5: The Doctor is Out

These days, I wasn't surprised to have an early morning visitor at the Society. I *was* surprised it wasn't Joe. Maybe five minutes after the day camp bus picked up Henry and Ava, the doorbell rang, and I found Dina's husband, Ben, on the porch.

"Come on in," I said. "I'm starting coffee."

"That'd be great. Dina's getting ready for the morning minyan, and I thought you might know how to find Joe this time of day."

"Um," I blushed, and cursed my Scottish fish belly white skin. "Actually, he comes by for coffee a lot—which Dina probably knows."

"She does." Ben did a pretty good Jimmy Stewart shrug. "I was trying not to be presumptuous."

"It's okay." I patted his arm. "We're kind of out after yesterday."

"Not a bad thing. Though you'll probably have to start fielding all kinds of nosy questions."

"Yeah. It's a small town." I sighed. "But it's not so bad. Connections ease everything."

"They do." Ben's spare, amiable face tightened. "That's actually why I'm here. I thought it might be better to have an informal talk with him. I'm not an expert on explosives..."

"But..."

"But the injuries didn't look like what I saw in Tel Aviv years ago."

"I wondered myself. The cannon didn't look seriously damaged."

Ben nodded. "I'm not sure, but I think I should say something to Joe."

"We'll both talk to him."

"To me, by any chance?" Joe asked as he opened the screen door.

He was in a pale-blue oxford and gray, summer-weight wool slacks, with his collar open and his sleeves rolled up, hair still damp, skin glowing from the morning shave. Despite the shadows under his eyes and tightness in his jaw, he looked good enough to eat.

"Yeah." Ben held out a hand for a shake. "Good to see you, Joe. I think I have something to add to the investigation."

"Thanks for seeking me out, then." Joe shook.

I played hostess: "Why don't I pour us all some coffee, and we'll talk in my office?"

On the way down the short hall, Joe put his hand on my back and gave me a slightly uncertain glance. Inevitably, last night was still in the room, for both of us. I patted his arm and held his gaze for a moment. All good.

As good as it needed to be, anyhow.

Ben, of course, didn't miss any of it, but was too polite to say anything.

Coffee poured and admired—it was dark roast from my Seattle cousin Jimmy, who'd started working at a small coffee company a couple decades ago while he was finishing his MFA and kept the whole family in the good stuff to repay the karma—we settled in to talk.

To their credit, neither Ben nor Joe made any snarky comments about the upheaval in my office, which was piled with cookware, sheet music binders, recipe books, and boxes of ephemera because my assistant Lewis and I were starting work on fall exhibits. I managed to clear the guest chairs by moving piles into the corner and securing them with a big cast-iron pot destined for a kitchen display.

"So," I said, nodding to the menfolk to get them started. "Ben has some insight on what happened yesterday."

"I'm sure you do," Joe said. "You really did a wonderful job helping the injured."

"Thanks." Ben squirmed a bit, exactly the way Joe would have if he'd been praised. "I spent two years working in an ER in Tel Aviv while Dina was studying there."

Joe's eyes widened. "So you know what bombs can do."

"Yep."

"That's why you told Garrett to watch out for concussion trauma," I said.

"Exactly. Bombs do awful things to the human body." He took a sip of coffee.

We waited. His story. His to tell.

"There's no way to say this without sounding like an insensitive jerk, okay?"

"I know you're not one," I said.

Joe nodded.

"Okay. The injuries weren't nearly bad enough. For a big explosion in the middle of a crowd, we should have more casualties, both deaths and serious injuries."

"I did wonder about that," Joe agreed. "Rowland Stark was the only one who died from the blast. One other man is still critical from a heart attack. Ambulance crew thinks shock."

"See, that's all wrong."

"Even with the distance between the cannon crew and the audience?" I asked. "They were extremely careful about it. I know, because they keep the cannon in the back shed at the Society, that they do drills every couple of months. Every time, they made sure to keep everyone several hundred feet back."

"No, I don't think it would be enough." Ben sighed. "I really don't think so. And there were almost no shrapnel or concussion blast injuries. Just about everyone I saw was banged up from the stampede afterward."

I nodded. "I was kind of surprised, too."

Joe drank some coffee. "There didn't seem to be a lot of damage to the cannon, but I figured that was because it's incredibly strong old cast iron."

Ben shook his head. "If the blast were centered anywhere in the cannon, it probably would have gone too. I think the explosion was outside it."

"Meaning what?" Joe asked.

"I'm not sure." He took a sip of coffee, contemplated. "Rowland Stark, what kind of shape was he in?"

"Not great." Joe flicked an apologetic glance at me. "Dr. Alexandre is still sorting that out. She called me last night to tell me she's not comfortable writing any kind of report until she talks to a friend who's an expert."

"Smart." Ben nodded approvingly.

"The expert's in Israel, as it happens."

Grim little smile from Ben. "Well, they have reason to know."

"That they do," Joe said.

"You'd also do well to talk to someone who knows munitions and explosives."

Joe looked to me.

"No," I said. "I did one summer internship in Williamsburg. There are people who do this for a living, and you need to talk to them."

"Do you know anyone?"

Oh, hell. I should have seen this coming. The armorer and I had exchanged emails over the years and stayed friendly, despite my crush. Come on, girl, be a professional. "Yes. I can ask the armorer I worked with—he's at a living history site in upstate New York now."

"I could reach out to a few friends in Israel if you think it would help," Ben offered.

"If you don't mind." Joe nodded. "I need to get educated about explosions. Yesterday."

"Good enough," Ben said. He drank the last of his coffee and checked his watch. "I'm sorry—I have a nine-thirty."

"Yeah," I looked at the clock. "Even on the day after a summer holiday, it's going to be ugly on the way into New Haven."

Ben dug his keys out of his pocket, shook hands with Joe, and cut his eyes to me with a little smile as he moved to the door.

"What was that?" Joe asked as Ben's footsteps faded.

"He's being diplomatic and giving us a moment."

"Oh."

"It's kind of sweet."

"It is." Joe closed my office door and reached for me. "I'd hate to disappoint the rabbi's husband."

I smiled, and leaned in. "It would probably be a sin."

"Give me my sin again."

"Juliet's the one who says that," I reminded him.

"You know I'm a Donne guy and not a Shakespeare guy."

Understatement of the year. Joe had picked up a love of Renaissance poetry in eleventh grade lit, and now he was involved with a woman who'd read most of the same stuff, he enjoyed slipping in the occasional quote when he could.

"What would Reverend Donne say about this?" I asked, moving close and putting a hand on his shoulder.

Joe's phone rang.

"Probably, 'get back to work, you heathens.'" He laughed, looked at the phone. "Spam. I have thirty seconds."

"It'll do."

"Sure will."

And it did.

Plenty of time for a pleasant but slightly cautious embrace—a return to the usual status quo after last night's wild moment. Reassuring, actually.

At the door, Joe paused. "How 'bout this?

'Love's mysteries in souls do grow,

But yet the body is his book.'"

I knew, because I'd paid attention in Lit Class too, that the line was from a very sexy poem…and Joe was using Reverend Donne's elegant Renaissance words to suggest what he'd like to do if we had the time—and a good kid-sitter or two.

He was also placing a marker. We weren't going back to last night, but we weren't forgetting it, either.

I smiled. "Nothing like starting the day with a little poetry."

And a lot of subtext.

His smile faded. "I'm afraid it's going to be the best moment of my day, *Dottore.*"

"We can hope for better."

"Always do."

Chapter Six: Morning Trainwrecks

I took a moment to watch Joe walk out of the building. Yes, this is an unapologetic female-gaze pause in the narrative to appreciate the fit of a good pair of tropical-weight wool trousers and a pinpoint oxford on male musculature. Sue me.

A pleasure, guilty or otherwise, for sure, but it was my last one for a while. As Joe pulled out from the curb, a high-end electric import pulled in.

Time to deal with my client.

In addition to running the Historical Society, I have a nice little side business in consulting film and theatre productions on period-appropriate props and costumes. Often, it's just a few emails or Zooms about what things characters use and how they handle them. I once spent weeks (and made a nice little pile of cash) explaining how three Victorian women would make a pie.

Occasionally, I actually work a set, like that benighted streaming production back in May.

Usually, it's a fun, low-maintenance way to share what I know, work with stuff, and bring in stupid money.

My latest client, though, was rather less than fun.

Jensen Brockway has a Master's in drama from Yale, and wrote one of those glossy thrillers, which sold only a few more copies than my own dozen-seller. (*Clothes Make the Woman: Dress and Female Power in 19th Century America,* if you're wondering.) A lockdown debut, a fare-thee-well from her agent, and the specter of a career as a very articulate barista led her to consider something more commercial.

That something is a reality show proposal with the scintillating name of *Regency Love.*

It's even worse than it sounds.

The proposal apparently is to lock about a dozen healthy young adults in a Regency mansion with only the technology of the time and see what happens. My job is to provide an historically accurate sense of what it would have been like to live in that house. Food, clothing, hygiene, and so on.

Jensen is listed as the creator/producer, which I'm pretty sure means she'll only make money if somebody buys the thing. Her earlier failures seem to have convinced her she needs to lean very hard (no pun intended) into the sexy stuff.

This, of course, is more than slightly problematic for anyone who knows how people really behaved in the time period. Not to mention, for anyone who expects producers to treat their cast with appropriate care.

So far, I'd managed to keep my advice to mantles, main dishes, and minuets. But I knew at some point, my conscience would get the better of me, and I'd end up pointing out that even though vulcanized rubber and antibiotics weren't invented for several more decades, they'd best provide some protection for their cast if they don't want all kinds of trouble, modern and historic.

In my current drained state, Jensen's bright-eyed excitement about exploring the "spicy side of history"—yes, direct quote—was the last thing I needed. But she was what I got.

Days ago, when I did not expect to be coming off death and disaster, I'd invited her to come over to the Society for a look at the 1806 bedroom this morning. Of course, in the newly minted United States, it wasn't the Regency Period at all, but no one would watch a show called Federalist Love. Or they'd think it was about sexy political extremists.

Anyhow, it was still a slow start at the Society, and still a fair time to bring in a client for a short visit. My board doesn't mind the clients at all, actually. We have an unspoken deal: they don't mind my consulting, and I don't ask for the big raise I richly deserve. It works.

"Christian! You look a little tired." Jensen gave me what I'm sure she believed was a naughty grin, but was closer to a rictus, and leaned in. "Hopefully, for a good reason. Who was that blond guy?"

"A friend."

"Ah." Her eyes gleamed. "With friends like that, who needs hookups?"

I just shook my head.

"Speaking of which, I can't wait to see this bedroom."

Fortunately, my assistant started up the walk right then, saving me from saying what I was thinking.

"Just let me talk to Lewis for a moment, and we'll head right up. You might want to take a look at the fainting couch in the front room—we've dated it to 1802."

I held the door for Jensen, then stepped off the porch to meet Lewis.

John Lewis Barnes, named, of course, for the Civil Rights hero, is the nephew of one of the grandmas in the pickup pen at Henry's school. He's just a few months away from finishing his PhD in History at Yale. He was looking for an understanding employer right when our longtime (I mean LONG time—Rose Marie Marzio was 92!) assistant retired.

Another wonderful example of how connections make good things happen in small towns. The job works for him, he loves the Society, we love him, and everyone's happy.

I won't be happy when he finishes his dissertation and leaves for a well-earned tenure track spot somewhere...but I'll be thrilled for him and glad we were a part of his life.

"Hey, Doc!" he said as he saw me, dapper as always in khakis and a summer plaid blazer with an oxford and bowtie. His new glasses have rims in the perfect light tortoise shade to bring out the glow in his sepia skin and brown eyes, and he's looking much better and happier these days as he gets a handle on his dissertation. "Looks like your day's off to a decent start. Probably the only good thing today, huh?"

"Yeah. Were you there?"

"Nah." Lewis shook his head. "Went to the New Haven fireworks last night, but I couldn't give up a free full day of writing and research time. Aunt Ruby went. She's okay—but it was pretty horrible."

"That it was." I took a breath. Put it behind us for now. "Research, huh? For the dissertation?"

"Yeah. I'm trying to document as I go along, and it can be a real pain when I find some interesting bit of info online and have to chase it down."

"It was so much easier in the days of libraries."

"No way, Doc."

Jensen was occupied in the front parlor, so we walked together toward my office. Lewis is handling one of the fall exhibits as part of his training, and he's started pulling things from the collection, same as I have.

"I had to move the music," I said as he followed me into the hall. "Dr. Aaron came over and needed a place to sit. I didn't take anything out of order."

"Not a problem. I need to get more efficient."

"We all do." I grinned. "You saw what I'm doing in the kitchen right now, getting ready for the fall cookery display."

"Yeah, but you run the place. You can be a slob if you want."

"I resemble that remark."

We laughed.

"How was the Glorious Fourth, Lewis?"

"New Hampshire!" He greeted Faith Stowe, one of our best volunteers, with a big, bright smile. They were close, and he always ended up helping her when she worked on crocheted afghans and other fiber art pieces. She comes from a long line of hand workers (yes, originally in the Granite State, hence the nickname), but she's not the best record-keeper in the world, and he's great at spotting and mapping repairs, so they're a perfect fit. "Pretty good. But glad to be back here to help you block out that new candlewick bedspread."

"Just what I want to hear. Can I borrow him this morning?" she asked me.

"Of course," I said. "I'm giving Jensen a look at the 1806 bedroom."

"Better you than me." Faith glanced toward the front and dropped her voice. "That one's a piece of work."

"She's trying to figure out a way to keep her dreams alive after a really ugly start to her entertainment career. I don't agree with how she's doing it, but I understand. I had to recalibrate pretty hard after I didn't get tenure at Shoreline State."

"Ah, but that was just God's little way of sending you here." Faith grinned. "Forgive me if I don't see any divine intervention in *Regency Love*."

"I can't argue that." I nodded to the office. "Coffee's fresh if you want to caffeinate before the bedspread."

"Not the worst idea," Lewis said, turning to Faith. "Did you hear what that fool Tom Brady posted online yesterday?"

"Oh, not again…"

They headed off, united in their disdain for the former Patriots hero. Jensen was studying the fainting couch with an expression that suggested she wasn't thinking about the upholstery. (Which was unintentionally funny because it was a late-19th century re-cover.) I wondered if I should point out that the front windows might have been at least a mild deterrent to misbehavior,but thought better of it.

As I steeled myself for the trip upstairs, the phone rang.

I was closest to the cute little dark-wood console by the stairs, so I picked up. "Unity Historical Society."

"Hello, Christian."

The crystalline high voice and crisp consonants, with the contrast of the swallowed "T" in my name, indicating a New Haven County native, tipped me off. It was Victoria Peters, the chair of the Society board. Descendant of one of Unity's founding families, retired librarian, and one of the cooler eighty-year-olds on the planet, she rarely contacted me outside board meetings and a scheduled monthly check-in over her 18th-century silver coffee set. It was her way of showing respect, and setting an example for other board members who might be tempted to micromanage.

Something must be up.

"Hi, Victoria. How are you?"

"Quite well. No trouble at all—and no concerns with you, dear."

Whew.

"But Elias Ruff wants to borrow you."

"Elias Ruff?"

"Ruff Construction, dear?"

"Right." I'd seen their signs across the area, and we had a volunteer named Ruff...though I wasn't sure how she was related to Elias or the business.

"He's Mary Grace's husband. Working on the strip mall site out on Route 70. You know about that."

Anyone who'd been living in New Haven County for the last twenty years knew about the strip mall site.

The late Rowland Stark's strip mall site, to be precise...the subject of years of ugly battles. It had started as a straightforward development wrangle more than a decade ago. A few years in, one of the opponents dug up records suggesting a Revolutionary War skirmish nearby, or possibly even on the spot, sparking a full-scale war over history, preservation, and Lord only knows what.

As if that weren't enough, last week, two skeletons had turned up on the edge of the site, stopping everything cold until it was determined who they'd been and what should be done with them. The cops didn't find evidence of a recent crime, so they followed protocol by sending the bones to the state medical examiner. At last call, she'd been trying to decide what agency should get them.

That, as the expression goes, is where we were when the lights went out. Or the cannon went off, to be more precise.

But I had no idea why Elias Ruff was trying to bring me in.

"I know about it," I offered tentatively.

"Apparently, some personal effects have turned up on the site."

"Isn't there a state archaeologist dealing with this?"

"The state medical examiner is still determining whom to call. Apparently, there's some question as to the provenance of the remains, and the Indigenous tribes want to be sure they don't have an interest. That's on hold for now."

"I bet it is," I said. "It will probably take an anthropologist and a fair amount of time to be sure. Though personal effects or grave goods can help."

"I'm told they're your kind of thing, Christian. They think it was some kind of campsite. They've found military buttons, a cooking pot, and other bits and bobs of stuff. Can you swing out and take a look?"

"Sure. My client is here, but in an hour or two…"

"Perfect. I'll tell him you'll be there while the crew takes lunch."

"Sounds good."

"And, Christian, dear?" she asked as I started to say goodbye. "Thank you."

"Of course."

As I hung up, I had a creepy feeling at the back of my neck. I turned to find myself staring into a pair of furious, bright-blue eyes. Empress Frederick, the Society cat, a tiny, elegant white puss who more than lived up to her regal name, was sitting on the stairs, impatiently awaiting her morning treat. Her generous serving of Good Kitty Salmon Surprise had already been delayed by my chat with Ben and Joe…and if I didn't want to get an ankle nip when I least expected it, I'd better serve Her Imperial Majesty at once.

But as I asked Jensen to cool her jets for one more minute, I knew the cat wasn't the reason for that weird little sensation.

I'm not really psychic like some Celts, but I do have radar. Mostly, it's just a gift for picking up the resonance from objects…but every once in a while, I get kind of a general sense.

And today, my radar was telling me there was an awful lot going on here…most of it anything but good.

Chapter Seven: Let (Regency) Love Rule

"This is some steep staircase," Jensen observed, as we headed up to the second floor. "My great-aunt still lives in an old family house, but it has a big wide one, like in *Gone With the Wind*."

"That's a bit later," I assured her, cringing only internally at the reference, "and in a much different kind of home. Early nineteenth-century New Englanders usually didn't want or need a house that big."

"No?"

"No." I kept my voice as neutral as I could. "Your great-aunt's home is probably Gilded Age, when even sensible New Englanders went a little wild. In the period we're discussing, even prosperous people lived in fairly small homes, often in pretty close quarters."

"Really?" A salacious sparkle in her eyes. "Close quarters?"

"Yes, indeed." I smiled. "Space and privacy as we know it weren't really a concept until later."

"Tell me more."

"Well, remember, in the days before central heating, bed-sharing wasn't just for fun—it was a way to stay warm. And everyone had far lower expectations of personal space and time than we do. Which doesn't mean they weren't extremely modest about some things. It just acted out differently than it does for us."

"Okay." Jensen looked confused. "Explain to me as we go along, okay?"

"Why don't you just absorb the setup, first?"

I opened the door to the bedroom.

Jensen stopped cold.

Oh, good.

I'd been worried she didn't feel it at all, but her reaction to the room was definitely encouraging. The whole *Regency Love* thing really bugged me on a lot of levels, especially because it seemed like Jensen was just slapping costumes on a modern hookup show and hoping for the best.

She probably was, honestly. But it was still my job to try to give her some sense of what it was really like to be alive then. I owed that much to the people who came before us. Even if I failed miserably, and it sure felt like I was going to, I had a responsibility to try.

"Wow." Jensen's voice came out in the soft hush people often use when they walk into our exhibits. "This is…"

"Yep." I allowed myself a small smile. "It's like walking back into 1806. You can go right in, it's fine."

She gingerly placed one of her buttery Italian moccasins on the hardwood floor. We'd set up the room so visitors could see the floral rug but not easily step on it.

"The bed's so small. Is that a single?"

"No. This is from before the Industrial Revolution so there weren't standardized sizes like we have now. But couples usually bought beds when they set up housekeeping—or were given them as a wedding gift—and there was a general idea of what a bed for two should be. This is it."

"No stretching out here, huh?"

"Nope. But you'd be glad of that in winter. Fires were usually banked and went out overnight, so your partner or your pet was the warmest thing in the room in the morning."

"That might be good." She grinned. "But I think they're going to have to scratch build sets to look like this. It's just too small…even if it's pretty. Can I touch the canopy?"

"Sure. It's cotton crochet. Faith—you probably saw her downstairs— restored it. The bed and canopy were found in pieces in a local family's attic. We had all of it, so re-assembling the wood frame was pretty straightforward, but saving the canopy was a real trick."

I smoothed a crocheted doily on top of the chest of drawers. It had required equally intensive work, despite the smaller surface area.

Jensen rested a French-manicured finger in the center of a flower on the canopy. "This is really from 1806?"

"Possibly. It might be a replacement, but it's no later than the 1870s. We know because everything was moved into storage in a barn when the house was renovated. So it's at least 150 years old...and maybe far more."

"That's wonderful." The next words had an unexpected edge. "We don't do nearly well enough preserving things."

I looked at her.

"You should know that. We're always building stupid things like the strip mall that got Rowland killed."

"How do you..."

"Well, what else would it have been? Half the town hates him. It's no surprise somebody finally just blew him up."

I stared. Never saw that coming. "Um, no one's sure it's not an accident yet."

"Well, if it wasn't deliberate, then karma got him." She shook her head, and blonde hair flowed in smooth waves. "It was absolutely wrong him trying to build that on an old Revolutionary site."

"It would be," I said carefully, "if we were sure it was Revolutionary."

"Come on. You know land records. The really old ones say things like 'three ropes from the big tree.' It's impossible to be sure, and we should err on the side of preservation. We'll never get that land back."

"That's true." I tried to keep the tone neutral. I might well learn something useful here. She clearly knew more about the project and the players involved than I did. Not that I was taking her as an unbiased source...but it would be good to have her insight when we got out there later.

"The site's been in development for at least 20 years. And people have been fighting over it for at least that long."

"Isn't some of it the usual Unity 'Not in Our Town' stuff?" I asked. "Town Council pretty much fights every potential development."

"And that's not a bad thing."

"Not when it's the Green and the Historic District, for sure. But some folks get pretty sick of driving to Hamden for a reasonably priced supermarket." And I'm one of them, I didn't say.

"Rowland never had a reasonably priced supermarket in mind. He was going for a huge outlet mall thing. Like that hot mess up in Branford."

The alleged hot mess in Branford was on a reclaimed factory site and looked like cute little clapboard cottages ranged across a village green. It was far from the usual eyesore strip mall. If Jensen considered that a violation, heaven only knew what she thought of real strip malls. I shrugged. "It could be worse."

"It could always be worse. But we know better now, or at least we're supposed to. And he shouldn't have been building that thing in this town."

"Not if feelings were so raw, for sure." I could agree there at least. I know folks at Town Hall, and I would not want to mess with them.

"Exactly. By now, it's become a sore spot. Probably anything short of declaring it open space and giving it over to the town would be controversial."

"No doubt."

"But," Jensen smiled dryly, "those skeletons will probably throw a wrench into everything."

"They'll certainly slow it down for a while." I was very happy to be on the safer ground of procedure. "The state has to investigate what they are and where they came from."

Jensen's face tightened. "What do you mean, where they came from?"

"The medical examiner has them now, but eventually, the forensic anthropology people will take over—they'll determine the age of the skeletons, and the ethnicity, if possible."

"That's right. You can always tell old remains, right?"

"You can always tell any organic thing before the nuclear era. Background radiation changed dramatically. It's stupidly easy to tell everything from bones to cloth to paint. It's how museums have discovered any number of fakes in recent years."

"Makes life tough for the forgers, I'd guess." Jensen chuckled. "Can't pass anything off anymore."

"Well, they can, but it's a lot more work. Remember that guy who faked wine from the 1700s?"

"Yeah. I'm still not sure why anyone would want to drink 300-year-old wine. I know the history thing, but it's pretty ick to me."

"Pretty ick to me, too," I admitted. I'm not saying I wouldn't like to see it, touch the bottle, and smell it…I'm just not going to DRINK it. "But he was really smart. He collected bottles from the real time period, and corks, too, when he could. So he had some pieces that would pass the historical tests."

"And he combined the real pieces with the fakes, and boom."

"Yep. Same way art forgers do. They get old canvases of minor or unknown works, create paint from the old recipes, and get to work. But art forgery is a little tougher now, because of the radiation thing. There are certain colors where that would show up."

"And our forgers would have a problem."

"Bigtime." I looked at her. This was the most extensive conversation we'd had. "Maybe you should be writing a thriller about art forgeries."

Jensen laughed, but her eyes were sad. "I don't think anyone wants to buy anything I write these days.

"Why not? Didn't you—"

"I got a huge advance back when those 'Girl Who' thrillers were big, and then the lockdowns hit, and I sold exactly a hundred and seven books."

"Oh."

"My now former agent diplomatically describes me as poison. I'm not going to be writing or selling books for a long time. Unless I can get platform in some other way."

"What's platform?" I asked.

A bitter bark of a laugh. "You don't know?"

"Um, no. My only book was an academic study, so I'm not a publishing girl."

"Well, platform is presence on social media, in your profession, in the world at large. How many followers do you have for your accounts? How many people are interested in you and your work?"

"Ah." I thought about it. "Three. Maybe four."

"Then don't try to sell a book. Publishing is really screwed up right now, and the only way anyone wants to buy a book is if there's some kind of built-in audience. So I'm figuring I establish myself as the *Regency Love* person, and then come back with a nice juicy historical thriller."

"Okay." I'd heard crazier things. Somewhere. Probably.

"I know it sounds nuts," she said, reaching out to gently run her fingers over the bedside candleholder. "But I just want to be a star at something. And I write better than I do anything else, so..."

"So you're producing a hookup show about the Regency?"

"The Regency is hot right now—remember that Flikkies series with the characters getting down and gossiping their way through the Season? And so are hookup shows. So, bang!"

"Bang." I sighed. I pointed to the candleholder. "See that?"

"Yes."

"That's the nightlight. When you went to bed, you brought a candle with you to light your way up the stairs, and then guttered it with the little cap when you were ready to go to sleep. Usually, pretty quickly. Candles were precious except in the most well-off families."

"So you'd take the candle, and say, your partner, and head up the stairs?"

Yep. I should have seen that one coming.

"Well, yeah," I said. "Though remember, people still weren't really going to make an announcement of their plans. A married couple might well go off to bed together, but an illicit pair would have to sneak around."

"In the dark?"

"Or possibly with a candle, or even a dark lantern."

"What's a dark lantern?"

"It has a panel to hide or limit the light from the flame. We have one downstairs—I'll show you."

"So we could have a Candle Ceremony, where you give your chosen partner the candle and head upstairs."

You could, I thought, if you want Jane Austen to spin in her grave. "I suppose."

"That would be very fun TV," Jensen said. "Better than that silly rose thing.

Think about it, you could light the candle and then…yes!"

So much for the pull of the past.

I cut my eyes to the far wall, where we had a pretty decent portrait of a woman from the original family. It was late-18th century, with lots of hair and flowing fabric, from the period where married women wanted to look beautiful and even a bit sexy to show they were a catch for their spouse. Wherever she was, I was sorry she had to hear this.

The clock on the landing chimed eleven.

Quite literally saved by the bell.

"I'm sorry," I said. "I have to be somewhere around noon. Why don't I show you that dark lantern, and we'll continue this another day?"

"Oh, that's fine." Jensen beamed and squeezed my arm. "You're wonderful, Christian. You've really given me a push in the right direction."

I would have rather given her a push into some other project, but I nodded. "Glad to."

It was, I thought as we headed down the stairs, better to keep my mind on Henry's college fund than historical accuracy. There was only so much I could do.

And an awful lot going on with this woman.

Regency Love, indeed.

More like a modern ego trip.

Chapter Eight: On Site Parking

As I saw Jensen out the door, the office phone rang.

Lewis got there first. "Unity Historical Society."

I turned.

"For you, Doc. Rabbi Aaron."

"Thanks." I took the receiver, hoping everything was okay. She'd had a pretty tough day yesterday, after all. "What's up?"

"I've been asked to weigh in on something, and I wonder if you'd like to come with me."

"Weigh in on what?"

"That strip mall site out on Route 70. Apparently, something turned up near the skeletons that looked like Judaica, and they wondered if I'd take a look."

"Interestingly, I've been asked to go too."

"Really?" Dina's tone had a dry, suspicious edge.

"Really. My board chair called and asked me to. Very unusual for her."

"Then we should definitely go for a little field trip. When are you going?"

"I'd planned to go around lunchtime. Does that work for you?"

"Sure. I don't have anything until a Torah class this afternoon."

"Great. See you in half an hour, then. Your car or mine?"

"Oh, mine, honey. There has to be some benefit to being married to a doctor." She laughed. She drives a shimmery pale-blue import, high-end and much spiffier than you might expect for a rabbi, but just about perfect for the wife of a brilliant and busy eye surgeon.

It's her one luxury. Complete with a tag reading "NACHES," a Yiddish word loosely translated as pride and joy. The sedan would surely be a joy for the haul out to the strip mall site on this steamy day. I far preferred the climate-controlled beige leather interior of Dina's ride to my own serviceable compact.

At eleven forty-five on the dot, she pulled up, and I stepped into nirvana. Dina's summer style tended toward linen slacks and loose sweaters, but for the site, she'd changed into khaki capris and a thin chambray shirt-jacket. Still professional and dignified, but washable.

As I climbed in, she looked at me and started laughing. "Same style memo."

"Yep." I'd traded my vintage linen blazer for a denim chore jacket I keep for messy days at the Society. "Just tell me you're not wearing Chucks."

"Perish the thought." She smiled. "Nice, sturdy hiking boots."

"That'll work."

The site was only about ten minutes away, and we spent the time in deliberately inconsequential chatter, about sunscreen, summer clothes, and the song on the radio, a far inferior remake of a Motown jam we both love.

Route 70, like many secondary arteries in Connecticut, is stretches of empty land interspersed with spurts of commerce. In Unity, those include the small grocery store, the Dairy Delight, and the Italian bakery, as well as a few businesses, like a lawyer's office, a beauty parlor, and the urgent care.

The strip mall site was almost the last parcel in town; there was one more stretch of open land before the town line…and then, in the welcoming precincts of Hamden, a sizable plaza with a big orange Home Warehouse and some fast-food joints Unity had huffily turned down a few years ago.

A big blue-and-white Ruff Construction sign marked the site driveway, with an overly optimistic, and quite well-weathered announcement: "COMING SOON: RETAIL AND RESTAURANTS!"

The low gate was open, so Dina turned down the gravel drive and winced a little as her tires crunched. "I don't think this is going to be good for the suspension."

"At least it's a dry day."

"There's that."

Just past the turn, a guy at a little guard shack waved us on and muttered into a walkie-talkie. He didn't need to bother. The drive, such as it was, might have been a couple hundred yards, leading up to a big flat gravel area with a trailer at the edge.

Around it, there were several piles of dirt that suggested work had begun, but the two pieces of heavy equipment on scene weren't moving, and there didn't seem to be many people around.

A heavyset guy in jeans, khaki shirt, and white hard hat got out of the trailer and walked to meet us at the car.

"You have to be the professor and rabbi," he said, a smile brightening his ruddy face. He probably looked a lot like a character from one of those Irish gangster movies when he didn't smile. And, from the determinedly friendly way he held out a hand, he probably knew it.

"We are," I said, nodding to Dina. "This is Rabbi Dina Aaron from Congregation Beth Shalom."

"Pleased to meet you, ma'am. That's okay, right?"

Dina allowed herself a little grin as she shook. "I hate thinking I'm old enough to be a ma'am, but it's entirely appropriate."

"Oh, jeez." The guy flushed. "I'm sorry—"

"It's fine. I was kidding," Dina assured him. "I didn't get your name."

"Todd Ruff. I'm running the site."

"Pleased to meet you. And this is Dr. Christian Shaw, Director of the Historical Society."

I held out my hand. "Christian is fine. I don't use the Ph.D."

"My wife doesn't use her Ed.D, but I keep telling her she should." Todd Ruff shook my hand. "I hope Dad didn't cause you any trouble with your board chair, but I didn't know anyone else to reach out to."

"We're all good," I assured him.

"Good." He motioned toward one of the larger piles of dirt. "I'll take you over to where we found it. We did the same thing we did with the bones, just put a tarp on top and started work in another area."

"That'll do," I agreed. "Preserving the site is important, especially if we end up calling in the state archaeologist."

"Apparently, we're already on the list because of the bones."

"Makes sense," Dina said.

"But these things turned up all the way across the site. They weren't with the bones."

"Two different sites." I didn't know what the rules were for these sorts of things, but finds in two separate areas suggests it's not a one-off, but possibly a more significant site. Or at least makes people who watch these things ask the question.

"Yes. If you want, I'll show you where we found the skeletons, too."

"That's a good idea."

"Over here."

We followed him through a valley between two piles of dirt to a flat space.

"How were they found?"

"Same as the skeletons." He shrugged. "The crew was setting up for the day, and somebody saw something catch the light. At least it wasn't a skull this time."

"Oh?" Dina asked.

"Scared the heck out of my workmen when they saw it looking back at 'em."

"Suppose so," I said. Pretty lucky that the bones and artifacts were just sitting right below the surface, I thought.

But I didn't train as an archaeologist.

Todd Ruff motioned to one of the workmen to roll back the tarp. He picked up a flashlight. "See?"

The light caught on dark metal. Corroded, but not entirely devoid of shine. I pulled the phone out of my pocket and got down. It was buttons. Eight of them, stuck in the ground in the configuration of a military uniform jacket…with more buttons at each side about arm's length apart. It looked like what might have happened if a jacket fell and the wool cloth decayed.

No residue at all of cloth, though, never mind anyone who might have worn it. Or anything but the buttons. Hmm.

I snapped off a few pics and pulled back to get a fuller shot of the rest of the scene.

Beside the buttons, a couple of pewter plates, and a round, dark object that looked like some kind of figurine.

"Interesting," I said.

A worker handed Todd Ruff something that looked like an antenna from an old boom box…and might well have been. Our host stretched it out a little further and pointed. "Here, Dr. Christian, get a pic of this."

I did. A dark silvery cup was peeping out—with engraving that was just barely recognizable as Hebrew.

"Oh, my," Dina said. "That looks like…"

"My guys knew it wasn't English letters, but they didn't know what it was. But my wife and I just went to my nephew's Bar Mitzvah, and I recognized the Hebrew."

"Yes," she agreed, bending down. "This looks like a kiddush cup. Actually, it looks a lot like one in the Jewish Museum in New York."

"Really, Rabbi?" Todd asked.

"Yes. That one's from the 1700s. Which I suppose would be about right… But I didn't know there was a Jewish community here at the time."

Dina held my gaze. I held hers.

I snapped a few more shots.

It all felt awfully convenient. Not impossible, of course, but very convenient. At least for the people who wanted construction to stop on the site.

"What's the status of the site," I asked Todd. "Are you still actively building?"

"It's tied up on appeal." He sighed. "I don't care all that much one way or the other—our deal with the developer is a retainer. We get paid to keep a minimum presence and do some basic preparation work while the case runs along. Mostly marking off space, clearing vegetation, that sort of thing."

"Are you having problems with protestors or anything?" Dina asked.

Todd laughed. "I wouldn't call it that. There are an awful lot of those keyboard warriors who whine online about how we're destroying history, but I've probably seen three people over the last year. Every once in a while, somebody just shows up with a sign and marches around for a little while, then probably goes up the road for a decent coffee."

To the Aurora Coffee next to the home store, he meant.

"But this has been going on forever."

"Oh, it has." Todd shook his head. "We're just the latest firm on the site. Dad wouldn't take Rowland on without a retainer and a bond, so whatever happens, we're fine. No big score, but no loss like some of the earlier guys took."

"Why, if you don't mind my asking?" Dina posed the question so gracefully he couldn't mind.

"Don't mind at all. Rowland was a terrible risk by the time he got to us. He had to offer special considerations, and Dad—who's as sharp as they come—struck a good bargain."

"If I remember correctly, Rowland just won the appeal on this last month, right?" I asked.

"He did. And we were ready to start when the antis went to court for an order pending the next appeal. This time, the court said no…and it was finally go time. Two days in, our bony friends popped up."

"So to speak." Dina's tone was just a teensy bit reproving.

"So to speak. Look, I've been on projects before where bones were found. Old cemeteries and suchlike. I believe in being respectful—I think about what I'd want if it was my grandma. Same for Dad…and he's a veteran. So if this is really a Revolutionary battlefield, Rowland would have had to find another contractor."

"Still a big if," I said. "Didn't that whole claim show up pretty late in the process?"

"It's been around for a while, but only got serious last year, right when the last appeal was falling apart." Todd nodded. "That's why we took the job in the first place. Figured there wasn't anything to it, and it would go away soon enough."

"But it didn't," Dina said. "Can we see where the skeletons were?"

"Sure. What do you think about the artifacts?" Todd asked.

"I think you leave them for now and ask the state archaeologist what to do." I said, pocketing my phone. "If they don't have a problem, the Society can certainly collect the pieces and store them until something else happens."

"You can?"

"My assistant and I can take more pictures, carefully remove the pieces and document everything if everyone is comfortable with that." I shrugged. "As long as the state archaeologist or any other authorities don't mind."

"I'll have someone call the state today. Probably take a while."

"Nothing with the state ever happens quickly."

"Well, we'll do what we can," Dina assured him. "Just protect the objects for now."

"We can do that. We'll bring in a couple more surveillance cams—right now, we only have them on the gate and trailer."

"That would be wise." I nodded. "Since it might be a while before the state decides what to do."

"Hurry up and wait." Todd shook his head. "And people wonder why folks don't want to deal with government."

He might have been offering a potential opening for a complaint session of a particular political nature, but neither Dina nor I are into that game, and we just moved on to the skeleton site. It wasn't much, just another flat spot, though it was closer to the parking area.

Within a few minutes, we were heading back to the car, now really dusty and hot.

Dina's hair had curled into a copper halo, and I was sure mine had gone full Cowardly Lion in the humid afternoon air. I'm not ashamed to admit I was having darn near romantic thoughts about her car's AC.

And maybe a stop for a cool drink before we get back to the Society. Are we too old to sneak off for a slushie?

"What are you two doing here?"

The high, brittle voice snapped around us like a bullwhip.

Dina and I turned to see Linley Stark clomping across the uneven ground from a big white SUV that was not so much parked as abandoned in the middle of the site.

"Hi, Linley. Some artifacts turned up, and they asked us to take a look." I kept my tone calm and even.

"Both of you?" Linley's glare sharpened on Dina.

"One of the pieces looked like Judaica," the rabbi explained patiently.

"Are you really going to help them destroy this project?" Linley actually wrung her hands. I'd read about it, but never seen anyone do it. "I don't know what I'm going to do—"

"Mrs. Stark, I told you there was no need to come down today." Todd Ruff came up behind us.

"But I—"

"I know you're worried about a lot of things right now," he said in a surprisingly soothing tone for a big construction guy, "but we're doing everything we can while we wait. I'm sure you have other things to do."

"I do." Linley preened a little. "Funeral arrangements and so on."

"Of course." Todd kept the soothing tone. "We've really got it under control here, Mrs. Stark. Dr. Shaw and the rabbi gave us what we needed to know for the moment, and a little direction about what to do next."

"What did you tell them?" she asked us.

Dina looked to me.

"We're not sure what they've got," I said. "We suggested the state come in and take a look before we do anything else. It's tough to tell what's going on without an expert assessment."

"Well, come back tomorrow and look again." Linley's eyes were wild and her tone brittle.

"I'm not sure that's the best idea," I began.

"Please. We need to settle this now."

"I'm willing, if I can clear it with the Society."

"Come out in the morning," Linley urged. "I'll call Victoria. She won't mind. You, too, Rabbi?"

"I can probably find an hour or two," Dina agreed. "After the minyan. Maybe ten or so?"

"Perfect!" Linley clapped her hands and smiled radiantly at us, then turned to the contractor. "Make sure they get whatever they need."

"Uh, sure, Mrs. Stark." Todd gave us an apologetic glance. "We'll see you in the morning, then."

Dina and I sent him apologies right back, and he held our gaze and nodded to Linley.

"Since we're coming out tomorrow," I started, putting a hand on her arm, "you really don't need to stay here."

"Do you have someone with you?" Dina asked gently. "At home?"

"Why would I need anyone?" Linley bristled. "I'm not going to sit there while someone pats me on the head."

Dina cut her eyes to me. "Well, if you need anything, I'd be happy to call somebody for you, or put you in touch with some support."

"I don't need support."

"Take care," I said, touching but definitely not patting Linley's arm.

Dina's face was neutral, and her goodbye friendly, but I knew she was at least mildly annoyed.

Our last sight of Linley: the woman haranguing Todd, as he listened with a carefully blank face. I suspected there was going to be a point very soon when Ruff Construction didn't care about that retainer…and there would be yet another contractor on the site.

"Amazing day," I said as she started the car.

"Getting more amazing all the time."

"Want to stop for slushies before we go back?" I asked. "I'm buying,"

"Best idea I've heard all day."

Chapter Nine: Pick 'em Up

The big payoff for parenthood may be having someone to take care of you in your old age…but putting the child's needs ahead of your own sometimes provides a more immediate benefit by allowing you to jump out of someone else's drama into the safety of kid stuff. On that particular day, after all the craziness, camp pickup time was a major relief.

Not just for me.

Tiffany, in off-duty wear of jeans and a cute fuchsia popover top, walked into the Society a few minutes before I had to leave, looking more than a little tired and frazzled. Jorge had dropped Ava at the bus because Tiffany was still winding down the shift, so she'd earned that exhaustion.

"I made fresh coffee," I said, reaching for one of the swag travel mugs my cousin Jimmy had thrown in with his last shipment from Seattle.

"Thanks. I could use it."

"Paperwork?"

"Oh, yeah. And talking to three different agencies about what I saw, plus sitting in with my guys while they told the officials what THEY saw. Just a mess."

"Ugh." I handed her the mug. "What do you think?"

"Thanks." She took a deep breath of the coffee scent and a small, careful sip. "I think everyone's worried about a lawsuit. You're the one who knows about cannons and such, and I can't really say about criminality…"

"I don't know that much. I've suggested an armorer for Joe…and Ben sent him to someone he knows in Israel who's an expert on bomb damage."

"That's good." She nodded. "But there's something else here. You know about Rowland Stark."

"I know enough. The whole strip-mall thing has become a huge issue."

"It sure has. You know the property is about half a mile away from Jorge and me, and a lot of the neighbors were up in arms. And Rowland Stark fought back—hard. He sued a guy who put together a petition against it. And his lawyers tracked down everyone who signed it."

"Really?"

"It wasn't directly threatening," she said. "But it was definitely intimidating. Something along the lines of calling everyone who signed the petition as a witness in a defamation suit…I'm pretty sure that's not legal, but it scared some of the neighbors."

"I bet it did. I'd heard he was a creep, so it fits."

"Well, you know his wife's a piece of work." Tiffany managed a rueful little smile. "Isn't she the one who made you fill out three different forms when she made a donation?"

"Plus photos."

"No."

"Oh, yes. Photos of the piece." I shook my head. "From four angles. She's a bit tightly wound."

"A little too kind, Christian." She patted my arm. "But that's you."

"Aw, thanks." I picked up my own mug. "Ready to walk over?"

"Yeah."

I waved goodbye to Lewis, who was in the front room with a notepad, mapping out his plans.

Outside, the sun was strong, and the air thick, but it was still fairly nice. I was glad I'd made sure Henry and I both got a good dousing in sunscreen before leaving the house. Of course, he'd needed it more, for a full day at camp, but I burn easily too.

"Pretty day," Tiffany said. "First I've seen of it. I crashed for a few hours when I got done."

"That's good. Family evening tonight?"

"Bachelorettes—Jorge is on a long hitch."

"Not a bad thing."

"Not at all." She smiled. "You're probably going to need to get used to the same stuff."

"Maybe."

"Maybe?"

"You know the Scottish. Hate to jinx things."

She looked at me. Tiffany has pretty good radar, too. "Yeah? That all?"

"I think so. But we came awfully close to…um, big and serious stuff last night."

"The big words?"

"Not talking."

"Ah." And this is how you know Tiffany is a really good friend. She didn't high-five, which a lot of girlfriends would. She just watched me. "Lousy timing."

"Yeah. That's what pretty much stopped everything."

"Don't worry, you'll pick back up."

"Yeah…I think so." I took a breath. "It's a little…"

"No," she said, holding my gaze. "It's a lot, with Frank and all."

"Yeah. And it's been a while." Suddenly, I had a horrible thought. "There's nothing—new—I need to know, is there?"

Tiffany chuckled. "You've been married, Christian."

"Married is 'Hey, the kid's asleep and we've got ten minutes before we both pass out from exhaustion.' This is kind of the big show. And with *this* guy?"

"Well, he is pretty fine." She smiled. "But he's definitely into you, so I wouldn't worry too much. Just let things happen."

"Things."

"There are diagrams in *Cosmo* if you need them."

We both dissolved in thoroughly inappropriate giggles.

"Oh, I needed that," I said.

"Me too." She drank a little coffee. "Seriously. You will be just fine whenever the time comes. Just don't overthink it."

"But overthinking is my best thing."

Another shared laugh. If there's anything better than friends, I don't know what it is.

"Hey, you two!" Ruby, Lewis's aunt, and her pal Lidia, who just happened to be Joe's mother, were walking toward us.

It was an unexpected summer treat that both had grandchildren going to camp for the same weeks our kids were. Everybody patched things together for the season, between family vacations, enrichment programs, and various specific interests, but most folks in town send their cherubs to Harmony Hills at some point, because it's the best day camp in the area, other than an insanely expensive one favored by New Yorkers, and it lets you pick different weeks.

We all know each other from the "pickup pen" at Phyllis Wheatley Elementary School, and we'd become close in a casually friendly way before we developed deeper connections. So it was definitely a pleasure, to catch up together while waiting for the bus.

Less of a pleasure was another member of the ladies of the pen, now striding toward us in full power walk, and full overpriced athleisure gear. Sally Birdwell, local Realtor, PTA princess, and generally perfect person (just ask her!) was the bane of our collective existence.

I doubt Sally deliberately tries to make everyone feel miserable and insecure. It's just her special magic.

We attempted to ignore her as long as we could.

"Terrible thing yesterday," Ruby said, then turned to Tiffany. "You holding up okay?"

"Yeah. Be fine. Thanks for asking."

"Of course." She patted Tiffany's arm and nodded to me. "Saw you wading in too."

"She ended up at the First Aid station," Lidia said. "Joe was investigating."

Her proud tone, and the smile strongly suggested that matters were settled for Lidia, even if Joe and I hadn't decided where this would ultimately go.

"It was ugly for everyone," I offered neutrally. "Joe's probably going to be up to his eyeballs with this for a while. They have to figure out if it's a criminal matter—"

"Oh, how could it be a criminal matter?"

Guess who?

We all turned to Sally, who was rocking matchy leggings and a t-shirt in pink and gray heathers, topped with a little bucket hat with a rhinestone heart and "Blessed" embroidered on it.

I suspect she's the only person who feels blessed in her presence.

"Well, really," she continued in that speedy, breathy voice of hers. "How could it be anything other than a horrible accident? Those old guys barely know what they're doing, after all."

"Well," Tiffany started. Even though Sally's social media feed gives her insecurity fits, she handles the actual woman far better than the rest of us, with the perfect combination of politeness and dismissal. "The authorities will have to determine what happened."

"Oh, the lawsuits will go on for years," Sally said with a flighty wave of her beige acrylics. "But it had better quiet down in time for Crafts on the Green in August. That's a marquee event and makes the town look so desirable."

Tiffany shot me a tiny eyebrow flick.

"Which is, of course, so good for property values and all of us."

We have a running bet on how many sentences it will take Sally, a part-time Realtor, to get to property values in any given conversation. This might have been the longest she'd managed to stay off the topic, ever.

Ruby and Lidia just listened with the careful blankness of women who've spent most of their lives dealing with far more serious problems than minor fluctuations in the mill rate. They've both come to the conclusion that the best way to handle Sally is to simply let her ramble, and she'll eventually go away.

I can't really argue.

"No doubt," I said. "But it's going to take a while to figure out what happened. There are a lot of technical issues."

"Well, I can tell you one thing. Linley Stark will sue everyone in sight."

The Grandmas' eyes widened. Tiffany scowled.

Oh, hell, I'll take one for the team. I asked: "Why?"

"Well, good heavens, her husband just got blown up on the Green. Somebody's got to be responsible for that mess. She'll sue the town, at least."

"Usually, there's some kind of liability protection for the town at events like this," Tiffany began. She knew about this because she'd had to give a deposition in a suit over a minor mishap at a church pumpkin carving event a few years ago. Guy was screwing around, almost lost a thumb…and tried to make it the town's fault.

I hadn't thought about the pumpkin thing in ages. It had been a huge donnybrook at the time, as well as a lesson for all of us who lead or host events—like, say Historical Society programs!—on how these things worked.

No one in Unity would hold an event without a liability policy now. Certainly not an event on town property.

"She's right," I said. "The town probably buys an umbrella policy just for the event."

"Well, you should know about the law these days." Sally's bright brown eyes lasered in on me.

"Excuse me?" I knew where she was going, but I was going to make her put it out there. See if the busybody has any shame.

She didn't. "Well, I hear you're spending a lot of time with Joe Poli lately."

"Oh?"

"Everyone saw you holding hands on the Green before it happened. So?"

Lidia shot Sally a glare.

I knew the look. I'd seen it on my mom every Thanksgiving for years when Great-Aunt Nettie asked, as she always did, when I was going to stop studying and get married. Somebody was about to get scorched. Verbally, I hoped…but Lidia *was* the woman who'd driven up the sidewalk when a bunch of rude parents had tied up the school traffic circle (after making sure no people were nearby, of course!) so anything was possible.

"Well," I said quickly. "We're seeing each other."

Sally's eyes gleamed at the prospect of juicy gossip.

"And that's all I have to say about it," I finished.

She pouted. "All?"

"All."

"But he's so—and you haven't—there must be…"

"Ladies don't talk about it in the street." Ruby echoed Lidia's glare.

"Oh, fine." Sally pouted more.

Fortunately, just then, the camp bus turned the corner.

Lidia and Ruby turned to me, and both winked. Tiffany chuckled.

"Kid alert," I said.

"Don't forget," Sally started, preening back into her perfect PTA princess form. "Tomorrow is Crazy Character Day. Sheridan is being Cinderella."

Sure she was. Five-year-old Sheridan, who has a more-than-mild crush on Henry, bounded off the bus covered in mud from head to toe, to an anguished howl from Sally.

None of the other kids was in much better shape, but filthy, happy, tired children are exactly what we want to see at the end of the day. It is, not to put too fine a point on it, why we pay stupid money for a good day camp.

We happily take them home, hose them off, feed them, and put them to bed early.

Parenting win.

Even with Sally fussing at Sheridan and nagging her older boy about keeping a better eye on his sis. Like he was going to somehow fish her out of the mud.

Anyhow, on camp days, I've arranged to do my last hour or so of work from home, so I can get Henry clean, make sure his numbers are good, and do whatever else has to happen for the night.

With everything else going on, a muddy kid actually seemed like a break.

Chapter Ten: The Bat Mitzvah Girl

Henry was freshly washed and freshly re-scented by Cookie, playing a video game, and nibbling on a chocolate square, an after-camp treat that had the added advantage of getting his numbers to a decent level until dinnertime, when Dina buzzed me.

"Got a few minutes to stop over? Amy Taylor would like to talk to you."

"Sure."

The bribe of my phone and Dragon Race was more than enough to convince Henry to leave his catch-up time with the cat, and we made the short walk in record time. Inside the gracious Victorian entry hall, I handed over the phone and parked Henry on the waiting bench, then knocked on the door of Dina's office.

"We're here."

"Come in."

Amy Taylor and Dina were sitting together on the couch with a book. Dina nodded to one of the side chairs, and I took it, and a quick look at Amy. For someone who was closing in on the century mark, she looked amazing. Her skin was lined, but a healthy pink, and her blue eyes still clear and sparkly. Her hair was the shimmery bright silver every aging person hopes for, and few get. My mother's coloring is similar, and I suspected Amy was using the same sort of purple brightening shampoo. Good for her.

Amy's lipstick was the perfect burgundy shade to harmonize with the thin pastel pink v-neck sweater she wore with khakis and loafers, all very good pieces, not new but well-kept. She had a classic platinum wedding set on her left hand, small diamond studs in her ears, and a pearl necklace with the deep, creamy luster that comes from long, careful wear.

Suddenly, I was keenly aware of the worn-down heels of my low-tops and the coffee mark I hadn't quite been able to get out of my tank top.

Amy gave me a bright smile, and then looked past me. "Is the little fella with you?"

She sounded as wonderful as she looked, her voice still clear and crisp with a faint trace of British accent.

"Playing video games on my phone."

She laughed. "My great-niece does that with her kids, too."

"I don't let him away with it very often," I started.

"Honey, we do what we have to do." Amy glanced at Dina and back to me. "If you're looking to get judged, go somewhere else."

"Thanks."

"I thought you two knew each other." Dina moved the conversation along.

"Yes." Amy nodded. "I volunteered at the Society until about six months ago."

"One of my best docents," I agreed. "I was sorry to lose you, but I understood."

"Oh." Dina looked puzzled—and a bit shocked.

"I took a hiatus from volunteering so I could focus on Torah study. Christian here encouraged me."

"Well, of course I did."

"Ah." Dina grinned. "Then we're all good here."

I nodded.

"So, Christian," Amy began, "Dina and I are discussing the Bat Mitzvah, and I wondered if you'd be willing to say a few words."

"Oh, wow," I stammered. It's not that I'm uncomfortable with public speaking…it's that I was amazed to be asked to participate in Amy's big day.

"Well, the Historical Society was and is a very important part of my life, and I'd like to make sure it's part of the ceremony."

"Of course," I said, recovering my professional demeanor. "I'm honored to be asked."

"And of course," Amy replied with a smile, "I'll be happy to return the favor and say wonderful things about you at your Bat Mitzvah one of these days."

"Thanks. I guess I'm going to have to get serious about that Torah study," I said.

"When you're ready," Dina said. She's very conscious of the rule barring Jews from proselytizing, always careful to keep her rabbinical ethics, even if she might privately think I should just make the time and get it done. (I know she does!) She turned to her computer, and I saw the screen: **Bat Mitzvah of Edit Taylor.**

"Is Edit your Hebrew name?" I asked, pronouncing it "Ay-Deet," since that made sense with Amy's Dutch background.

"No, honey. It's my real name." She chuckled. "When I came over here, nobody could pronounce it—I bet you know something about that, Chris'shun."

She exaggerated the New Haven County swallowed "T" with an impish gleam in her eye.

"You bet she does." Dina grinned. "So they couldn't do any better with Edit?"

"Worse. People called me Eddit when they saw my name, and Amy when I said it, so I finally just gave in to the Amy." She shrugged. "Easier than trying to correct people."

"I suppose," I said. I'd learned to grit my teeth and accept it, but it didn't seem fair for Amy, considering everything she'd been through to get here.

"Gerry calls me Edit, and it's rather nice to hear it again."

Gerry? I caught a hint of something.

Dina cut her eyes to me. *Don't ask.* "Anyhow, she wanted to ask you in person."

"Always a good thing," I agreed. "And always good to see you."

"You too, Christian. As soon as I've successfully read my Torah portion, I'll be back at least one day a week. Not giving up study entirely."

"I'm glad to share you," I assured her.

"How are things at the Society?" she asked.

"Oh, the usual. Lewis and I are starting work on the fall exhibits…he's handling the front room himself."

Amy grinned. "You are going to miss that fella when he leaves."

"Terribly."

"Lewis is wonderful," Dina agreed.

"And I have a new client," I continued, knowing Amy would get a kick out of the hot mess in the 1806 bedroom. "Working on a really bonkers reality show idea."

"*Regency Love?*" Amy asked.

"What?" My jaw dropped.

"Oh, that Jensen gets crazy ideas. Always has, ever since she was a little girl trying to dress up the cat."

"You know Jensen's family?" Dina asked.

"She's part of mine, Rabbi." Amy gave a ruffly little chuckle as her eyes took on an amused sparkle. Nothing she likes better than putting one over on the youngsters. "Great-niece, same as poor Linley. Used to be like sisters, before they went to college and grew apart."

A knock on the open door made us all turn.

"Edit?" A small man with big, bright gray eyes behind large glasses stood in the doorway.

"Oh, Gerry!" Amy rose from Dina's couch with surprising grace, her face lighting up. "Looks like my ride's here, Rabbi."

"Looks that way." Dina grinned. "Good to see you, Gerry."

"Good to see you, Rabbi." Gerry Diamond, a synagogue board member, and morning minyan regular—not to mention standup guy and general good egg—shook Dina's outstretched hand, adding a friendly pat on her arm, and turned to me. "Hey, Christian."

"Hey, Gerry."

"You know, you could just go with Chrissy…"

Gerry's eyes gleamed. We had a long-running joke about my name and my plans to formally convert.

"I think I'd prefer Giant Redheaded *Shikse*," I said. "What's Hebrew for that?"

"Too long for you," Dina cut in, shaking her head at us both.

Amy grinned.

"You're coming to the Bat Mitzvah, aren't you?" Gerry asked.

"Wouldn't miss it for the world," I assured him.

"Neither would I." He beamed as Amy crossed to him. "The most beautiful Bat Mitzvah girl ever."

"Go on, now." Amy laughed.

We watched them leave, arm in arm, and chatting happily.

"They're wonderful," Dina said.

"Nice friendship."

"Or something."

"Oh?"

"Both have been widowed for decades, and he's taken to hanging around when she's studying Torah." The gleam in her eye suggested more.

"You think…"

"I think there's something very nice going on here. I'm not sure of the exact details on that…and I'm not sure it matters. Or that it's any of our business."

I nodded. "Whatever it is works for them."

"Exactly. They're clearly happy together, and they've clearly found some kind of happiness."

"It's sweet. Nice to see." I realized I was twisting my wedding ring.

Dina noticed, too. "Everyone grieves and recovers differently."

"Uh-huh."

She glanced out into the hall, where Henry was still busy racing a dragon around some kind of urban roller-coaster course. "He's going to be busy for a while. Sit and talk for a minute."

"Maybe—I…"

Dina held my gaze. "Maybe you're not so cool after yesterday?"

"Not yesterday. Last night."

An eyebrow flick. "Last night?"

"Joe was over, and things got…intense. Just a little, before he had to get back to work."

"Ah. And now that you've had some time to think about it, you're feeling guilty and maybe just a bit nervous."

"Yeah. This feels big and serious, and I'm not sure I'm ready for that."

"It *is* big and serious." Dina smiled. "That's a good thing. You know he's a good man. And I'm pretty sure he loves you."

"I'm pretty sure I love him."

Her searching gaze held. "And you feel like you're betraying Frank."

"Not exactly. It's not about him…and that's what's really awful."

"Because it means he's really gone." She rested a hand on mine, ran a finger over my wedding ring.

"Yeah."

"He's still a part of you, you know. A part of you and Henry. Helped make both of you who you are. But life moves forward."

"It does." My eyes were full.

"And part of that is finding someone to love. Really love." She patted my hand and pulled back. "It's okay to enjoy that…to enjoy being with him."

"He's serious about me. And Henry."

"You're serious about him."

"Uh-huh."

"So see where it goes." A grin. "I do a mean interfaith wedding."

"Okay."

"Okay?"

"Well," I said, "not tomorrow or next week, but it's not impossible."

"Good." Her eyes took on a wicked gleam. "And have fun, huh? This boy-girl stuff is supposed to be fun."

I nodded.

Dina nodded, briskly. "Now go get the little fella off the screen and get some rest. If I'm going to spend tomorrow morning playing archaeologist with you, I don't want you tired and cranky."

Chapter Eleven: We Love Norm!

Out on the Green, Garrett was walking Norm.

Sometimes, the guys just "happen" to be around when Henry and I need them…but this time, it was a genuine coincidence.

"NORM!" Henry yelled, and Garrett let the dog loose so he could run right over, setting up a little canine-human lovefest that would get me in even more trouble with Cookie.

Garrett and I watched for a minute or so, enjoying the little-boy giggles and uncomplicated happiness.

Then I took a good look at him.

"How are you holding up?"

He shrugged. "What about you?"

"Not my best day, but far from my worst." I gave Garrett the hard look. "What's up?"

"Ed's driving me nuts."

"Nuts, how?"

"Solicitous, following me around. Too nice." Garrett winced. "It's weird. We generally manage on a sort of benign, loving neglect."

What a sweet, low-key way to describe a comfortable, committed marriage.

"He was scared for you," I reminded him. "I used to do the same thing to Frank after a really dangerous assignment."

"Ed was a cop. He should know—"

"And he's always been the one in danger, not the one worrying."

Garrett just looked at me for a moment. Then shook his head with a rueful smile. "For a woman with no online presence, you're pretty savvy."

"People I can figure out. Social media, no way." This was a long-running, well-worn and, honestly, comforting, argument between us. Garrett has become a social media maven in retirement, maintaining quite a footprint, including a snarky historical/political Flutter feed under the name of an obscure member of Lincoln's cabinet. He believes the Society needs a significant presence.

Widow of a newspaperman that I am, I believe the platforms are neither media nor especially social, and I've done my best to hold the line. Though even I will admit it's possible we might draw in more interest and support with a carefully done page on one of the photo sites.

"Well, too bad." Garrett gave me the usual exasperated glare. Today, it was strangely soothing. "Flutter has a lot to say about the bomb. Most of it's garbage, but even a stopped clock is right twice a day…"

"Yeah. Stopped clock for sure."

"Seriously. Some folks seem to think Stark deserved it."

"Why?" Even for the online cesspit, the idea that someone deserved to be blown to bits on the Town Green in front of his family seemed a bit much.

"Apparently, there's an awful lot of bad will over that strip mall project, especially since the bones turned up last week."

"The bones again."

"Again?"

"Got called out to the site early today to look at some other old stuff found near them—the bones are the state M.E.'s problem."

"Interesting." Garrett's eyes gleamed. "Got any thoughts?"

I shrugged. "Something doesn't feel right but I'm not sure what yet. Dina was called too because there was some Judaica."

"Judaica?"

"A kiddush cup. A small pewter piece with Hebrew inscriptions. She says it looks a lot like an eighteenth-century piece in the Jewish Museum in New York."

"Really. I didn't think there were Jewish settlers this far inland until later."

"Neither did we. We're going to take a closer look at everything tomorrow. There was a pewter plate and some other stuff, too."

"What doesn't feel right?"

"I'll know it when I see it." I looked ahead at Henry and Norm. "What else about Rowland Stark?"

"General shady business dealings." Garrett shrugged. "A few hints of #MeToo things, but mostly, it seems to be cheating subcontractors, holding up towns for tax breaks, and promising far more than he delivered. Sounded like he was just barely skating inside the lines."

"That wouldn't surprise me," I said. "Joe said he was unethical. But I didn't realize any of this was enough of a thing for people to talk about online."

"Anything, no matter how miniscule, is enough to talk about online." Garrett smiled. "He would have been marginal…but the explosion got a lot of traffic, so folks are looking at him."

"I guess that makes sense."

"It does. There's video."

"Ugh."

"Yeah." He shook his head. "I'd guess someone with authority is trying to get it pulled, but right now, it's everywhere."

I sighed. "Lovely."

We turned the corner to my street, with Norm dragging Henry all the way. Both of them were having a wonderful time.

Watching them was just what Garrett and I needed.

"You okay?" he asked as we closed in on my driveway.

"Yeah. Yesterday was a little rocky." Meaning the bloodshed on the Green of course. As much as I love Garrett, I would never be comfortable talking about the little incident with Joe.

"It's okay if you feel awful," Garrett said. "Probably even healthy. Processing and all."

"Same for you."

A shrug and a wicked little grin. "Oh, but I'm the big macho man. I'm supposed to be the strong, silent type."

"That works so well."

"Tell me. I'm married to it."

"You going to give Ed some rope?" I asked.

"To hang himself with," Garrett said with a small, snarky grin, then paused. "Nah. He is just processing yesterday, too. Weird for him to be watching instead of responding."

"Uh-huh." I didn't point out that I'd said the exact same thing to him just minutes ago.

"I believe someone already made that observation."

"Did they?" I asked with a faint smile.

"They did." He smacked my arm. "Nice catch."

He whistled for the dog, starting the usual round of hugs and pats and goodbyes.

As Garrett turned to leave, he grinned. "Ed was able to freeze the sausages, but I have to get rid of some of these tomatoes and zucchini. How about a big garden dinner tomorrow night?"

"I like it."

"Good. I'll call the rabbi. You call Tiffany and ask Joe if he's free. Guy has to eat."

Joe and his eating habits weren't my concern for the next couple hours. Once again, the sheer weight of daily tasks kept me out of the emotional muck. Dinner, cat maintenance (Cookie's claws were approaching lethal weapon status), and laundry made for a consuming whirlwind of distraction.

It was only around eight-thirty when Henry was down, and I'd finally managed to pour myself the promised wine when I started to think about things again.

And the phone rang.

Joe.

"Hey."

"Hey. Miss you."

"Same here."

For a moment, we let that hang between us in the faint crackle of cellular ozone. It was nice to miss and be missed, I thought.

"Actually, kind of nice to have someone to miss," Joe said.

"Mind reader."

"Oh, I like that. Let me concentrate a little..." A teasing, naughty note crept into his voice. "Why, Dr. Shaw, I'm on duty!"

"I'm not."

"I'll take a break. Guess where I'd like to be right now. And what I'd like to be doing."

"Oh, my. You make me blush," I said in my best Jane Austen heroine tone.

"I can only hope." He laughed, the kind of low, warm rumble that raised the temperature a couple degrees. "Imagine the possibilities."

"I'd better not." This was well down a road that neither of us had the time to follow at the moment. Too bad, too. "Not sure I can anyhow. Too much noise right now."

"True, but way too bad." A rueful sigh. "I thought you Celtic types had the Second Sight."

"I have a hard enough time figuring out what I see with my first two eyes, never mind the third one."

"Oh?"

"Dina and I were out at Rowland Stark's strip mall site today. They say they found artifacts with those bones from a few days ago."

"And…"

"I'm not sure." I didn't want to give Joe anything until I had more. "We're going out to take another look tomorrow."

But he heard it in my voice. "You think this is something?"

"I don't know. Do *you* think it's something?"

"I know Dr. Alexandre is still trying to decide which agency gets the bones, and she asked me if I thought the explosion had anything to do with them. So please keep me in the loop."

"Will do."

"And keep your eyes open and your guard up." Joe's voice was gravelly. "I don't know what's going on, and I don't want you at risk."

"Okay."

"I'm not big-footing you, am I?"

"Not really. Ed's done worse."

"Fair enough." He chuckled a little. "Why do you need another look?"

"Linley Stark's trying to get them out of the ground as soon as she can.

We're trying to slow her down a little. And you know that site is a huge bone of contention."

"Which may be part of Stark's murder."

"Yep." This was a great time for a subject change. "I've been invited to speak at a Bat Mitzvah."

"Really?"

"Amy Taylor is finally getting hers, at 90-something. Girls didn't get bat mitzvah'ed when she was growing up in Holland in the 1930s, so she's having it now."

"That's neat." Joe was one of the few people who could use the word and not sound too geeky. "Like that lady on Long Island."

"Exactly like her. Probably like me someday, too."

"You think?" Joe knew, and respected, that I was raising Henry in his father's faith and planned to formally convert eventually.

"It's a lot of work and study, the kind of thing you can only really do as a kid—or a retiree."

"Or a PhD with some very supportive friends, maybe."

"Maybe." I couldn't stop a faint smile. "So anyway, since she's a longtime volunteer and supporter of the Society, she asked me to say a few words. A real honor."

"When?"

"A week from Saturday."

He paused for a moment, and then asked in an almost tentative tone. "Can I come, too?"

"Well, yeah…invites are usually by family, so Henry and I could bring you."

"I'd like that." A breath. "I want to know more about your and Henry's religion."

"Yeah?"

"Yeah. It's a big part of your lives, and if I'm going to be, too…"

He trailed off, clearly realizing how far he'd just gone.

"I'm impressed," I said. "You get it."

"I try to. I know this is a lot for you."

"I know *I'm* a lot." I couldn't help a little uncertainty. A guy like Joe could be with anyone. A single, bodacious, uncomplicated thirty-year-old with a simple job and no crow's feet.

"That's the best thing about you, *Dottore*. You're the whole box of chocolates, not just one piece of candy."

"That's not Donne," I said because I had to say something.

"Nope. That's me."

Wow.

The signal cut out for an instant right then.

"Of course," Joe said, his tone irritable. "More emails. I'm waiting for bank records."

"Back to work, then." I was almost relieved. Things were as settled between us as they needed to be—until we could talk it out in person. Or maybe not talk.

"Yeah. Sorry."

"No apology needed."

"Thanks, *cara*."

It was entirely safe to allow myself a few exceedingly naughty thoughts on the strength of that little Italian endearment. After all, he'd be too busy to read my mind.

Chapter Twelve: Another Morning at the Ranch

No surprise I didn't sleep well, considering everything. I woke at four and couldn't get back out, so instead of lying there fretting, I went out to the living room, did an extra-long yoga video, and took the time to condition my hair and do a good facial scrub in the shower. Even put on some of the nice rose and honey body oil instead of the usual basic lotion from the big box store.

By the time Henry woke up, my hair was curling in smooth copper springs, and I was dressed. Even though I was wearing old khakis and a chambray blazer, both easily washable in deference to the return to the construction site, I'd finished the outfit with a lace-trimmed peach tank. Just a little saucy.

Saucy made me think of Joe. And the bridge, just a short distance down the road. Probably a little closer, considering last night's big and serious discussion. The bridge a lot of healthy single adults would have probably crossed by now.

I'd joked about it with Tiffany, but I really was more than a little nervous about the whole thing. I hadn't exactly been the belle of the ball before Frank, and I certainly hadn't been studying up on the current dating rules. If there even were any.

Joe, I was sure, had all the offers he could handle, and it was none of my business if he'd taken some of them to get back in practice after the divorce. Really. Whatever happened before we got together was a closed topic.

Unless we were supposed to have some kind of very adult talk about it, before.

I sure hoped not. I honestly didn't want to know. And I wanted even less to confess to my own pathetically short rap sheet. I hadn't been a Victorian maiden when I married Frank, but I definitely hadn't cut a swathe on the hookup scene.

Embarrassing.

I hadn't felt this inadequate since my third date with Frank. That had kind of taken care of itself, thanks to good wine and better chemistry, so maybe this would, too.

As I made Henry his nutritious pre-camp egg and cheese scramble for breakfast and slapped together my summer-standard Greek yogurt and berries, I tried to force my brain onto more important matters, like the mess awaiting me at the site, the unexpected connection between Jensen and Linley, and Rowland Stark's unfortunate end…and kept returning to Joe.

A guy who's conversant with Donne probably spends a fair amount of time thinking about the things the good Reverend wrote about—and might have some expectations a scruffy girl from Mars, PA, couldn't meet.

Not that I had time to worry about it. Henry's camp is terrific, but there's a big difference between packing for the camp day and having him just up the street at Phyllis Wheatley Elementary. He'd gone last year, too, and the most stressful moment of my day was checking his bag.

I knew, because Tiffany and I had commiserated about it, that it was a chore to pack for Ava, too. But Ava didn't need a testing kit, an assortment of snacks, and a bunch of other items that were just part of Henry's day. So, while Henry ate breakfast, I went down my list, double-checked everything, and then made sure the other ordinary camp day things were there, too.

The camp day is an hour longer than the school day, plus about twenty minutes each way on the bus, so it's almost an extra two hours of work time. But you pay for that time with organizing on the front end.

Not to mention hosing off when the little angels get home.

It's all worth it, though. The prevailing opinion in town is that a camp isn't doing its job unless the kids come home filthy, happy, and exhausted. And Harmony Hills is very good at that.

Despite the early start, we were still a little tight on time as we headed for the door, Henry hoisting his backpack and me grabbing my purse, a big sensible mom-tote, despite the status brand and soft metallic leather. I bought it with the proceeds of an early consulting job, and even though metallics go in and out of style, I'll use it forever. Probably hand it on to some future granddaughter, too.

My phone buzzed with a text as I locked the door.

No time to talk, but thinking of you, Dottore. Not entirely appropriately.

Of course, all my worries vanished like a popping soap bubble. Well, at least I'm aware that I'm a cliché.

Back at you, Counselor. Miss you.

I was smiling like a fool as we started walking for the Green. Harmony Hills runs a little bus route through town, and the Green is one of the first.

Tiffany was parked on a nearby side street, climbing out of the driver's seat as Ava bounded from the back.

"Henry!" Ava crowed. "Are you ready for the Gaga tournament?"

Gaga, for the non-camp crowd, is Israeli volleyball, a very popular summer sport. Please don't ask me to explain how an Israeli game caught on in an area with a strong Italian cultural flavor. Just accept it as part of the fun of New Haven County and keep moving.

"SO ready!"

They scooted over to the bus stop, where the Grandmas and Sally were already waiting. Ruby and Lidia both shot us a wave, with Lidia adding an extra little grin to me.

I realized I had no idea how much Joe discussed with her.

I knew someday I wouldn't want to hear anything from Henry other than he was being safe and responsible, and the girl (or guy, if it went that way) made him happy. But who knew what Joe's arrangements were?

"How are you two?" Tiffany asked. She was in uniform, ready for another busy day of saving lives. Well, this time of year, it was more taking overly enthusiastic home renovators to the ER and the occasional ugly crash, but still.

"We're good. How about you?"

Her jaw tightened a little, and I knew.

"Just heard—the man we took in with a heart attack didn't make it."

"I'm sorry."

"It happens, but I don't have to feel good about it." She shook her head. "I know we should be glad we got through that disaster with two fatalities, but…"

"Two isn't zero."

"Yep. Especially that guy. As far as I could tell, he was in the back minding his own business and was just sent into shock by the blast."

"Real innocent bystander."

"Exactly. We had a lot of that in New Haven, back in the day. Stray bullet shootings and such. Probably why it's bothering me."

I patted her arm. "Happens."

"I really don't have a good feeling about the whole thing. I know you're the one who knows about cannons, but it just seemed weird."

"Hinky?" I asked. She and I both spend enough time around cops to know the word—and the very specific meaning, the police officer's sense that a crime's been committed.

"Yeah. I don't know how it's even possible. And I can't point to anything."

"Well, I know just enough to be dangerous, and I agree with you."

Her face relaxed a bit. "Yeah?"

"Yeah. I'm still trying to figure it out."

"Did you tell Joe?"

"I've pointed him in the direction."

"Point him a little harder and tell him I'm suspicious, too."

"Okay. Next time I talk to him."

She smiled, with a bit of her usual sparkle. "I bet it'll be soon."

"Sure hope so."

Tiffany caught something in the way I said it, but both of us had work to do, and girl gossip would just have to wait. "Dinner at Garrett and Ed's tonight?"

"Oh, yeah. Somebody has to eat the zucchini."

"And that somebody is us."

Chapter Thirteen: Back to the Dig

Lewis was in my office when I got there, holding his coffee mug and looking dazed. Not slow-roll morning daze—something else.

"What's up?" I asked. "Something with the dissertation?"

"No. Mrs. Peters just called and asked if I'd go out to the strip mall site with you and Rabbi Aaron."

"Great! Why should we have all the fun? Faith can watch the store for an hour or so."

"Yeah, but it's why I was asked to get involved that's a little weird."

"Weird, how?" I motioned to the one clear side chair and slipped behind my desk.

He sat, his posture and face tight. "It's not that I'm not happy to be asked."

"But..."

"Apparently, there may be something at the site that suggests free people of color or the formerly enslaved."

"Okay." I met his gaze. "But you're an early twentieth-century guy, not a Revolutionary War expert."

"Right. And I *am* the only Black guy in the picture."

"So, of course, you're going to know about Black stuff." I sighed. "Ugh."

"Yeah. What do I do, Doc?"

"Well, since our board chair specifically asked for you, and since it might be useful for your career, I'd suggest you go if you're comfortable doing that. But I'm going to have a word with Victoria…and turn her loose on the construction people."

A small smile. "Nice."

"Not even a little nice. Rabbi Aaron happens to have some expertise in antique Judaica, but she wasn't thrilled to be treated as the ambassador from Judaism, any more than you want to be the representative of Blackness."

"That's it, exactly."

"Okay, so we're due at the site in about an hour. Give me a bit of time to call Victoria and finish the morning stuff, and we'll round up Rabbi Aaron and head out. Wheels up at 9:30."

Victoria Peters, to her credit, was as repulsed as I'd been when I explained.

"Oh, no, dear. I knew Lewis was studying African American History, and I assumed…" She trailed off. Took a breath. "I need to stop assuming."

"We all probably do."

"Well, I'll have a word with Elias Ruff. A little consciousness-raising, as we used to say during my hippie phase."

"You had a hippie phase?"

A musical giggle. "Christian, dear, I was at Woodstock. Rather muddy, but otherwise quite delightful. And everything people say about Jimi Hendrix is true."

"Everything?" I asked with only a little subtext.

"I was between marriages and enjoying myself a bit at the time." The tinkly giggle turned into a richly naughty laugh. "Yes, indeed. Everything."

"Well, then."

"Anyhow, if Lewis wants to come to the site for the experience, of course he should. But he shouldn't feel obligated."

"Thank you for understanding."

"If we're lucky enough to still be here, dear, we should try to make it a better place."

As it turned out, that was the only win of the day.

When we pulled up at the site, once again in Dina's baby blue chariot, Todd Ruff walked out, with a big bankers' box and a sheepish expression.

"What…"

"Mrs. Stark. Ordered us to get back to preparing the site where we can. I discouraged her, but…" He shrugged. "She's the boss now."

Dina shook her head.

Lewis kept his expression neutral, but a little twitch at his jaw suggested he wasn't thrilled.

Me? I wanted to hunt Linley down and beat her senseless with the box. Well, at least we still had pics. They might just end up as evidence.

That was the real problem. If my suspicions were correct, Linley hadn't done much harm to history, but she'd done serious damage to any criminal case.

Which, I thought, could have been the point.

"Well, then," I finally managed.

"Anyhow, folks, I'm sorry." He turned to Lewis, hand out for a shake. "I don't think we've met."

"Lewis Barnes, assistant curator at the Society."

"Good to meet you, Dr. Barnes."

Lewis gave him a shy grin. "Not quite Doctor yet, but I appreciate the thought."

"I'm sure you'll get there." Todd released his hand but held his gaze. "My dad told me he and Mrs. Peters brought you in…and why. I'm sorry about that."

"Oh." Lewis looked a little stunned.

"My foreman, Gary Harden, is Black. We've worked together for thirty years." He nodded to a burly man supervising a piece of heavy equipment. "And I still sometimes miss things."

"As we all do," Dina said. "And we can always do better."

"Good to bring it in the open," Lewis said. "And I'm glad to get a look at the artifacts, even if they're really before my time period."

"It would be better in place," Todd admitted. "Wasn't my call."

Something in his tone suggested it had been quite a scene, which, indeed, it had been even when Dina and I had been leaving the previous day.

Why was Linley so hell bound to get some movement on the site?

Was it just some kind of grief thing? Lord knew I'd been a bit crazy in the first few weeks after Frank's death.

Not that kind of crazy, though. Just kind of dazed and unfocused. And keeping Henry within reach until Ed very gently pointed out to me what I was doing, and why it was a problem. He told me he'd done the same with his kids in the weeks after his wife's death, all those years ago.

But I sure wasn't Linley's kind of crazy.

I wondered if there was something else going on.

"Do you want to look at these things here?" Todd asked.

Dina and Lewis turned to me.

"Honestly," I said, "since we don't have the site anymore, we might as well look at them in the workroom at the Society."

Todd nodded.

"Of course, we'll sign for them," I continued. "Do you have a standard form or…"

"Let me quickly print up something." Todd motioned to the trailer. "C'mon in and enjoy a little AC while I take care of it. There's a water cooler, too, if you need a little hydration."

Ten minutes later, we were in the car with the bankers' box carefully settled beside Lewis on the backseat. And twenty minutes after that, we were in the workroom at the Society, gloved up, and getting to work.

Dina snickered slightly, as she put on the purple nitrile gloves we all wear for handling artifacts.

"I guess I'm really part of the team, now."

"Got that, Rabbi." Lewis grinned.

"I doubt the fellas at the construction site used anything, but at least we won't make any damage worse. Or ruin anything that isn't already ruined."

Dina gave me a sharp look. "Like what?"

"Better I don't say anything. I want you to come to your own conclusions."

"Okay."

The buttons, out of place, were reduced to a couple of sad handfuls of corroded metal. I took them out and put them aside. Dina reached in and gently extracted the kiddush cup.

"Wow," Lewis said. "That's beautifully made."

"The design is lovely," Dina said. "It looks exactly like one on the Jewish Museum website."

"Exactly?" I asked.

Lewis and Dina met my gaze.

Dina silently handed it to me.

I picked up the magnifying glass. The piece was beautiful, with a design of vines and Hebrew lettering. It was dark, corroded, the way silver or a silver alloy should be after some time in the ground. But it didn't seem dark enough for as long as it had been.

And I knew it was possible to fake the patina. There were scene shop tricks I'd seen on movie sets, and silver was really easy to tarnish, after all. This piece, after a couple of centuries in the ground, should have been almost flat black.

"I'm not sure how it would have gotten there," Dina said.

"What do you mean?" Lewis asked.

"This was a pretty rural area back then," she explained. "And most Jewish families were in settled places. Yes, almost any Jewish family would have a Kiddush cup, but not many would have such a fine silver one. They'd have to be fairly well off. And it's an awfully big coincidence for them to be living right near a battlefield."

"Good point." I nodded, turning the cup in my hands.

"Would a son have taken it with him to battle, so he could practice his faith?" Lewis asked. "Or might there have been a rabbi?"

"It's a good thought," Dina said. "But highly unlikely. Among the many things we Jews are good at is recordkeeping. I did a little nosing around last night to see if there was a congregation or a rabbi in the area at the time."

"Why am I not surprised?" I smiled at her.

"It's me." She shrugged. "I figured I might be able to find some background."

"And?" asked Lewis.

"And there were no Jewish congregations this far inland until the 19th century. So yes, we could have had a Jewish soldier, but it's highly unlikely that a family would send him to war with their finest silver kiddush cup."

"One that looks exactly like the one in the Jewish Museum," I added.

"Exactly like the one on the website." Lewis looked at it.

"And which is available as a solid-silver reproduction." I turned it over, showed them a rough spot on the bottom. "Does that look like something was filed off?"

"Somebody salted the site," Lewis said.

"Let's look at the other pieces before we draw any conclusions," I said, nodding to Lewis.

A pair of twinkling sounds from opposite sides of the room startled us all.

"Oh, that's me," Lewis said. "My dissertation advisor is in Ghana this summer, and we've been trying to connect for days."

"I've got to get back to the *shul* to prepare for a Torah study group," Dina said, pulling her phone out of her purse. "Can we talk more later?"

I nodded, as they took off in opposite directions. "The stuff's not going anywhere."

Chapter Fourteen: Afternoon Delights

The rest of the day was normal, or at least as normal as it could be, with Lewis working on his front-room exhibit, Jensen texting me, and the usual assortment of small but desperately important crises associated with running a local non-profit. Aside from those issues (how *was* that play, Mrs. Lincoln?) summer is pretty quiet at the Society, and we're informally closed in the afternoons.

The good news was, I had time for a phone call with Joe, who ducked out of an arraignment to get an update on the scene at the site.

"How'd it go?" I asked.

"Enough bail that the mope will think twice about violating his conditions on the D.U.I. You?"

"By the time we got there, the stuff was in a box—on Linley Stark's orders."

"Really. What do you make of that?"

"Could just be asserting control as the new boss. Could be trying to move the project ahead. The moving the stuff was interesting…but the stuff itself was a lot more."

"How so?" Two very curious syllables.

"Suspiciously perfect. Possibly not consistent with the local history of the time. Questionable at the very least."

"Think they faked it?"

"To be determined," I said. "I don't want to prejudice your investigation… so nothing more till I have a really good sense."

"That's fair. Thanks."

"Of course." As much as I enjoy playing with him, I like working with him, too.

"Only good thing about this case, *cara…*" Joe started.

"What?"

"Working with you."

"Jinx."

"Jinx?"

"It's what I was thinking."

He chuckled, with just a tiny kick of naughtiness. "I like reading your mind. Wonder what else is going on in there?"

"Mostly work right now, sad to say." I sighed.

"Pick up anything else that might be useful?"

"Not right now, but I'm keeping my ears open."

"Good. You see most of the witnesses every day."

"Well, if you're curious about everyone's impressions, you can join us for dinner in the garden at Garrett and Ed's tonight."

"Dinner?"

"Somebody has to eat the zucchini," I reminded him.

"Not me."

"You're not a fan of the zucc?"

"Gotta get moving," Joe said briskly. "What can I bring?"

"Your adorable self…and maybe berries from the farm stand on Route Ten?" I knew he'd pass it on his way home from New Haven, so it was an easy ask.

"You want berries, you got berries. See you tonight, *cara.*"

After we exchanged goodbyes with just a little spin, it was back to work.

And a pleasant surprise.

Just as I finished uploading the documentation on a couple of newly donated items—a late 19th-century crystal vase and silver card case, both Tiffany pieces from someone's great-aunt's estate—I heard a knock on the doorframe.

"Christian?" Amy Taylor poked her head in, with the warm smile she always gave me.

"Hi, Amy." I always felt a little weird addressing a *grande dame* by first name, but it was what she preferred, and I told myself I was showing appropriate respect by deferring to her choice.

"Had a moment to drop by on my way back from my Bat Mitzvah dress fitting at Miranda's."

"Wonderful." I stood as Amy moved aside and revealed that she wasn't alone.

A much less pleasant surprise.

Linley Stark was behind her, in a navy cotton shift, looking pale, gaunt, and jangly. All of which was absolutely her right. There's no one right way to widow.

I reminded myself that even though she's an entitled pain in the pantalets, she's grieving and deserves some space. "Hi, Linley."

"Hi, Christian." Her tone was listless, her expression pained.

One of those, I thought. The people who wear their losses like a crown and expect everyone around them to bow before it.

Amy glanced at her, and her mouth twisted ever so slightly. She turned to me with a little eyebrow flick that said it all. "I thought it might be a good idea for Linley to get out of the house for a bit."

I wasn't sure if it was classic New England getting on with it—or perhaps just a teensy bit of irritation at Linley's attitude, considering the incredible difficulties Amy had survived to get here—but either way, she clearly wanted to give Linley a shove in the right direction. And it was my job to help.

"Well," I said. "I think that's a great idea. We can always use more volunteers. Why don't you call me tomorrow, and we'll set up some times?"

"Um, okay." Linley shrugged. "I guess it would be good to do something."

"It would be very good," Amy said briskly. "If she doesn't call you by ten, call her."

"I'll do that," I promised. For Amy, I would. I'd be happy to let Linley rot in her living room till the mail piled up, but letting Amy down was not an option.

"Well, thank you so much, Christian. Linley is going to take me home and perhaps stay for some tea."

"I don't like tea, Aunt Amy."

"Coffee, then. It won't be as good as Christian's, but it'll do just fine." Amy gave me a grin and herded Linley to the door.

Just before she hit the foyer, she turned back. "Thanks, Christian. I appreciate it."

"Always glad to give back." I actually kind of was, considering I had a pretty deep cosmic debt from all the support my circle gave me after Frank's death.

"Thought you might be." She winked.

I winked back.

Chapter Fifteen: Somebody Has to Eat the Zucchini

There's nothing like a big family dinner in the garden.

Climate change notwithstanding, summer is still short enough in New England that we prize warm evenings when it's comfortable to eat outside. Outdoor grilling is a consuming seasonal passion for almost all males in the Nutmeg State and some of the females.

Ed and Garrett are no exception. As soon as it's warm enough to sit outside in the evening without layering up, they start inviting everyone over—and it continues into November. Though, usually, they're cooking on their own late in the season. It becomes a running joke as we all look for ways to not get stuck eating in the garden on cold nights—or trying to convince them to cook outside and eat inside.

But in July, it was high season, and nobody was looking to skip the party. Especially since they'd invested in both electric bug killers and citronella lanterns to give them a fighting chance against the evil bloodsucking invaders.

It's hard to argue. Their house is a truly beautiful old saltbox Garrett bought for a song decades ago. Ed is the handy one, and Garrett is the gardener, and between the gorgeous deck and the lush plantings, their backyard is wonderful. It's not elegant in a pretentious, Martha-Stewart-y way, but rather comfortable and welcoming. A perfect hangout for family and friends.

So it's no surprise we end up there at least once a week in warm weather.

Summer evenings like this are a bonus for New Englanders. I suppose people who live way down South take them for granted, but to us, the ability to gather in a backyard and eat fresh tomatoes with family and friends comes as a massive treat.

Especially since we didn't have to do much of anything.

The cookies Tiffany and I had made for the Fourth were still good, though the lemon meringue pie probably hadn't seen July 5th—Garrett and Ed are both stress eaters, though they'd deny it to the skies. Good, too, the sausage and peppers. Garrett picked new tomatoes, and I stopped at the grocery for more fresh mozz. Tiffany brought more chips and salsa, and we were all set.

Since it was no longer a giant Fourth feast, but a weeknight break, Dina and Ben brought a case of the New Haven-made soda that everybody loves, and Italian ice (regular and no-sugar-added!) to go with the cookies.

Hey, everything's better with Italian ice.

Even zucchini. That's the other great risk of dealing with home gardeners: you never leave their house without eating zucchini—and taking some home. Fortunately, I've discovered that Henry will eat them with ranch dip. Unfortunately, I made the mistake of telling Garrett and Ed, and now, whenever we're in the garden, there is zucchini with dip. Also, a separate shredded zucchini salad, because, as I said, there is much zucchini—and somebody has to eat it.

Garrett's prized Japanese irises were in bloom, nodding in a nice little breeze as Henry and I walked down the path. Joe had sent me a text that he would be late, but he'd be there as soon as he finished talking to his boss.

"...but I still think they're going to fall apart before the playoffs," Ed was saying to Ben, one of the three Mets fans in Connecticut.

Neither Ed nor Garrett is a serious baseball fan, but both can talk a good line during the season. Just about everyone can. Connecticut is right between New York and Red Sox Nation, and the split is just north of New Haven. Below that line, it's all Yankees...above, Sox. And baseball, along with weather, is one of the great social topics. Being able to talk a little light trash eases any conversation or event, and most of us learn very quickly how important it is to have something to say about the season.

Henry, a legacy Mets fan like his dad, is a proudly unusual bird, and usually disappointed. But, in common with all Mets fans and those who love them, he understands the heartbreak is the point.

You go into the season with the Mets knowing they will ultimately disappoint you, but they'll give you some wonderful moments along the way. There's some kind of life lesson in there. Plus, of course, the obvious expedient of learning to lose gracefully. A lot of grownups—not all famous ones—never do.

Henry jumped right into Ed and Ben's baseball talk, running over to join them as Ed supervised the sausage and peppers. Garrett was at the island on the other side of the deck, slicing some gorgeous tomatoes, red, green, and deep purple. He looked up and smiled at Henry, then turned to me.

"Now, this is more like it."

"Definitely." I handed him the container of mozzarella and watched as he laid the colorful tomato slices on the old china plate. Garrett's grandma's wedding set—he was the only son and last of the line, so he ended up with a lot of family pieces. "Gorgeous tomatoes."

I took a slice of zucchini from the platter beside it, skipping the ranch dip because I actually kind of like the taste, or at least texture, of fresh zucc.

"They're good this year. This one's Mortgage Lifter, that one's a Cherokee Purple, and those are Green Zebras. So far, the bunnies haven't destroyed them...Norm is doing a pretty good job of being menacing."

The alleged rabbit menacer was happily sprawled in the shade, watching Ed and making sure no stray pieces of sausage escaped.

"Sure," I said. "As long as it's working."

He laughed. "Oh, sooner or later, the deer and the bunnies will win. And we'll be back to the farmers' market."

"Yep. But that's life. And in the meantime, we have these. You should take a pic or two for one of those social media things they do."

"Already put up a nice display of today's crop, thanks." Garrett grinned. "Thinking about getting more active out there?"

"No, but I'm wondering if anything's happening in the virtual ozone."

"Nothing you don't already know about. Connecticut Flutter was pretty shocked by the explosion, figured Rowland Stark was a nasty person who deserved it, and by the way, there are a lot of folks out there who don't know how cannons work—or don't work."

"Pretty harsh," Dina said, walking over with two bottles of sugar-free lemon soda and handing one to me. "Henry isn't interested, as usual."

"Neither am I." Garrett had a glass of red wine waiting in the far corner of the butcher block.

"Do I see lemon soda?"

Tiffany was walking through the gate, Ava a half-step behind her.

"Indeed you do." Dina handed her the second bottle and turned back to the cooler for another one. "Nice to see you two."

Ava ran over to Henry, and the two quickly moved over to Norm, leaving Ed and Ben to the baseball talk. It had been a whole hour since they'd seen each other, not to mention hours since they'd petted Norm, and much catching up remained.

"How was the day?" I asked Tiffany, who'd traded her uniform for capris and a loose coral scroll print polo, her expression a good bit less stressed than that morning's.

"Actually, pretty simple. A few transports and one minor crash. Nothing too serious. Nice break after everything we had this week. Even got out on time. Too bad Jorge's doing a double. He could have used a break, too."

"That's right." I nodded. "They had that ugly crackup at the I-91/95 split today."

"Fuel spill," Tiffany shook her head. "He's going to be out there for hours."

"Well, we'll send you home with some sausage and peppers and, of course, zucchini."

"Of course." Tiffany's eyes sparkled. "Perfect."

"Perfect indeed." Garrett is in on the zucchini joke. He picked up the platter of tomatoes and mozz, a truly perfect caprese. "Why don't we head over to the table with our veggies and watch Ed show off his grilling prowess?"

"Sounds good." I picked up the plate of zucchini and dip, and Tiffany took the bowl of shredded zucchini salad. It was actually pretty decent, with a nice herby vinaigrette. It was just that there was an awful lot of zucchini these days.

"Well, what a lovely sight you all are," Ed said, as he dished sausage, onions, and peppers into a giant platter. Father to two daughters and honorary dad to me, he more than understood that a good compliment is always a perfect way to start an evening.

Everyone smiled.

None of us had done anything beyond adding an extra swipe of tinted lip balm, but we all smiled and thanked Ed, who beamed.

"How do you feel about sausage and peppers?" he asked, holding up the platter.

"Yum!" called Henry, echoed by Ava, as they ran over, with Norm trailing right behind them.

"Woof!" Norm was clearly hoping for more stray sausage. Well, he's a New Haven County native. Why not?

"Take a roll and pass 'em down, Doc," Garrett said to Ben, as he sat beside Dina. "Dinner, as they say, is served."

"Oh, good, I'm not too late."

Everyone turned to see Joe and Cannoli. The human had a leash in one hand and a big basket in the other.

"Well, hello, Counselor," Garrett said, rising to shake his hand. Ed was still up and turned for an equally friendly greeting.

"I was told berries would be a good thing to bring, and these were the best of the bunch."

He held out the wooden basket of large, perfect blueberries, the kind you only see in high summer, deep blue black with that nice little frost on them.

"Oh, don't those look good," Dina said.

"Delicious." I reached for one.

"Not till they're rinsed." Tiffany smacked my fingers.

I looked at her.

"You want to know how many people I have to drag over to New Haven with dehydration from e-coli from unwashed fruit?"

I sighed. "You're right."

"Of course I am." She grinned. "But once they're clean, they'll be wonderful with the cookies and Italian ice."

"Nice choice, Joe." Ed, who was closest to the cooler, handed him a soda. "We've got stronger stuff if you want it."

"Better not. I'm going back to looking at Rowland Stark's financials after this. No rest for the wicked."

He subtly cut his eyes to me, clearly a low-key way to explain that the evening was not going to end in any fun way.

"Or anyone else," Ben chuckled, raising his soda bottle. "I have to work on a journal article this evening."

"So do I," I added, with a nod to Joe. "Roughing out a piece on corsets."

Ben and Joe's eyes lit up. Garrett and Ed chuckled.

There is something about straight men and corsets. Even progressive, modern-minded ones can't help being drawn to the idea.

"Well," Ben said. "Mine's about ways to heal corneal abrasions in older patients. Probably not quite as much fun."

Everyone laughed.

"Then, since there seems to be a lot of important work to do this evening," Garrett said, "we'd better get down to dinner."

And so we did.

During the meal, we kept the conversation determinedly light and social. It's an unwritten agreement that when kids are at the table, we include them and keep the content as clean as possible in a busy modern world.

It's good social training for the kids, and the grownups, too. Not to mention fun and relaxing. There's nothing wrong with taking a break from death and destruction—or politics and religion, for that matter—while you're attempting to enjoy a good meal with your family of blood and/or affection.

And I'll happily take a nice friendly argument about *Frasier* versus *Cheers* or Sayers versus Christie with my caprese anytime.

It was only after everyone (including Norm and even Cannoli) had their fill of sausage and peppers, caprese and zucchini, and we'd adjourned to the chairs under the trees, leaving the kids at the table with their ices and Norm, that topics returned to the uglier end of the spectrum.

"So, how's the Rowland Stark investigation going?" Ed asked Joe, handing him another soda.

"Could be worse," Joe replied as he gave Cannoli a scratch behind the ears, the sort of careful acknowledgment everyone expected from a prosecutor. We were all savvy enough not to ask him questions he couldn't answer—but he might need a little while to realize the fact. "Could be a lot better, too."

"Social media seems to have decided that Stark was asking for it," Garrett observed.

"What a terrible thing to say." Dina glared at him.

"I didn't say I agreed with it. I just said it exists," Garrett shrugged. "Surely you're not as out-of-touch as Christian about this stuff."

"Sadly, no. I have two twenty-year-olds." Dina nodded. "I know people say, and believe, the most dreadful things out there. So it's no real surprise that folks are saying that."

"Still ugly," Tiffany said. "If the family sees of it..."

Quiet nods.

"Is this just the usual social media snarking, or is there something else involved?" Joe asked.

Garrett took a sip of his wine—the same glass he'd been nursing all through dinner. It's fair to say he is not a heavy drinker. "I think there may be more going on...but it's hard to say."

"Can you send me some screenshots?" Joe asked.

"Sure. I'll get my phone."

Ed scowled a little. In addition to the conversational standards, we have a strict no-tech rule at dinner.

"It's a criminal matter, which is an exception," Garrett said, reaching for the phone, which had been parked behind one of the bug snuffer lights. "Let's see what we've got here..."

Chapter Sixteen: Cannon Fodder

Friday morning found Lewis and me busy at the Society, with him working on his front room exhibit and me sifting through a pile of papers.

He'd been on the porch when I walked over after seeing Henry to the camp bus, reading a book, and trying to look nonchalant, not that anyone is nonchalant before their first exhibit.

No surprise, Lewis had at least a mild, and insanely early, case of pregame nerves, but he was handling it in the best possible way: focusing on producing a good display, rather than sitting around vexing.

I expected the morning to heat up a bit, no pun intended, once the volunteers started arriving, but it began with some rare quiet time. After Lewis was settled in, going over inventories to find pieces that fit his ideas, I slipped back to the office, made a pot of good coffee, and started in for a little work on that journal article on corsets, with the Empress supervising from the bookshelf.

"Hard at work, *Dottore*?"

Joe stood in the doorway, in his usual morning look, of mostly-buttoned oxford with no tie, damp hair, and a few shadows under his eyes.

Wonderful as always.

If I spared a passing thought for the idea of waking up with him, it was entirely my business. Entirely.

"Not that hard at work," I said. "Always have time for you. Coffee?"

"Yes, please. Up way too late trying to sort out Rowland Stark's financials."
He poured himself a cup and sat down in one of the side chairs.

The Empress jumped down, gave him a sniff, accepted a pat, and flounced on to her next important engagement.

"That difficult?"

"Yeah. Wife isn't being forthcoming—keeps getting fluttery and claiming she doesn't know anything. There are at least two different accountants involved, and one of them died from the blast."

"What?"

"You didn't know?" Joe asked.

"No. The heart attack victim was Stark's accountant?"

"Yeah."

We stared at each other long enough for me to become aware of the grandfather clock ticking.

"That can't be a coincidence…can it?" he asked.

"Cops and prosecutors hate coincidences," I said.

"But how can it be anything else? Even if he had a weak heart—and I haven't seen the autopsy yet, so I don't know—someone would have to make sure he was there."

"Someone who was in on it and who had something to gain by removing the accountant."

"Tiffany's right about hinky, isn't she?"

I nodded. "There are more questions here."

"Just what I need." Joe sipped his coffee and contemplated for a few comfortable moments. "The good news is, that armorer pal of yours surfaced this morning."

"Already?"

"Something about a dawn re-enactment somewhere? No idea. Anyhow, he got my email and thought it was important, so he called right after seven."

"That's great."

"Yep. Going to send him my pics from the scene and get an idea of what he thinks. He's pretty sure the problem wasn't in the cannon."

"I thought so," I said. "If it were, the cannon—and most of us—would have been in smithereens," I reminded him. "As bad as it was, it wasn't nearly as bad as it could have been if the whole cannon had blown."

"Right." Joe nodded. "Even a blank load has plenty of gunpowder."

"No boom without it." I took a sip of my coffee. "But I'm sure Blake Talley told you it has to be carefully calibrated."

"He did. He explained the process very well. I think something happened with the linstock."

"It's just a fuse."

"Unless it wasn't." Joe studied his coffee. "I'm not sure if it's even possible. Could the linstock somehow be rigged to explode?"

"Not with any of the usual things on the setup." I thought about it. "You should probably run that past Blake."

"I will. Just thought you might know."

"Blake's better," I said.

Joe looked up from the coffee. "Is he, now?"

Oh, hell. Blushing, and couldn't stop it.

"Something you want to tell me?"

"No." I sighed. "Okay. I had a crush on the guy when I interned there. Nothing ever came of it—and it was almost twenty years ago, anyhow."

"Ah. You like men with big guns, huh?" His eyes sparkled. "Nothing wrong with that."

The problem with Scottish fish belly-white skin is that a blush isn't a flush, but an eruption. "I do like my weaponry."

"Good to know." A grin. "Blake sends his compliments."

"I bet he does."

"No, really. He's pretty impressed with your work. And you." Joe didn't sound jealous, just factual. "Kind of neat. It's nice when someone you knew as a kid succeeds. Once in a while, I find myself going up against people who were junior associates at Magen and Renzulli. Always good."

"Especially when you win."

"Oh, always then." He drank a little more coffee. "Blake's married with four kids, oldest starting college, if you were wondering."

"I wasn't."

"Good." He held my gaze. "Really good."

"You know…" I started. I wasn't really sure what to say, or how.

"I know." He drank some coffee. Smiled again. "We've both had lives before this. I won't ask you about Mr. Big Gun Blake Talley, if you don't ask me about Anna-Maria Righetti and homecoming night."

"Fair enough." I drank a little coffee. "Should we go look at the cannon?"

"You can check my weapons anytime."

A pause. A grin I felt down to my toes.

"I'll take you up on that soon." I got up, put down my coffee cup, and picked up the key. Joe unfolded himself from the side chair, towering over me a little. For a moment, we just stood there, enjoying each other. Frank had a huge heart and presence, but he wasn't a big man. Joe's sheer size is different and somehow both comforting and exciting.

I'm not sure why, but it's helpful that he's the opposite of Frank in the visual. He's more like Frank than I'd ever tell him in other ways: both smart, standup guys and very comfortable walking the line between protecting a woman and respecting her independence.

Joe was watching me, too.

"What?" I asked.

"Nothing. Just like looking at you."

"I like looking at you looking at me."

Joe laughed. "I like—"

"I like both of you." Faith Stowe said with a laugh of her own as she walked into the office.

Joe and I stepped back a bit, and he blushed a little, too.

Faith gave us an indulgent look, as if we were adorable children. Oh, no...we're not cute, are we? Ugh.

I tried for a professional demeanor. "I'm just taking Mr. Poli out to see the cannon in the shed for a moment, and then I'll be back."

"Nice to see you, Mrs. Stowe," Joe said, holding out a hand for a shake.

"Nice to see you, Mr. Poli." She shook and very lightly cut her eyes to me. "Glad you are taking an interest in local history."

"Well, when it's so beautifully presented, it's hard to resist."

They smiled together, both enjoying the play.

"See you when you get back from the shed, Christian. Make sure you get a good look at the cannon." She shot me a wink behind Joe's back.

Outside, Joe gave me a wicked little smile. "Cannon."

"We're all very into armaments around here."

"Bet you are."

The shed, a real old wooden shack, not one of the cute little house thingies that pass for sheds these days, belonged to the town public works department, but they kept a collection of vintage seasonal things there, like the Colonial flag from the Bicentennial, the World War One-era posters they put up for Veteran's Day, and the old pewter lanterns that decorate Town Hall during the holiday season. Because they were old things, someone decided the Historical Society should have access to them and gave us the keys.

I supposed I should be flattered, but honestly, it was no thrill to have to let the cannon guys, the VFW Auxiliary, the Lantern Ladies (yes, their real name), and any number of others into the shed whenever they needed something.

I unlocked the door and held it for Joe.

"Whoof! Hot in here," he said.

"Tin roof concentrates the heat—even this early in the day. You don't want to be here in the afternoon."

"No." He glanced at the boxes and rolls and banners. "Do they keep everything in here?"

"Everything they can't find another home for." I shrugged. "If you notice a resemblance to an Ancient Egyptian tomb, you're not wrong."

"Right." He nodded. "That picture of King Tut's tomb with everything just thrown in any which way."

"Yup. A month or so from now, we'd have to excavate to find the cannon— they'll throw the summer light-pole banners in here and who knows what else."

"Well, then, it's a good time to be here." He unclipped his phone from his belt. "Let's take a look."

The cannon, as it had when I walked past it on my way out of the Green that afternoon, looked surprisingly undamaged. There were some scratches on the barrel and a little charring by the fuse hole, but that was all. I moved toward the end.

Joe grabbed my arm. "Careful."

"It's not like a gun. It doesn't just go off without the whole long process."

"Still. Please be careful."

"Of course. Give me your phone. I'll take a pic or two of the inside."

He handed it over. "I don't like this."

"Duly noted." I aimed the camera and light inside. And saw something surprising. "It's been unloaded."

"What?"

"Somebody unloaded this."

"They did?" He leaned down to look. "Get a pic."

"I am. I'll zoom it to the back."

"Please."

I snapped a couple of shots. As I got to my feet, Joe put an unnecessary, but welcome hand on my arm to "help" me up.

"Here you go." I handed him the phone. "Make sure you send the one of the back of the barrel to Blake. I don't think there's anything to see, but he's the expert."

"Which means what?"

"I'm not sure. It could just be that the cannon guys unloaded and cleaned it up before putting it away earlier this week."

"Can you check that out? I know they hang around the Society."

"Sure. Not a problem. I wanted to ask them about the strip mall dispute anyhow."

"Why?" Puzzled glance.

"They've been here forever, so they'll know everything there is to know about it."

"Good idea. What do I have to offer you to get an update later?"

I smiled. "Call me before you pick up Aly this afternoon."

"Come see us this evening." His tone was casual, but his gaze was serious. "It's a legitimate excuse for you and Henry to drop by for a few minutes. Say hi, everyone meets?"

"Could work," I said carefully.

"Good." He beamed. "Why don't you just come over after *shul*? We'll be done with dinner and into father-daughter movie time by then."

"Works for me."

Our eyes held.

The little dust motes in the hot air of the shed suddenly seemed more like glitter, and the temperature went up at least a couple of degrees.

It was the literal definition of one hot second.

And then Joe's phone rang.

"Um, yeah," he said. "Gotta get back to work. See you tonight."

"Yeah." I cleared my throat and pulled the shed key out of my blazer pocket. "I have to find something to do with Linley."

"Why?"

Back to business. Safer.

"Amy brought her by yesterday. Apparently trying to keep her busy. Probably good for the construction crew, anyhow."

"Yeah. Why did she jump in like that?"

"Doing something—anything — sometimes helps after an unexpected loss," I said, surprised to hear my voice softening a little on the last two words.

"You know this." He put a hand on my arm, just reassurance.

"Yeah. Everyone handles it differently, but some people need to be a whirlwind."

"Even just a couple days after?"

"If you keep moving, you don't have to stop and acknowledge the loss. For some people, it's a really good coping mechanism…right up until it's not."

"So I shouldn't take anything from this."

"No." I shrugged. "I don't think so. Let me get a sense of her and get back to you."

"Fair enough." He patted my arm. "And find out about when the cannon was unloaded."

"Will do."

As I locked the door, he put a hand on my arm again and leaned in for a quick kiss on the cheek. "Later, *cara*."

"Later."

Back at the Society, the pile of papers had gotten no smaller. Not that I was going to get to it—for a very happy reason.

Chapter Seventeen: Bundles of Joy, Parcels of Trouble

My three fiber artists from Town Hall came over at lunch that day, fizzing with excitement. Allie had asked me to get out some whitework, but she hadn't told me why. Something in the sheer happiness of her tone pointed me in a direction, though, and I made sure to mix a couple of christening dresses and caps in the half-dozen or so pieces of bright white lawn embellished with various tiny flower and vine designs in equally pristine thread. Lovely stuff, but still relatively easy to keep clean, since it's all cotton and thus bleachable.

Allie and Deborah arrived first, practically bouncing like little girls. It was comical on Allie, a dark-haired twentysomething trying for dignity in her first big job…but really funny on Deborah, the Registrar of Voters, cool ash-blonde, and normally supremely professional.

"So…is there news?" I asked, pointedly smoothing a christening gown with a daisy motif.

"Yes, there is!" Allie motioned to the door, as Bethany walked in. "Meet the grandma to be!"

"Oh, congratulations!" I walked over to her, holding out my hands. We're New Englanders and not huggy, after all, but this was a special moment, and she pulled me right in.

"I'm so happy." Her black eyes were sparkling, and her ebony skin shining with a glow no highlighter could produce. "My son told me last night, and I told these two this morning. So of course, we had to come over and start looking for ideas."

"The christening gown is probably the most elaborate piece," I said. "So you'll probably want to make that first, and then start work on other things, like blankets and perhaps other clothes."

"Makes sense to me." Deborah held up the other gown and cap set. "These little roses are amazing."

"That was for a girl named Rose. Somebody put a lot of thought and love into it," I told her. It was probably our prettiest one, donated by Rose herself, when she was a grandmother moving into a smaller place more than sixty years later.

"Do you know…" Deborah started carefully.

"Girl!" Bethany announced. "They decided they wanted to know, and I'm glad for that, too."

Henry had been a surprise, though Frank and I had had a side bet. He won. But whatever works—and Bethany's absolute joy was wonderful to see.

She took up the rose gown. "This is a real beauty…though the daisies are pretty too."

"You could also use the leaf and vine motif on this shirtwaist, or the lacework on this collar," Deborah said. "Or any combination."

"No bad choice." Allie held up a handkerchief with an especially elaborate pattern. "You could take some of these here and combine them with the others."

"Can you move the patterns around, Christian?" Bethany asked.

"Sure. Remember that nifty software I used for the pattern for Allie's wedding gown?" The three had worked together on a unique and gorgeous forget-me-not decoration for the bride, giving her something incredibly special for her big day.

"Two weeks!" Deborah said, elbowing Allie.

A shared laugh.

"All I have to do is take some photos and load them into the computer, and I can pretty much come up with anything you'd like."

"Wonderful." Bethany studied the pieces. "So, we could copy that beautiful rose design from the bodice, and do the daisy sleeves, and maybe edge it all with some of those swirly leaves?"

"Sure can."

"Ladies, we have a winner!" Deborah proclaimed.

"We've still got half an hour," Allie said. "Can we watch you use the program, Christian?"

Indeed, they could. The four of us happily worked up the pattern for Bethany's grandbaby, and I was delighted to send them home with it.

As I walked them out to the porch, I slowed down beside Deborah, remembering her husband was not only on the cannon crew, but the assistant chief of the volunteer fire department. Sometimes, these small-town connections come in handy.

"What's up?" she asked.

"You're maddeningly good," I said.

"Honey, I'm a town official and a mother of four. If I didn't know when someone wants to talk to me, there would be something wrong."

"Too true." I laughed. "Nothing too serious. Just wondering if I can borrow Charlie's expertise for a few minutes."

"Got a friend who needs a little insight on the cannon crew?"

"Yep." Of course, I was blushing. "He's trying to get a sense of what was supposed to happen, and what did…and I don't know enough about cannons."

Deborah's friendly smile widened to something naughty. "Probably better I don't say what I'm thinking about cannons."

"You're awfully kind."

"Nah. I've already made every imaginable comment to Charlie about Dr. Freud, to no avail."

I joined her naughty smile. "I bet it's hard not to."

"Sure is. And the guys make it just too easy. But after a quarter-century with those crazy Paul Revere boots under my bed, I'm used to it." She sighed. "Anyhow, Charlie has help at the store today, so I'll send him over."

"Thanks. I'll make sure there's coffee."

"He'll appreciate it…and he'll love schooling you about the cannon crew."

"I appreciate it."

"Of course." Deborah smiled. "Always glad to help."

Half an hour later, I was busy prowling around the internet looking for ideas on my corset article, when Ted and Mike, two of the three members of the VFW's Historic Equipment Committee, appeared. At least a couple times a week, they showed up to maintain our excellent collection of uniforms and assorted other donated items. Both retired businessmen, and both infantry vets, they didn't have much patience for the cannon re-enactment, or much insight on it. But, thanks to their local connections, they had many useful thoughts on Rowland Stark, and, surprisingly, Amy Taylor—which I'd be happy to share with Joe.

Once the VFW guys headed upstairs, I went back to the office and returned to corsets. There's actually a lot more going on with them than you think; styles evolved over the years, with silhouettes to shape the wearer's body for the current fashions and materials that were often state-of-the-art. Starched fabric augmented by whalebone stays, and eventually thin steel ones. Steel reminded me corsets were seen as a form of armor, often a woman's defense against assaults on her virtue. During the Russian Imperial Family's final captivity, Empress Alexandra ordered her daughters to keep their corsets on at all times. Yes, some of it was because their jewels were sewn into them…but some of it was the daily contact with swaggering Bolshevik soldiers.

Not that a corset would have been much help to those poor young women…

"Dr. Shaw?"

I was more than glad to return to the present, with the friendly face of Deborah's husband, Charlie, at my door.

"Hey! You know I don't use the title," I reminded him. While we didn't know each other very well, no one other than the occasional hopeful telephone solicitor, calls me Dr. Shaw. But Charlie, who ran the cast-iron stove store that had been in his family for at least three generations, was old-school. Each time we met, he opened with the title, and I told him not to use it, world without end, amen.

Formalities covered, I stood up, shook his hand, and waved him into the office.

"Thanks for coming over," I said. "I've got coffee."

"Good. I need it. Nasty little brush fire over at the Corderos' last night. Kept us up all night, but we knocked it down."

"Terrific."

Low-key grin. "Good night's work. So Deb tells me you want to talk a little about the cannon and such?"

"Yes, please." I reached for the mugs. "I'm sure you won't take this as a bribe."

"Encouragement." Charlie happily accepted the mug. "And I don't mind clueing you in on Rowland Stark. Not a bit."

"No?"

"Nope. Don't mind this getting back to that nice young State's Attorney."

He gave me a significant grin, much like Deborah's. "Bout time both of you had a little happiness."

"Thanks."

"'Nuff said on that. It's neither here nor there right now." Charlie's friendly face turned deadly serious. "That SOB Rowland almost got us all killed. Sorry, Christian."

"What?"

"I'm sure it was no accident. Half the town has been gunning for him over the strip mall for years. And then he screwed over Brad Majeskie and Greg Collier."

"What…"

"Didn't pay them for the work they did on that plaza up in Ansonia. Brad could lose his house. Greg's mom is going to end up in some public home because he can't get private dementia care. Those are just the ones I know about. Probably cheated a bunch of other folks, too."

"Awful." I didn't know the Majeskies well—their Saint Bernard was legendary for destroying bedding plants, but I'd probably only met them once or twice. The Collier kids were a few grades ahead of Henry and absolute hell on wheels. Neither family deserved to be run into the ground by Rowland Stark.

And Charlie was probably right. There might well be any number of people who had cause to kill Rowland.

"Yeah, it is." Charlie drank a little coffee.

I waited.

"Honestly, Christian, I know it sounds awful, but maybe we don't need to know if it wasn't an accident."

"You know, for fire scenes. What do you think?"

"I'm not an explosives guy. I'm a get the people out and hose it down guy. It looked to me like the linstock went up, and I don't know how that happens."

"I studied cannons," I said. "I don't either."

"Right. But the cannon seemed okay. We unloaded it after the scene was released. Seemed safest."

"I agree." I thought of something. "Where did you put the ball?"

"Should be in the shed. One of the guys took it. Don't remember who."

"Ah." I didn't think he'd lie to my face, but he might shade it to protect a friend. Especially if he thought Rowland's death was justified. Or at least deserved.

"Understandable. It was traumatic."

"It was. Even for me." Charlie shook his head. "I've seen some bad scenes but that was different."

"Yep." I drank some of my own coffee. "Anyhow, on a much happier topic, did Deborah tell you why they dropped by here at lunch?"

"No. Figured more embroidery stuff, whatever."

"Yeah…but Bethany is going to be a grandma—to a girl."

Charlie smiled, grateful for the subject change. "Thanks for the heads up, Christian. I can warn Junior. Poor guy only just got a job at UCONN Medical Center. He deserves to have a little fun before he gives his mom a grandbaby."

"Figured." After Deborah's wistful comment about having to wait, it was only fair.

"Gonna have to distract her."

"Well, maybe she can take out her frilly impulses on Bethany's granddaughter for a while."

"Good thought." He drank the last of his coffee. "I'll try that."

"Good luck." *To both of us.*

The rest of the day was a whirlwind.

I never did get back to the corsets, between Lewis hitting a research snag, the Empress having a spectacular hairball attack in the middle of an 1870s Turkish rug, and a call from Victoria Peters, who wanted me to find a "smart but not overly woke" anti-bias training program for the board.

I've never been so grateful for camp bus time.

Tiffany walked up just as I did, looking absolutely lovely in a bright pink print dress in the perfect shade to make her skin and hair glow. Plus, it hit just above the knee, showing off the warm gold of the spiffy new self-tanner she'd found a couple weeks ago.

"Well," I said, "I hope Jorge is off tonight."

Her face lit up. "Oh, he is. It's family dinner—and mom and dad private time later. The first words I expect to hear when he walks in are *'Ay, mami.'*"

"Nice." I joined her grin. "That's right. He's bilingual."

"In the best possible way."

"I think Joe is too." I could feel the start of a blush, but if anyone could give me a little insight on Joe's unexpected slips into Italian, it would be Tiffany.

"Really?"

"Well, the other night, at first, I thought he'd called me by the wrong name—Cara...and then I realized he was saying *'cara mia.'*"

"Oh, that's nice."

"It threw me a little, but I thought so."

"Chill, Christian." Tiffany chuckled. "It *is* a very good sign. Jorge switches to Spanish when he's happy and comfortable. Or...interested."

"That's it, exactly."

"More than that, though," she said. "He feels safe with you. One more sign that he's serious about you."

"I'm serious about him, too."

"Figured."

"Henry and I are swinging by his house this evening, just for a couple of minutes, for me to give him a little info on the cannon crew. And to meet Aly, very low-key."

"I like it." Tiffany grinned. "Nice idea to keep it very casual—so it doesn't seem like a major deal to the kids."

"Definitely."

Ruby and Lidia turned the corner.

"Looking pretty."

"Love the dress."

Tiffany got maybe a full thirty seconds to enjoy the compliments before Sally minced onto the scene. She was in a thin beige sweater dress and nude patent pumps, her hair blown out to humidity-defying smoothness, her no-makeup-makeup perfect.

"Oh, I hope the bus is on time tonight. We need to drop the kids off with the grandparents. Malcolm and I have a getaway weekend at the Saybrook Inn."

Of course, they do.

Everyone managed to feign interest for the minute or so that it took for the camp bus to make it down from the corner. Much longer, and we would have had a hard time hiding the eye rolls.

Apparently, Sally and the accountant hubs were marking their engagement anniversary with a special night. Or something like that. I didn't pay too much attention. The only thing that did stick was her comment that the town was looking for new ideas for the site originally planned for Rowland Stark's outlet mall boondoggle…and people in the neighborhood—like Tiffany— might see their values going up.

It always comes back to property values when Sally's around.

No one betrayed even a trace of amusement when her son Douglas threw himself at Sally and left two giant dirty handprints on her back. She'd earned it.

Henry was every bit as much of a mess as his campmates, but dust doesn't show as badly on khakis, and I'd been smart enough to leave my cream linen blazer at the Society. Ava, as girly as her mom is off duty, held up hands for a high-five and praised the dress. All good.

The next few hours were feeding, cleaning up, and getting to *shul*, and then the spiritual and social comfort of the service. Especially nice after the week we'd had.

After the service, Dina and Ben were busy talking to some folks they hadn't seen all week, and Henry and I settled for quick hugs and a couple of words. There would be coffee and a good long conversation sometime in the next few days.

And with a visit to Joe and Aly next on my agenda, it was entirely possible we'd have something to discuss.

Chapter Eighteen: Happy Family Moments

We drove, even though my little cobalt-blue compact was probably embarrassed to be seen here in the McMansion district. It's maybe a fifteen-minute walk, or a shorter jog, from the historical area, but it's a whole different world. Long ago, New England farms gave way to suburbia in most of Unity, with developments of varying style and quality surrounding the center of town.

Many, like Tiffany's neighborhood, are nice, comfortable middle-class homes. Nothing fancy, but definitely a source of pleasure and pride for the folks who live there.

The McMansion area is different. These are the showplaces. Many of them have been featured on those Sunday morning real estate shows that keep the local TV stations in business. Whatever the particulars of a given house, they're all big and elegant—and you can *see* the money.

I'd known Joe lived on Trelawney, and if I'd wanted to, I could have driven by his house anytime in the last couple of months to see what it looked like. I hadn't because it wasn't especially important to me. He'd been a high-end lawyer married to a particular kind of woman, so I had a rough idea of what it meant.

The actual reality, though, still came as something of a shock.

Joe's house was vanilla brick, with a big bay window on one side, a huge, two-story window on the other, a curved driveway, and a golden-wood door with a large half-moon of stained glass. The silver sedan with the TRUBILL tag (a witty reference to an indictment, a "true bill") was parked in front, so I knew I was at the right place.

Henry whistled. "Looks like AlysDad has a nice crib, Ma."

"Well, remember, he worked at a big fancy law firm in New Haven for a while. Probably needed the space for parties with his co-workers and things."

"Yeah, okay." He looked around as we walked up the path to the door. "Awful big house. Bet he gets lonely when Aly isn't here."

"I'm pretty sure he does, sweetheart." I ruffled his hair, and then rang the bell.

The door opened before the little electronic jingle ended.

"Hi, Henry, Dr. Shaw. Dad's on the phone. He'll be right out." Alyson Poli, fifteen and feisty, gave us a cheerful greeting. She has her dad's smile and brown eyes, and wavy caramel-colored hair, probably from her mom. Since it was a warm Friday evening, she was wearing leggings and a rainbow "How Dare You Assume I'm Straight" tee with the logo of the Southport High Gay-Straight Alliance.

Her dad, who had become a Justice of the Peace just so he could marry his sister and her wife, would have no trouble with the allyship...but he might take issue with the way she expressed it. Or not. None of my business either way.

"Hey, Aly," Henry said. "How's high school?"

"Pretty great so far. I'm doing a sleepaway music camp program starting next week. You know I play sax, right?"

"That's very cool," I said. "Band is a lot of fun."

"Jazz band sure is." Aly grinned. "I love to improvise."

"This girl can blow a horn, in case you didn't know," Joe said, as he walked into the foyer. He'd unbuttoned the top two buttons of his oxford and rolled up the sleeves, and his hair was a little mussed. I'd forgotten how attractive that whole after-work loosening-up thing can be.

I was very glad I'd worn a pretty coral-and-white print skirt and matching sweater and neatened up my hair and lipstick for *shul*.

"Come in and stay a bit," Joe said.

It was only then I realized the two-story window was behind us, spilling warm evening light into the room, and noticed the huge staircase winding down from the second floor, blond wood polished to a radiant sheen. There was a big mirror on one wall, and a huge modern light fixture made of wavy creamy-white pieces of glass dangled from the ceiling.

The inside was as expensive and intimidating as the outside. At least to me.

"Henry, I'm guessing Aly would happily play a round of Uno with you while Dr. Shaw gives me an update on the cannon crew."

Aly, who was clearly informed and on board, shepherded Henry into what looked like a very beige living room.

"This is all Amber's decorating," Joe said, waving to the foyer. "It makes me itch, but I haven't had time to get rid of it, and I don't know what I'd do anyhow."

"It's a lot of beige," I admitted.

"It is." He smiled. "But I wanted the house because Mama's here in town, and Aly still has friends."

"Makes sense."

"Besides, she was moving to Southport anyhow." He shrugged.

The shrug suggested he didn't want to talk about it. Fine by me since I had no idea what to say.

"C'mere," Joe said, moving on, and resting a hand on my arm. "Take you to the best room in the house."

Of course, it was the kitchen.

Yes, it was large, and the appliances were well out of my price range, but there was an assortment of kid-friendly snacks on the island, a school calendar on the fridge, and two mugs and a fresh pot of coffee on the big farmhouse table. It reminded me more of my grandma than Martha Stewart.

"This is a lot more comfortable," Joe said, motioning to one of the chairs, which had soft blue-check padded seats. "Only room where I had some say."

"Yeah?"

"Yeah." He sat, too. "I left the rest of the house to Amber—she knew what she wanted, and it wasn't worth fighting over. But the kitchen? I wanted something like Mama's, even if we had to have the big-name appliances."

"I like it," I said. "It definitely hits that."

"I think so, too." He poured coffee into one of the mugs, plain, thick white china—an upgraded version of diner standard—and handed it to me. "Figured a little coffee is never a bad thing."

"Nah. I'm not one of those folks who drinks decaf at night."

He poured his own cup. "Me either. And I have to get back to work once Aly's down."

"Do fifteen-year-olds actually go to sleep on weekend nights?"

"No, but she dismisses me at about ten and heads off with a book. Which she actually reads—so I can't complain too much."

"Not at all. Sounds like you have a grounded one."

"Mostly. Despite everything." Joe turned the coffee mug in his hands for a moment. "It's that old Jacqueline Kennedy saying—if you screw up raising your kids…"

"It doesn't matter what else you get right." I nodded. "I agree."

We shared a smile.

"So I'd like to enjoy the happy family moment for a while," he said, "but I bet you have useful info—and a night with your boy to get to."

"The only thing on Henry's and my schedule is a planet documentary…and letting Cookie re-scent him after being over here with Cannoli. But yeah. You need your time with Aly. That's important."

"Incredibly. When she was born, it never occurred to me that I might someday have to sleep in a house without her in it…at least not until she was grown."

"Tough stuff." I reached over and patted his hand, and he twined fingers with mine for a moment.

"Uno!"

The call from the living room pulled us both back, and we shared another smile.

"So before we have to stop a war, what did you learn from the cannon guys?" He slowly pulled his fingers away and picked up his coffee mug. Almost like he wanted to have something to do with his hands.

Hmm.

"Well," I said, picking up my own mug, "they did indeed put the cannon back in the shed after the Staties released the scene. They also unloaded it."

"Was that really safe?"

"Apparently, there's a safe way to do it, and a couple of the guys are volunteer firefighters, so it wasn't as insane as it sounds."

"Only slightly reckless."

"Something like that." I took a sip of coffee. No surprise, it was good Italian dark roast. "You'll still want to get Blake's opinion on the cannon."

"I've sent him the pics, so that's in progress."

"Good."

"Did Charlie the cannon guy have any further thoughts on the strip mall thing?" he asked.

"No, but my two fellas from the VFW did."

Joe waited.

"You know we have a few guys from the VFW who maintain our military artifacts."

"Right."

"We actually have a pretty good collection for a small museum—from Civil War stuff to a whole lot of World War II pieces." I shrugged. "The important thing here is that most of the cataloguing and curation work is done by a small team from the post. Military history isn't my field."

"Makes sense. If you have good volunteers, use them."

"Exactly. And these guys are good. Motivated to preserve their legacy. That was just a little background. Probably more than you needed."

"It's okay. I like listening to you talk, *Dottore*."

"I like listening to *you* talk. Sometime, I'm going to come to New Haven and watch you do opening or closing arguments."

"Yeah?"

"Yeah. If that's okay with you."

"More than okay. Amber never—um, sorry. Not fair to do that." He squirmed a little and took a sip of coffee.

"I understand. There's stuff sometimes." I shrugged. "Part of being grownups who aren't doing this for the first time."

"Not a bad thing."

"Nope. Just a thing."

"Okay." He reached for my hand again. "So you have an open invite to watch arguments, and I really do need to know about this whole strip mall battle."

"Sound good." I squeezed his fingers and released them. "Well, Rowland bought the land maybe ten years ago, and it's been a fight ever since."

"Right."

"And there's a pretty well-organized opposition who's been studying records for years to prove that it's a Revolutionary War site."

"How organized?"

"There's a formal group, and they have enough money to use a lawyer off and on, and enough time to comb over all the adjacent properties. And here is where it gets interesting."

"Interesting?" asked Joe.

"Potentially interesting anyhow. Turns out the next parcel is part of the Taylor family trust."

"As in Amy Taylor, the Bat Mitzvah girl?"

"None other. Also as in Linley and Jensen's great-aunt."

"So she—and presumably they—have a direct interest in what happens to that site."

"Yep." I nodded. "I'm not sure what Amy's plans would be…but I'd guess she would lean more toward open space than to a strip mall."

"You mentioned a trust."

"Apparently, the Taylor family owned much of the land in town at one point, thanks to getting here first and making a few advantageous marriages."

"Um, advantageous marriages?" Joe blinked.

"Remember, until at least the early 19th century, marriage was a property matter and not a personal one."

"It still is for some people."

Ooh, lots of subtext there.

"No doubt," I said, trying to skate it. "But the modern idea of marrying the person you love instead of loving the person you marry didn't take hold for a long time. So it wasn't unusual to see families marrying to protect their holdings. And it's not really a surprise that the Taylors did."

"Old New England family and all."

"Exactly. Something interesting—apparently, Amy did not get that warm a welcome into the clan."

"No?"

"No. War brides are romantic to us today. To an old New England family, the idea that their prized oldest son would go to war and come back with a foreign wife? Especially one who didn't even worship their God? Not a great start."

"Ugh." Joe took a sip of his coffee. "Pops and Nonna ran into some of the same thing when they came over here to get away from Mussolini."

"Right. America may accept the huddled masses, but we don't necessarily want them at our dinner table."

"I'd like to say we're not like that anymore…"

"But you have a television." I nodded. "Yeah. Anyway, Amy, thanks to a crisp English accent, a willingness to fit in, and boatloads of charm—that last is a direct quote from one of the VFW guys—overcame the concerns to become a pillar of the community. And here in the land of a good streaming movie, we might have stayed. Except for an interesting quirk in the Taylor family."

"What's that?"

"The guys weren't sure of all the details, but there is some kind of family trust involving the land. Apparently, they had to vote to agree on the use of any given parcel. Even more interestingly, there is also apparently a lot of money. This is New England, so no one is going to talk numbers, but it's fair to say that Amy, has some level of control over the land next to the strip mall…and possibly a good chunk of money, too."

"She's the great aunt of Rowland Stark's widow?"

"Yep."

"Do we think something is going on here?"

"I'm not sure what we think."

"Information is always useful." He smiled.

"Better than nothing, anyhow." I shrugged.

"Nicely done, *Dottore*." He raised the coffee mug like a toast. "A good day's work."

"Do my best." I clinked my mug against his. "Information gathering is better than dealing with my client, for sure."

"Oh?"

"She's making me crazy—imposing her modern thriller writer mindset on nineteenth-century life."

Joe chuckled. "That's got to be fun."

"Not even a little." I sighed. "I don't know how long I can keep my mouth shut about the sex thing."

"What sex thing?"

"Well, it's a hookup show, so…"

"Really?" He let out an explosive laugh.

"It's supposed to be some big bodice-ripper. It's not to period, and honestly, it's pretty irresponsible."

"I can't argue the irresponsible, considering that they didn't have any of the modern ways to prevent disease or other things." He sipped some coffee. "Not to period? Weren't they good and saucy in the Regency?"

"They were less prudish than the Victorians, but they weren't getting any busier." I took a sip of my own coffee. "There's a reason it was called the Sexual Revolution."

Joe's ears turned pink.

"There just wasn't the kind of hooking up that the *Regency Love* people are hoping for. People just—didn't. The casual stuff we see now didn't happen in that time. Sex was a big deal."

"It's still kind of a big deal, ask me."

"Speaks the father of a daughter," I replied with a teasing grin.

Joe didn't grin back. He held my gaze with an intensity I hadn't expected.

"Speaks a man with, for lack of a better description, honorable intentions." He reached for my hand, laced fingers across the kitchen table.

"Yeah?"

"Yeah." He leaned over and kissed me lightly. "Not the time, but there's a conversation."

"There is. A good one."

"I think so, too."

We sat there enjoying the warmth between us for a moment.

Then, he asked: "Do you hear that?"

"I don't hear anything."

"Exactly. That's never a good sign."

We put our mugs down and headed into the living room, which looked like it had been furnished by someone who wanted hot cocoa and marshmallows. The furniture—two couches and a chair-and-a-half—were all poufy and just off-white, floating on a dark-stained hardwood floor. There were shelves built into the walls, but they sported nothing but a few rather generic pieces of porcelain.

No books?

I was sure that was Amber's doing.

At the far end of the room was an impressively large TV, currently showing a spectacular space documentary. Henry was transfixed, and Aly wasn't far behind. Cannoli was sitting on the couch, about as happy and relaxed as a tiny dog could be.

"Nat Geo?" Joe asked.

"Yeah," Aly turned to her dad with a big smile. "I haven't seen this one in a while. Turns out Henry's into space too."

"Pretty cool TV, AlysDad," Henry said. "You can even see the rings of Jupiter."

"I like it." Joe smiled. "Well, maybe your mom will come over for dinner sometime, and you can watch a couple of videos."

"Ma?"

"I think we can schedule that." I smiled at Joe. "In the meantime, these two have a father-daughter evening to enjoy, and Cookie is waiting for us."

"Good seeing you, Dr. Shaw," Aly said, shooting her dad a smile. "Glad you and Dad are spending time together."

If I'd been waiting for a formal endorsement (I honestly hadn't thought that far!), I'd certainly gotten one.

Sure didn't hurt, though.

"Thanks, Aly. Really good seeing you, too."

A weird little twinkling noise came from the couch, and Joe and I both glanced over in concern for Cannoli, who was jumping to the ground and waddling toward his daddy.

"Really, guys." Aly shook her head at the clueless olds. "That's my update alert. There's a new post on the Jazz Band page. I've been waiting for this."

"Well, we've been dismissed," Joe said. "Glad you two had time to stop over."

Cannoli snuffled at his ankle, and Joe picked him up.

"Glad we got to see you, too," Henry said, giving Cannoli one more pat. He would pay for that later with Cookie.

"Goodnight," I said. "Thanks for the coffee."

"Thanks for the info."

"Always a pleasure." He leaned in and gave me a small kiss on the cheek. Entirely appropriate, even with kids around. "Goodnight, *cara*."

"Goodnight."

If I spent some of the time when I was supposed to be writing my article on corsets thinking about what might happen if Joe and I had our promised conversation, well, it was entirely my business.

Chapter Nineteen: The Mad Knitters Weigh In

We sometimes go to *shul* on Saturdays, if it's religiously or socially important, like a holiday or bat mitzvah, or if we just feel like it. But we always have another engagement on Saturdays: the Mad Knitters, AKA my mother and her two best buds.

When I was expecting Henry, Mom retired from teaching in Mars and moved up here, settling into a nice senior building near the water in West Haven.

Close enough to be involved but far enough away so we aren't all up in each other's business.

But one weekend morning is always Mom's. We meet her for brunch at Pokey's, the diner near the shore, and let her show off her brilliant (hah!) daughter and adorable grandson. She's earned it; she raised me alone after my father took off for a temporary separation that became permanent thanks to a bad flu outbreak. Single parents weren't cool back then, especially in the Western PA backcountry, but she just kept going.

These days, she's enjoying a very late adolescent rebellion with her partners in crime.

There's a constant level of middle-school drama in the complex, and sometimes it erupts into something a lot like gang wars, only, thankfully, with glares and snarky comments instead of bullets.

Not to mention the romances. The oldsters make soap operas look positively restrained.

Mom's pal Peggy Wolfe, an adorable bottle redhead and the belle of the ball, is sneaking around with Old Man Holman, who's in the same age cohort as everyone else, but has been at the complex longer.

The only reason they're sneaking around is because it's fun; both are widowed, and everyone actually thinks it's cute. Well, that might be another reason to sneak—I wouldn't want everybody commenting on how cute my relationship is.

The other knitter, Suzanne Luciano, is one of the few women who's still married, and she parks her retired insurance agent husband, Sal, at the fishing pier every day before setting off for a full day of crafts, granddaughters, and gossip. The fishermen, who are sort of the Y chromosome version of the Mad Knitters, may—or may not—catch anything, but the one sacred rule is they are NOT permitted to bring fish home.

As for my mother, she's just starting to dip her toe in the dating scene. The Sarge, a retired Marine who most of the ladies in the complex have been eyeing for years, always seems to be around when she has packages or needs a hand across the icy parking lot. And lately, they've started walking together.

I'm not supposed to know, but Peggy very happily informed me of the fact when Mom took a bathroom break at the last family brunch. So far, I've kept it close to the vest, as advised —verbatim!

This week, Peggy and Suzanne arrived at the same time as Mom, which almost never happens, and we were able to get an umbrella table on the patio, which *really* never happens at Pokey's. I assumed it was because Henry and I were running just a little late.

We'd stopped at the old stationery store near the complex to pick up a few school supplies and spent too long chatting with Mr. and Mrs. Dae, the New York couple who recently bought it, giving them some tips on settling into the New Haven area.

Maybe the secret to a good table is hitting at the very end of brunch.

Or maybe it was just that day. There were a couple of big events in New Haven proper this weekend, and people might just be out enjoying them instead of doing the usual at their local.

Whatever it was, we were all happy to take our seats, place the usual orders, and enjoy our routine. Pokey's has had the same waitresses since the dinosaurs crawled out of Long Island Sound and ordered steak and eggs, so they know us—and everyone else.

"Getting big, isn't he?" our server Alma asked me as she looked Henry over.

"Taller every day." I grinned.

"And you're looking pretty happy, too, Nice to see you smiling again."

"Aw, thanks."

"You know," Peggy said, inspecting me, "you do have a little color in your cheeks."

"It's a sunburn."

"And a boyfriend," Mom said. "Or wasn't I supposed to mention that?"

"That lawyer?" Suzanne asked. "Are you exclusive now?"

"We're seeing each other," I confirmed, blushing. And, honestly, wondering how a woman whose last date was in the Eisenhower Administration knew the slang. "As far as I know, he doesn't have time to see anyone else."

"But you never know with men, honey." Peggy gave me a canny look. "Don't get too far into this, until you're sure."

"He's a very good guy," Mom said, giving Peggy a glare. "I'm sure he's on the up and up. She's even going to let me meet him soon."

"Wow. He must rate," said Suzanne. "Do we know him?"

"You've seen him in the paper," Peggy told her. "That State's Attorney who just won the conviction in the Markov murder."

"Oh, him. Joe Poli. Italian." There was a note of clear approval in Suzanne's voice. "Nice looking guy, and I think Sal knows his mom—Lidia, right?"

"Yes." I stared.

"Don't get weird, honey. It's not that all Italian people know each other— it's that New Haven County is a small place. He went to church with her years ago…and remembered Joe when he saw the story on the murder trial."

Mom chuckled. "See, Christian? It's just like Mars, only with better food and a water view."

She was more right than I wanted to admit. New Haven County is a major population center, but it does have a lot of small, close communities embedded in the larger area. So it seems like a tiny town at times.

And unlike Mars, which was in the middle of nowhere, more than an hour away from Pittsburgh, which was the closest I came to civilization growing up, we had New Haven—and a train to the REAL big city.

Fortunately, just then, Old Man Holman walked past, sparking a chain reaction of glances across the table. And after him, a bunch of women from the other building, who sent the Mad Knitters into a territorial frenzy. While I was afraid they might start sticking their needles in the sand as a warning, I've never been so grateful for the craziness of the complex.

Conversation stayed mostly on weather, grandchildren, and social matters for most of the meal, but I knew that was going to change.

And indeed, it did, as soon as the poached eggs and hash were demolished.

I suspected that Peggy, the whodunnit fan of the group, had also held back because she planned to interrogate me thoroughly on the incident on the Green, and no decent person would expect another to discuss it over oozing poached egg yolks.

Kind of her.

"All right, so tell me, what on earth happened on the Green?" Peggy asked, taking a clearing sip of coffee.

"One of the cannon guys blew up," Henry told her. "Ka-boom."

"Horrible," Suzanne said. "Do they know why?"

"Joe and State Police Major Crimes are looking into it," I assured her. "Still unclear if it was accidental…or what."

"Did I hear that it was Rowland Stark?" Peggy asked.

"Yeah."

"What a creep," Peggy said.

"Creep," agreed Suzanne.

"How do you…"

They exchanged glances, and Suzanne gave Peggy the "you first."

"I was at a party with my late husband years ago, and he got grabby. You'd probably call it a #MeToo thing now…but back then, it was just being a jerk."

"Ugh." I shook my head. "I'd heard there might be some stuff like that out there."

"There was all kinds of that stuff out there," Suzanne said. "Guy was known for grabbing a handful—and not paying his bills."

"Not paying his bills?"

"You know I did the books for Sal until he retired," she reminded me. "Well, I can't tell you how many times I had contractors asking for extensions because Rowland Stark hadn't paid them, and they couldn't pay us. Not a good way to do business."

"No. I knew he played the edges, but I didn't realize he was that bad."

"He was. Even with his wife's money."

"Linley?"

"Linley came from money on both sides—her father was a Taylor, her mother was a Barnwell."

"Barnwell Stone?" I asked. I knew about the quarry and the stone business because the Society had looked into replacing flagstones at one point. Barnwell was the best, and most expensive—and the family still owned its original quarry.

"Yeah. They're good people. Rowland isn't—wasn't." Suzanne's nose wrinkled. "Just not a nice man, dear."

"I'll second that," Peggy said. "Understand, I think we've gone too far in practically criminalizing innocent flirtations...but there was nothing innocent about Rowland."

"Nothing," Suzanne agreed. "So, does Joe think somebody blew him up?"

"I'm not sure what Joe thinks right now," I said. "And it wouldn't be right for me to say."

"Oh, of course, honey." Peggy patted my arm. "I wouldn't want you to talk out of school."

Suzanne and Mom exchanged little grins.

"Well, it wouldn't be a surprise if somebody had blown him up," Suzanne said with an emphatic nod. "If it was bad enough that people outside his business knew about it, you know it had to be pretty crazy on the inside."

"True," I said. "I do think I need to suggest Mr. Poli take another look at the victim's financials."

"After he takes another look at you," Mom teased. "You're being responsible, right?"

"MOM." I wanted to dive into my egg cup.

"Well, it's been a while, dear, and your mother is right," Peggy reminded me. "The largest increases in sexually transmitted diseases are in older age groups."

Make it stop!

"Um, honey," Suzanne said, "the CDC meant over 50. I don't think that's Christian…quite yet."

"Thankfully, no." I picked up my coffee. "Not that there's anything wrong with people over 50 having a vibrant and interesting romantic life."

"Oh, she's got your number, Barb," Suzanne grinned at my mother. "Has she had the little talk with you?"

"Talk about what?" Henry resurfaced after spending the last few minutes watching an interesting-looking boat go by.

"Homework," I said quickly. "Grownups sometimes get stuck with it in the summer."

"It's true, you know," Henry agreed, immediately distracted by a contentious issue. "Ma's writing some article on corsets."

"Corsets?"

Two of the three Mad Knitters, with the merciful exception of the one I'm related to, turned to me with considerable interest.

"Um, yeah. There's a lot going on there."

"A lot going on everywhere, sweetie." Peggy smiled and raised her coffee like a toast.

Chapter Twenty: Weekend Work

Normally, we do our weekly grocery shopping on the way home from West Haven, and then I make some kind of special dinner. The idea is that it should be more elaborate than our simple weeknight meals. This time of year, I often do zucchini lasagna, which is great for Henry because the veggies take the place of the noodles—and their carbs.

Not to mention a good way to dispose of some of Garrett and Ed's ubiquitous zucchini. Ubiquitous Zucchini will be the name of my alt-rock band.

We were putting away the frozen stuff when Lewis phoned and asked if I could meet him at the Society because he wanted to look at the artifacts from the plaza site.

Henry grumbled a little because he'd wanted downtime with Cookie, but the promise of games on my desktop was enough of a bribe to restore his usual sunshiny mode for the short walk. He'd had a snack on the way home, but I made sure to turn his pump to the higher activity setting so his blood sugar wouldn't dip too low.

Life's a balancing act.

Lewis was in the workroom when we got there. He has keys and the alarm codes, as do most of the board members and a few longtime volunteers. Our security system is pretty old, but serviceable. It doesn't have fancy cameras, or the email connection. Basically, all it does is ring the call center for a break-in or unauthorized entry. Since our collection is valuable in an historic and social sense, but not especially in a monetary one, it was just fine for the purpose. At some point, we should probably look into the little doorbell cams and such, just because we should…but this wasn't that day.

At the worktable, Lewis was turning the African figurine from the site in his hands. He was as casual as I'd ever seen him, weekend-comfortable in a navy Yale polo and well-worn but not sloppy jeans.

"Hey, big guy!" He greeted Henry. "Doc."

"Hey, Mr. Lewis!" Henry chirped back, going in for a quick handshake. I smiled to myself, seeing the echo of his dad. From the time Henry was barely able to walk, Frank taught him to shake hands and talk to other men the way he had, in that casual but respectful way old-school fellas do. He'd settled on 'Mr. Lewis' because it was polite—and Lewis loved it, because it recalls his full name: John Lewis Barnes.

"Why don't you take the phone and go play Dragon Race in my office?" I suggested.

"Cool."

I sat down beside Lewis. "So what's up?"

He turned the figure to me.

The piece was a heavy black material with a dull sheen. I'd assumed either pottery or stone, of a woman holding a basket. It was small and rounded, the woman's curves exaggerated a bit, her hair worked in braids.

"This is right off the Met website," Lewis said. "It's exactly the same as one they have. One that you can easily download a photo of."

"Okay."

"Well, I was telling a friend in the Engineering School about this whole thing, and she said there might be something else going on."

The way he said the word 'friend,' I suspected there might be more than one matter of extra interest, but this clearly was not the time. "What did she think?"

"She's into CAD—computer-assisted drafting—3D design…and 3D print-ing."

"Cool stuff."

"Cool girl. Not that we need to talk about that right now." He shot me a shy smile.

"Uh-huh."

"Uh-huh." He ran his fingers over the piece. "She tells me there's a way to use photos to 3D print a piece. The printers are good enough now that they can extrapolate to build a piece that's a perfect reproduction of the image…or the thing in it."

"So if someone wanted to 3D print an artifact…"

"They could easily do it."

"But what about the materials?" I asked. "Isn't 3D printing just plastic?"

"Not anymore. Apparently, there are a lot of ways to formulate the material. And you might be able to come up with something pretty similar to stone. They didn't do any tests on this, did they?"

"No."

"It looks like basalt to me," Lewis said. "You know, the black volcanic rock."

"But?"

He turned it over. On the smooth bottom of the figure, at the very base, was a tiny, barely noticeable scuff. If you hadn't been looking for it, you'd have assumed it was some sort of minor damage.

"What's this?" I asked.

"It could be something from the 3D printing process that was sanded away." Lewis rubbed his finger over it. "Without a chemical analysis or radiocarbon dating, we can't be 100% sure."

"But it sure looks like somebody salted the site," I said.

"Yeah."

"And in an especially nasty fashion, coming up with a fake African artifact to bring in the whole concern about enslaved people—or free people of color."

"That's the one." Lewis's normally amiable face tightened. "Someone put a fair amount of thought—and malice—into this."

"I'd say." The box of artifacts was sitting beside him, and I reached inside and pulled out the kiddush cup. "Rabbi Aaron said this looked like something on the Jewish Museum website. Maybe we should talk to her, too."

"Is she free?" Lewis asked.

I looked at the clock. Three-thirty. Late enough that Sabbath services and the meal afterward were done…early enough that she wasn't yet getting ready for the couples' dinner that had become her tradition with Ben since the twins left for college. "She may have a few minutes for us."

Not only did she have a few minutes, she was there in less than two. Turned out she'd been taking a post-service walk to relax, so she just turned right onto our porch.

The Empress glared at her from the stairs as I opened the door for her. Her Imperial Majesty has never met Rugelach, the big tortie temple cat, and she never will, but she can smell her.

Dina, weekend casual in dusty-blue joggers and a white shirt probably borrowed from Ben, just shot the angry little kitty a smile and greeted us.

"So you think the figurine is a 3D print?" she asked Lewis.

"It's at least possible. A friend in the Engineering School—" again with the little spin- "tells me that it's pretty easy now to take a 2D image of something, like a figurine from the Met website, and turn it into a 3D piece."

"Do a lot of people have access to that now?" I asked.

"Probably more than you think," Dina said. "The kids have friends in some of the high-tech programs at their school, and there are a lot of 3D printers running around now."

"I don't think there's a way to 3D print metal, though," Lewis said. "Or at least not one that could make a really good copy of an antique piece."

"Which means something else is going on with the kiddush cup." Dina nodded, carefully picking up the piece. I handle things carefully, of course, being an historian, but Dina has a whole different level of reverence when she works with Judaica. I'd seen it before in the way she lays out Torah scrolls in the sanctuary, or even just carefully returns a book to her shelves. "Let's see about this."

"Did you tell me it's extremely similar to one on the Jewish Museum website?" I asked.

"It's not similar. It's the same."

"Then you know that's a problem, right?"

Dina looked sharply at me, but Lewis, with more than a year of working with the pieces at the Society, knew precisely where I was going.

"If it's 18th century, it's pre-industrial," I reminded her.

"Before assembly lines and consistent production," Lewis added.

"That's right," Dina said as she processed it. "No two items were ever exactly the same because they were handmade. We need to look at the Jewish Museum website and see how similar it is."

"Let's go." I pointed to the office.

With only a little squawking from Henry, who was not pleased to be kicked out of my big black chair, even with the bribe of my phone, we fired up my office desktop and pulled up the Jewish Museum collections. They'd done a masterful job of photographing and uploading their pieces.

"You should do something like this with the Society collections, Christian," Dina said as we combed through photos of kiddush cups.

"We should," agreed Lewis. "It would be a huge project, but seriously worth it."

"Huge project for sure," I said, scrolling.

"There!" Dina pointed. "That's the one!"

I brought it up on the screen, and with the zoom and the magnifying glass from my desk, we had no trouble discerning that the two pieces were indeed identical.

"So this one's a fake, too," Dina said.

"How…"

She tapped one pale pink nail on a little symbol at the bottom of the listing for the kiddush cup, and the page jumped to something new: A Museum Shop page offering a Reproduction: 18th Century Kiddush Cup, sterling or sterling plate.

"So somebody just bought a reproduction?" Lewis asked. "Shouldn't there be a mark of some kind?"

Dina ran her fingers over the bottom, carefully, gently. "Look. A tiny rough spot."

"Just like the figurine," I said. "Only this time, it was the makers' mark sanded off."

We all stared at each other for a moment.

"Somebody made a really serious effort to salt the site," I said.

"And to bring in a bunch of different concerns, too," Dina added. "Jewish history, the experience of formerly enslaved or free people of color...this was no accident."

"Not at all," Lewis's soft voice came out almost like a growl. "Insulting to everyone."

"Unbelievably." I shook my head. "But why? And what did they think would happen? Eventually, artifacts are put through chemical tests and often carbon dating, so sooner or later, the fraud would be exposed."

"Maybe just another delay?" Dina asked.

"Or maybe to delay it long enough for something else to happen," said Lewis.

"Something else like what?" Even before I finished the question, I knew one possible answer...as we all did.

"Yeah, well." Dina put the kiddish cup back in the box. "We've had our hands all over this stuff, so I'm not sure how much use it is as evidence, but..."

Lewis put the figurine in. "Should we call Mr. Poli?"

"Oh, I think Christian can handle that." Dina gave me a brightly innocent yenta smile.

"He's with his daughter right now," I said.

"And you're with your son." An expansive shrug. "I just walked past Kule's Ice Cream, and the sign for fresh strawberry sorbet is up."

"It is?" Lewis asked. "My aunt loves that stuff. Guess I'm stopping for a pint on the way home."

"An ice cream stop is a very good thing." Dina shot me a pointed glance.

"I'm not horning in on the guy's dad time. But I do need to hand over the evidence," I said, turning for the office. "Henry, I need my phone..."

Chapter Twenty-One: Strawberry Zucchini Surprise

Joe quickly brushed off my apology for interrupting family time and offered to come right over and collect the box. And then:

"Do you and Henry have plans right now?"

"Well, you know it's my night to iron…" I teased.

"But…"

"The shirts aren't dry yet, and Henry could use a snack."

"So maybe we take the kiddies to Kule's for some of that fresh strawberry sorbet."

"Oh, you saw the sign too?"

"They sent out an email blast. I'm on their list."

I laughed. "Nice."

"Very nice. We'll be right over. That is, if Aly doesn't brain me for referring to her as a kiddy."

From his tone of voice, I could tell he was on the receiving end of a teen glare at that exact moment.

"We'll buy the YOUNG PEOPLE some frozen refreshments," I said.

"That's probably better. See you in a few."

By the time Joe and Aly arrived, with Cannoli in tow, Henry and I were on the porch with the box, after filling the Empress's water and food bowls and setting the building alarm.

Joe was looking delightful in a red polo and jeans, almost a match for Henry. Aly was leaning full into teen scruffy, with peach space-dye leggings and an oversized tee with a big glittery flower on it, her caramel hair back in a harmonizing silk scrunchy. Who knew those were back?

"Hey, Aly, AlysDad." Henry shot Aly a wave and exchanged a manly handshake with Joe. Then, he bent down to greet the real star of the show, getting a good licking from Cannoli.

We were *so* going to pay for that when we got back to Cookie.

"Ready for some sorbet?" Joe asked.

"Not strawberry." Henry wrinkled his nose. "Cocoa."

"Your treat, your call," Joe said.

"I like that shirt, Dr. Christian," Aly said, shooting her dad a glance. "Doesn't she look nice, Dad?"

"She always looks good, Alyson." If Joe's tone weren't warning enough, his return glance should have been.

"Well, thank you both," I replied, picking up the box, "Where do you want this?"

Joe handed the leash to Aly and clicked the lock on his trunk. "Hold it for a second. We'll stop at the police station because they have an evidence locker, but I have to seal and label it first."

Ten minutes later, the box was safely dropped off at the PD, and we were happily perusing the flavor board at Kule's outside window. After crossing paths with Lewis on the walk—and getting a teasing grin as he scooted off to his aunt with a pint.

"So, we know this guy's no-sugar cocoa," Joe started with a nod to Henry. "Miss Alyson, what's your pleasure today?"

"Chocolate pretzel ice cream," she said. "Strawberries are ick."

"Of course they are. *Dottore?*"

"I'd do the fresh strawberry, but they have my all-time favorite: birthday cake."

"Birthday cake? Really?" Aly looked at me, as stunned and impressed, as if I'd announced a fondness for K-Pop. (I actually don't mind it, but I'd never say so publicly.)

"Yep. Really. I am an overgrown tween." I shrugged. "Some of us don't get all hung up on grownup dignity."

"Well, I am going to have the fresh strawberry sorbet," Joe said. "Somebody has to."

"Is that like somebody has to eat the zucchini?" I asked.

"No." Joe shuddered a little. "And I'd appreciate you not bringing up zucchini in the middle of something much tastier."

Suddenly, I realized I'd never seen him eat zucchini. He'd arrived late for dinner at Garrett and Ed's, so he hadn't been there for the dip, and now that I thought of it, he had just passed on the shredded-zucc salad. Plus, I'd never made my zucchini lasagna for him.

"Do you have a problem with zucchini, Counselor?" I asked.

Aly giggled.

So did Henry.

Cannoli looked up at his person as if offering some support.

"I hate them." Joe wrinkled his nose.

"How does a New Haven Italian guy not like zucchini?"

"Easy. I don't." He shook his head, exaggerating a little for the benefit of the kids. "Big ugly green things. Yuck."

"Seriously?" I asked.

"Seriously. I'll eat any other vegetable you put in front of me. Even brussels sprouts, if they're those nice roasted ones. But not zucchini. They're disgusting. Especially when they're all overgrown. They don't taste like anything."

It took everything I had not to howl with laughter at the sight of a grown man holding forth on his hatred for zucchini.

"Good to know. I make zucchini lasagna a lot in the summer."

"Not for me, you don't."

"See, Ma?" crowed Henry, "I told you everybody doesn't like every vegetable."

"Dad's just weird," Aly said. "Most people like zucchini."

"Most people also like strawberries, and yet…" Joe shot back, taking the bait for the play fight.

"Fruit is good. Chocolate is better."

"Aly wins that round!" crowed Henry.

"What is this, kids pile on grownups?" Joe asked.

I held up my hands. "Okay, people. Why don't we leave the zucchini for the moment and just enjoy our treats?"

Cones duly obtained, plus a mini-size "Kules Kompanion Kookie" for the dog, we walked back toward the Green. The kids took Cannoli and went on ahead, and Joe and I lagged back a bit.

"So we know for sure that somebody planted those artifacts," Joe said.

"Definitely. Somebody salted the site."

"That's the term of art in archaeology?"

"I'm not an archaeologist, but yeah." I shrugged.

"Good to know. Never know what you'll need."

"True."

"The skeletons are real, though, right? You can't 3D-print a skeleton, can you?"

"I'm pretty sure you can't. Or at least it would be obviously fake." I took a little more of my ice cream. Kule's birthday cake is as close to heaven as we poor mortals can get. "Maybe the skeletons are from some modern unsolved crime, and the enterprising opponents of the plaza decided to throw in the artifacts to slow the process."

"You mean they just got lucky with the skeletons?" Joe licked his sorbet. "Wow. I don't even like strawberries all that much, but I like this."

"Uh-huh. This is me not saying anything about you and zucchini."

"Nice." He laughed. Took another lick of the sorbet and noticed me watching him. "Want a taste?"

"Umm…sure." I took a very careful, very PG-13, taste of the sorbet. "Delicious. Want to try the birthday cake?"

"Nah. I'm not into sprinkles." He leaned closer, glanced to be sure the kids were well out of earshot. "But I wouldn't turn down watching you take another taste of mine."

I blushed. I was probably redder than the sorbet.

"Kidding." Grin. "Mostly."

"Yeah." I hid behind my cone for a moment, hoping to cool my flush. A Scottish fishbelly eruption doesn't just go away in a blink.

Joe watched me for a moment, obviously enjoying the play.

"Anyhow," he said finally, "I have a really hard time believing the skeletons are a coincidence."

"So do I," I agreed, returning to balance, and taking a quick glance to Aly and Henry, who appeared to be talking happily as Cannoli led the way. "Cops and prosecutors hate coincidences."

"Might be the only thing Ed and I agree on."

"Oh, stop." I smacked his arm. "Ed thinks you're a standup guy. He even likes you. He just has some reservations about my dating a prosecutor."

"It's not *his* reservations that worry me." Joe held my gaze.

"Well, I don't have any."

"Glad to hear it." He took my hand.

Aly glanced back right then and shot her dad a smile.

He smiled back, then squeezed my fingers.

"All right," Joe said. "So, nothing to worry about here."

"Nope. But I've got plenty of concerns about those skeletons."

"You're not the only one." He nodded. "I'm going to check in with Dr. Alexandre and see if she has any insight. They're hers until she calls in someone else."

"Like who?"

"I think UCONN has a forensic anthro specialist. There's also a group from the Indigenous tribes who take care of their people if there's any question of that. I'm not sure there is, in this case."

"The anthro people will probably be able to tell. They'll be able to determine the age of the skeleton, how long it was in the ground, and get a sense of whether it could be Indigenous. And, of course, there's DNA."

"Right. Joe nodded. "Dr. Alexandre will know where they are on that."

"Good place to start. Very smart idea."

"And one that'll have to wait till Monday. Barring true emergencies, she takes the weekend off. She's got small kids, and I don't think this qualifies."

"You're right. Family time is too important."

He took another lick of sorbet. "No question."

"And speaking of family time, you're going to drop Henry and me at the house and go on with whatever you had planned with Aly tonight."

"I was, actually." Joe smiled. "I'm glad you get that."

"Of course." I leaned over and took one more lick of his sorbet. "I get plenty."

"Well played."

"Gotta come to play, Counselor." I grinned right back. "Have a great night with your girl."

"And you with your fella."

"And my ironing. "

He laughed again. "That too."

Henry and Aly were laughing too, just ahead of us on the Green, happily playing fetch with Cannoli.

Just before we stepped onto the Green, Joe stopped and looked at me for a moment. "*Dottore*, we might just make this work."

"We might indeed."

Chapter Twenty-Two: Mini-Golf and Major Twists

Our Sundays used to be quiet. Since Garrett and Ed have a bunch of grandchildren, they're usually brunching and going to activities in various corners of the state, depending on who has a birthday, game, or performance. It sounds exhausting (it would exhaust me!) but they love it.

Henry and I used to do yard work, and then just stay in and relax—Henry with video games and his favorite TV shows, I with books and a nap, in the living room so I would wake up right away if anything happened. Lately, though we'd kept the yard work and slow pace, we'd added an early evening event with Joe.

Aly spends most of the weekend at her dad's, but she has to get back to her mother and the new stepdad in Southport Sunday afternoons so she can prepare for the coming school or camp week. The hand off was always depressing for Joe, and one week, he called me and asked if Henry and I might like a round of mini golf.

It's turning into a nice little new tradition for the three of us.

We usually go to the small but well-done miniature golf course tucked away on a back road just out of town, which even has a snack bar with no-sugar-added ice cream treats. When it rains, we hit the bowling alley.

Either way, Henry and Joe end up in a friendly, teasing competition, and I lose miserably. I'm truly terrible at both golf and bowling, but I have a great time, and more importantly, Henry does.

A lot of the fun for me, is watching Joe and Henry together.

Henry and his father had a wonderful relationship. Frank, like me, hadn't expected to marry and have children, and he considered his son the greatest gift of his life. For Henry, the sudden loss of his dad was a large, horrible trauma…but also just a hole in his day-to-day.

Everything changed. It wasn't three guys (counting Cookie) against one girl. And it wasn't nearly as much fun anymore.

We'd worked out new routines and treats and traditions in the two years since and made our peace with life as it was. Joe was nothing like a replacement.

That would have been impossible.

But these Sunday outings were definitely fun. Which was the point.

Light, fun, and friendly, and everyone kept it that way, even though everyone also knew there was some big serious stuff in the background.

Anyhow, on that particular Sunday, it was a thick and sticky afternoon, but the thunderstorms weren't projected to hit until nightfall, so we decided to take our chances on mini golf.

Low-key, friendly, and fun the outing might be, but I was still going out with the guy I was seeing, which gave me an excuse to bring out the pretty clothes. Even though I'm most comfortable in the slim pants, vintage oxford shirts, and blazers I wear for work, I have a wide and deep girly streak. So it was a joy to bring out a long floral skirt and thin coral sweater, and even little metallic ballet flats, since mini golf was not exactly a hike through the underbrush.

Joe was off-duty adorable in a navy Yale Law Alum polo and khakis, the kind of outfit that could make some men look seriously dumpy. On him, though, it emphasized that he was in pretty terrific shape—mainly because he balanced out the Italian home cooking with those late-night jogs. He had faint smudges under his eyes, and there was a tiny hollow at his jaw that hadn't been there before the murder trial and seemed a little more pronounced now.

It occurred to me that if we stayed together, I'd end up joining forces with his mother to make sure he ate during trials. Not the worst outcome.

"Don't you look pretty," he said, holding the car door for me, as Henry climbed into the back. "You're a secret girly-girl, aren't you?"

"Ma is SO girly," Henry called from the back, and then started giggling as Cannoli greeted him with a thorough licking.

The mini-golf is pet-friendly, so Joe brings Cannoli because the poor little fella gets lonely.

"Nothing wrong with girly," Joe said, leaning in for a respectful and low-key kiss on the cheek. And a whisper: *"How about a short skirt sometime?"*

He had to expect a blush, and I absolutely delivered.

I held his gaze for a moment before he put the car in gear.

Big and serious, indeed. And hot.

The mini golf wasn't nearly as crowded as I'd expected. People in Connecticut have a weird relationship with weather, even in the summer. They completely lose their ability to drive in the rain, and the threat of a line of thunderstorms can lead folks to buy bread, milk, and hunker down like they're bracing for a month-long blizzard. Let's just not even talk about winter.

"Think we're missing something?" Joe asked as he parked. "There was a small chance of thunderstorms this evening."

"I think we're the only sane people in New Haven County."

He laughed. "I won't argue that."

"I am going to kick your butt this time, Ma," Henry announced.

"You both kick my butt every time," I reminded him.

Joe smiled innocently, his eyes gleaming in a way that made clear he was holding back an appreciative comment about my backside. "I'll remind you that I won last time, Master Glaser."

"By one stroke."

Cannoli recognized where we were and let out a happy little yip. Joe got out and leashed him up, as I did my best not to giggle. Cannoli liked to waddle down the paths, and the sight of tall, manly Joe with his mite of a black mop dog on a red nylon leash was unintentionally hilarious.

"Yes," Henry said, after patting Cannoli, "I'm going to win tonight."

"Winning isn't everything," I reminded them.

Henry and Joe looked at each other.

"You want to tell her, or should I?" Henry asked.

Joe gave him an 'after-you' nod.

"It's the only thing, Ma."

Cannoli pulled on the leash, and we proceeded into the shack.

The match, in the sweetly landscaped fake-country glades of the course, unfolded in the usual fashion, with Henry and Joe quickly jumping out into a close game and me racking up extra strokes with my terrible putting.

As for Cannoli, he was having the time of his life, surrounded by people he liked, all those interesting smells and the occasional stranger coming up to admire him. He didn't mind a bit when Joe handed the leash to Henry when he took his shots.

Good time for all—even me, since I honestly didn't care about winning.

"You didn't golf much before now, did you?" Joe said after my three-try tap-in on the fourth hole.

"Never have I ever." I grinned back. It was not a new conversation. "Not a big thing in Western P.A."

"Not a big thing in my old neighborhood, either, but I learned in law school."

"Social reasons?" A guess, but a good one.

"If you're going to run with the pack, you'd better be able to play with them, too." He landed a long putt, giving him a one-stroke lead over Henry, and smiled. "This is much more fun."

"Don't get used to it," Henry said. "I got a hole-in-one on Eleven last time."

"I'm not taking anything for granted," Joe assured him.

I lagged behind the guys and Cannoli a bit to give them some space, enjoying the shade and the evening air. Nice to see both of them happy and relaxed after the last couple of awful days.

"Well, Dr. Shaw. Fancy seeing you here."

I turned at the sound of the voice, which was somehow familiar. Gerry Diamond, Amy's friend, was sitting on one of the little side benches. He was dressed almost the same as Joe, though his polo said Columbia Alum, and he had a walking stick, which he hadn't had the other day with Amy.

But as old as he had to be, it was no wonder he would use one now, for walking around the course. "Why, hello."

I held out a hand to shake and he took it with the double-handed grip of a friend. Fine by me.

"Here with my grandson and the great-great. Fun way to spend an afternoon. And we all need a break after this week."

"I couldn't agree more." I nodded with him. "Been a pretty wild week."

"Too true." Gerry studied me for a moment. "I've just got a bad feeling about all this. And you know, Amy's right in the middle of it."

Which put him in the middle of it. And maybe in a position to know something useful. "Gerry, I'm here with a good friend, who happens to be Assistant State's Attorney Joe Poli."

"The one who just won the Markov case?"

"The very one." I motioned to Joe.

Joe's face was tight as he walked toward us, pulling Henry along. "What's up?"

"Gerry Diamond, may I introduce you to Joe Poli," I began a bit formally. He's an Assistant State's Attorney in this district."

"Pleased to meet you, sir." Joe handed Cannoli's leash to Henry and stepped forward for a shake.

"He's on the board at Beth Shalom. And a friend of Amy Taylor." I held Joe's gaze, making it clear what kind of friendship I meant.

Gerry's ears turned pink, but he didn't say anything.

"Wonderful place, the temple," Joe said. "So good to see it staying in use."

"Definitely." Gerry smiled. "You interested in preservation?"

"A little. I'm mostly interested in making sure we keep track of who we are and where we come from. All of us—however we got here."

"Smart guy." Gerry shot me a smile. "Nice fella, Christian."

"I think so." I cut my eyes to Joe, enjoyed the flash of warmth before moving onto serious matters. "Gerry's a little concerned that Amy's in the middle of this."

"Really. Perhaps you and I should have a word while Henry kicks his mother around the next few holes."

"If she doesn't mind, I would really like that."

"Glad to, sir." Joe sat down beside him on the bench. Cannoli trundled over to him and looked up at Gerry with the unerring aim some animals have for kind people. Joe picked up the little dog, and the older man smiled and patted him.

"What a nice fella," Gerry said. "What is he?"

"Not sure. Probably some Scottie and some Pom—as far as I know, he's just Cannoli."

"Works for me."

Cannoli sat down, and Joe cut his eyes to me.

"C'mon, Henry. I think I might be able to get the next one only one stroke over."

Henry looked at the grownups for a moment and decided that it wasn't worth the effort to figure out what was going on when the pleasure of besting his mother was available. "You are SO toast!"

Joe didn't catch up with us until the last three holes, and he didn't say anything about his conversation with Gerry other than to offer the older man's compliments. But he was a tiny bit distracted and didn't fight Henry nearly as hard as he might have on another day when Henry insisted on a forfeit because of his absence.

Joe made up the ground by buying the no-sugar-added chocolate ice cream, and by coming in for a serious drubbing at Demon Race on the computer afterward. Cannoli hid in the kitchen, as he usually does at times like this, and Cookie parked himself in the bay window, glaring in the direction of dog smell.

Cookie despises Cannoli. He likes to jump in front of Cannoli and hiss, which is truly terrifying since he's twice the size of the poor little thing. As they get more used to the idea of each other, the hissing has started to taper off a bit...but Cannoli is still terrified, and Cookie is still menacing.

The humans do their best to keep them separated—and ignore the tension. There's not much else to do.

And although I obviously do not endorse any kind of cruelty to living creatures, I can't help finding the whole situation hilarious. Cookie, who is normally a giant furry ball of goo, turning into the lion defender of the house because of a tiny little mop of a creature—it really is pretty funny.

After Henry took off for bed with a book, and Cookie followed, with one last hiss in Cannoli's direction, I poured Joe a glass of the chianti I'd taken to keeping in the house for him.

My idea of house red is anything fruity and not too strong, but I'd never offer a New Haven Italian man Big Shopper Box Wine. No more than he'd offer a Scottish woman generic shortbread.

"So, Gerry." Joe's long fingers were tense on the balloon as he held up the glass to the light.

"I know you hate coincidences, but I do think meeting him there really was one."

Joe took a sip. Savored it. There's an old theory that a man who is good with food and wine is also good with other things because sensuality works across the board. I don't know why I thought of it just then.

Oh, of course, I do.

I sat down on the other end of the couch with my own glass, not too close. Neither of us needed to be distracted at the moment.

"The meeting probably really was a coincidence…or just a function of the probabilities of living in a small town," I said. "It's the only nearby place to play mini golf, and if you've been hanging around with kids all day, you might want to burn off a little energy."

"I suppose."

"Garrett and Ed take Jana's kids to a mini golf in Fairfield a lot." I took a sip of my wine. It really was good. The guy knows his way around a nice red.

"Mama takes Jamie's, too. So that's not really a coincidence…or especially troubling." He drank a bit more. "But Gerry's right— Amy's smack in the center of all of this, and it's worth a look at everyone's financials and property records."

"Property records?"

"Amy apparently has control of the Taylor trust, which owns the land. There are some details to work out, but it's possible that her interests could be part of this."

"How?"

Another sip of wine. A thought. "You have friends at Town Hall, right?"

"I do."

"Maybe you ask around a little about the Taylor land."

"I will." I nodded. "Add it to my list for tomorrow."

For a moment, we sat in comfortable silence.

Joe lowered his glass.

I lowered mine.

Henry's door was still cracked, with a bar of light coming through that meant he was still awake.

Our eyes held.

No question what was in the room. The only question was what we'd do about it.

And that light from Henry's door suggested it was not a good time to do much of anything.

"So, *Dottore*," He picked up the glass again, took a sip, and studied me for what seemed like an hour. "*If ever any beauty I did see, which I desired and got, 'twas but a dream of thee.*"

"Ah, Reverend Donne has arrived." It was the same line he'd quoted weeks ago when he asked me out for the first time. Special to us.

"Indeed he has." He took my hand. "Don't think I haven't pushed because I don't want…um, you."

I waited. One of his fingers slipped over my wedding ring.

"If it's a religious thing, I'm okay with that."

"Huh?"

"Well, you're—observant-ish, right? I don't know what the rules are."

Honestly, I didn't either. Dina had seemed pretty supportive of the idea, though. I managed to keep my voice steady. "I'm not really sure there *are* rules for single grownups with, as you put it, honorable intentions."

"Okay." He held my gaze. "I'm trying to be careful here. I'm pretty sure you haven't been with anyone since your husband."

"Nope. Not even a snack."

That got me a grin. "A snack?"

"Yeah. You know, something fun and not serious."

"Uh-huh." Joe squirmed a bit. "There was a little snacking right after Amber left…but nothing serious."

"Only fair," I said. Please, no details.

"Neither here nor there. I'm serious now." His fingers tightened on mine. "And if you want to wait until we settle things in some way…if it's important to you religiously, then I'm absolutely fine with that."

"Oh. I'm not that observant." I took a breath. Am I? "Settle?"

"I know where I am." He laced fingers with mine. "I also know it's not fair to push you."

"You've thought about this."

"I have." Slow, wicked smile. "And other things."

"So have I." I smiled back. "And I'm hoping to do more than think one of these nights."

Joe's smile faded a little, still sexy, but rueful too, with a warmth I felt down to my toes. "So, one of these nights…"

"Yep." I leaned in and kissed him. "Not a snack."

He pulled me closer. "You, *Dottore*, are the whole Thanksgiving buffet."

"You're a pretty big smorgasbord yourself."

A shared laugh, and a light kiss with more than a little intent before he pulled me in and held me.

Not the worst way to end the day.

Chapter Twenty-Three: Monday Morning Blues

Thanks to that good Chianti, I actually managed to get to sleep without thinking too hard about death and destruction...or Joe. Didn't even have a nightmare.

I should have enjoyed the rest while I had it.

From the moment I opened my eyes, it was just that kind of day. My alarm didn't go off for some reason, and I woke up half an hour late and thoroughly behind the eight ball.

The next hour or so was a lot like being in a blender: something always moving, somebody always wanting something, something forgotten that had to be fixed *right now*.

A new camp week meant new activities and accouterments, which I'd thankfully had the minimal brain power to assemble before we went out with Joe...but I still had to get all of it neatly organized into the backpack. Not to mention fishing a camp t-shirt out of the dryer when I realized I'd been too distracted to fold, throwing together a nutritious breakfast for Henry, making sure he had snacks and a properly set meter, and that his shoes were relatively mud-free.

Then there was me.

As was my habit on boring Saturday nights alone, even now because Joe was with Aly, I had washed and ironed all my vintage oxford shirts and pressed my beloved reclaimed and refurbished linen blazer, so everything was ready. With the temp expected to spike 90 this afternoon, I didn't need a long-sleeve cotton shirt, but the linen blazer was about to come in very handy.

I threw it over my silky green tank top and put a pin in my pocket to dress myself up when I got to the Society. In the one minute I had before we went out the door, I slapped on sunscreen and a smudge of eyeliner. I had tinted lip balm in my purse—and desk, too, let's be honest—so I could finish off later.

As I dashed out of the bathroom, Cookie squawked.

"What? I gave you breakfast."

Another squawk.

"Fine." I grabbed a handful of Tuna Sardine Surprise treats and tossed them down. The surprise, if you're wondering, is that no one threw up from the smell.

"Let's go, fella," I called to Henry, grabbing a few drops of lemon-scented hand san.

"Ma! I'm building a wall—" he squawked, sounding an awful lot like his best friend.

"The wall will still be there tonight," I assured him. "Save and get moving."

Henry's annoyed growl as he turned off his tablet was almost the same as the noise Cookie was making as he snarfed the treats.

There's something to be said for a soundtrack.

I couldn't help chuckling a little as I herded Henry out to the path. We had just over two minutes more than it would take to walk up to the Green for the bus. We were going to make it.

Whew.

Tiffany and Ava were already there, and so were Ruby and Lidia, and their respective grandkids. This was a really big summer for Ruby's granddaughter, D'Andrea. Harmony Hill offered a MiniCampers program for pre-K, so she was getting to go along with her big brother on the bus for the first time. And he got to watch out for her.

All good.

Lidia was at the other end of the spectrum—the girls, Joe's nieces, would soon be middle schoolers with all that entailed.

Sally and her two blew in from the other direction. She was moving at the same speed as me, but somehow looking so much cooler in a cream linen shirtdress, her hair beautifully pulled up in a twist. Just another day when I hated her perfection.

Tiffany, in uniform and clearly counting the seconds, too, shot me a grin. "Made it."

"Barely."

"Happens," Ruby said. "Everybody's patching it together."

"Isn't that the truth," Sally huffed. "Such a busy day. I'm going over to take a look at a parcel near the strip mall. I'm hearing it might actually be a go, so why not?"

"Nothing ventured," I offered neutrally.

"Exactly. If that project finally moves, it'll bring up the value of all the empty land out there."

"Well, good luck," I said it, everyone else nodded, and we were, gratefully, done with Sally for the moment.

Once the campers were loaded and waved on their way, the parents scattered with the efficiency of a military operation. Sally blasted off toward her SUV, Tiffany to hers, on the other corner, and the grandmas started walking toward the café for their morning break.

As I turned for the short walk to the Society, I heard a bark. Garrett, Ed, and Norm were just crossing onto the Green.

"Aw, we missed Henry," Garrett said as I greeted them. "Too bad."

"You can join us at pick up," I reminded him.

"True." He smiled. "So, how was mini golf night?"

"Very nice." I looked to Ed. "Joe took a break from sorting through financials to spend time with us and ended up finding a clue."

"Did he now?"

"Who should be mini-golfing with his grands but Gerry Diamond."

"Now that *is* interesting," Ed said. "He sometimes joins the fellas at the diner in the morning. Standup guy."

Ed has a regular Monday morning coffee date with a bunch of retired military and police guys. It was probably his next stop after walking Norm.

There's a core of about five, but other men drift in occasionally. I hadn't known Gerry was one of them, but it fit.

"That was the sense I got." I nodded. "And really protective of Amy."

"I think he's sweet on her," Ed said.

"At least," Garrett agreed.

"I thought so, too. Kind of nice."

"Aren't you the little matchmaker?" Garrett smacked my arm. "Hoping they'll follow the Bat Mitzvah with a wedding?"

"Maybe."

"Don't get all hung up on that cute old couple thing," Ed warned. "People do what they do at their own pace, you know."

"I do." I held his gaze. "And I'm not a fan of rushing things."

Both got the subtext.

"Not rushing is good," Garrett said. "Hiding because you're scared isn't."

"Got to admit, that fella of yours has been around an awful lot more than most prosecutors in the middle of a big case," Ed observed. "I might have to revise my views."

"Yeah?" I asked.

"Just sayin."

Garrett cut his eyes to me as Ed walked on. Nothing like having a couple of dads to watch out for you. Joe deserved an awful lot of credit just for putting up with them.

We turned onto the street before the Society, and I saw Jensen's small electric car.

"Oh, no," I said. "Not again."

"Your happy little client?" Ed asked, a wicked gleam in his eyes. "More *Regency Luuuve?*"

"Oh, fine. Jensen's driving me nuts," I admitted. "I have come to hate *Regency Love.*"

"You don't need the money."

"No. But I hate dropping a project. And I keep thinking I might be able to—educate?—her."

"Not hardly." Garrett scowled. "She wants you to give her some kind of patina of accuracy for that ridiculous hookup show idea. It's how she's going to redeem herself. The book sure didn't go anywhere. You read it, right?"

"I had to." I shot Garrett a sharp glance. "You didn't."

"First ten pages at the library when you said you were working with her." His nose wrinkled.

"Crap," Ed pronounced. "He made me read it, too."

"It did seem to be pretty basic, under the lurid stuff. She's really good at writing vivid detail, whether it's violence or sex. But there's not a lot of structure."

"That's why I prefer the classics," Garrett said. "Dorothy Sayers couldn't just have Lord Peter and Harriet throw their clothes off when things got boring."

"Might have done them good." Ed chuckled. He's an old-school shoot-em-up fan—probably because Spenser can do all kinds of things he never got to do—and thinks Sayers and Christie are just a little too precious. Once in a while, Garrett makes him watch the David Suchet Poirot series just to see him squirm.

"Anyhow," said Garrett with a squashing glance to his husband, "the fact remains that you've been drawn in to help a middling thriller writer reinvent herself with a little costume-drama porn. A damn near impossible task."

"Reinvent herself? Isn't that a bit much?"

"If you ever troubled to visit Writer Flutter, which we have already established you should, you would know publishing is a huge mess right now, thanks to Covid, e-publishing, the economy, and Lord knows what else." Garrett glared. "Your client is right in the middle of it. She wasn't enough of a sensation to weather the pandemic—though she probably did better than any poor schmo who debuted in the spring of 2020."

"I don't think anyone noticed anything but fear of immediate death right then."

"Exactly. But Ms. Brockway did not live up to the promise of her big advance, so she has to find something else to do…and she has to sell it like it's a new evolution."

"Hence the historical project."

"Hence." Garrett nodded. "I would be very careful of her. Desperation and entitlement are a nasty combination."

Norm woofed. We were at the Society stairs, and the Empress was in the window. Hissing.

"We can take this up later. Lewis is probably here already, working on his exhibit."

"He's doing the whole front room for fall, right?" Garrett asked.

"Sure is."

"Good for him." Ed didn't spend a lot of mental energy on Society exhibits, but he likes and respects Lewis—and the effort involved in getting a PhD. He'd better if he doesn't want to wake up strangled with a different doctor's academic hood one of these days.

Chapter Twenty-Four: Dangerous Patterns

Jensen wanted to go back to the 1806 bedroom to, as she put it, "absorb the ambiance." As long as she was quiet, out of the way, and didn't damage anything, she could absorb the paint from the walls for all I cared. Probably, I should have been more cautious, but I didn't have the mental energy for her just then, and anyhow, if she was dumb enough to steal, I'd know right away. In addition to the comprehensive notes I make when I set up a room, I memorize every piece. I'm not as good as Henry, with his photographic memory, but I know my exhibits. Jensen couldn't move a cosmetic jar without my knowing it. I waved her on her way and headed to my office.

The phone started ringing as soon as I put my bag down on the desk. Bethany, asking if I could print up the original rose pattern in case she wanted to do a dress in that pattern for her grandbaby, too. Such an easy request I could knock it out before the rest of the day, and I decided to do just that.

Especially since I'd promised Joe to do a little nosing around about the land. Sometimes, it's better to be lucky than good.

I left Lewis in charge, sitting in the workroom with coffee and a little map of the front room, gaming out his fall exhibit, while the Empress watched from one of her favorite perches on a file cabinet. She doesn't particularly like Lewis and never engages with him unless bribed, but she does seem to enjoy watching him.

Bethany, Unity's Registrar of Deeds, was in her office when I came in with the pattern.

She looked up and smiled. "Thanks."

"Glad to…it's nice to be involved in something sweet and happy right now."

"No kidding. Too much negativity." A sigh. "No surprise, I suppose, considering it was all around Rowland Stark."

"Yeah. I've been hearing a lot about him."

"I heard a lot before it ever got to you, honey." She gave me a wry grin.

"The strip mall site?"

"Oh, yeah. That site was trouble from the drop, and Stark never helped himself."

"No?"

She shook her head. "Came in all hard like Mr. Big Businessman. Alienated folks."

"Weird. His wife's from a local family. You'd think they'd know better."

"Her?" Bethany snorted. "Even worse. A few weeks ago, she was in here looking at the parcels. Demanding to look at maps like we were her staff."

"Not cool." Town Hall employees work hard and there's no faster way to annoy them than attitude.

"Nope." A shrug. "Whole thing is pretty silly, Christian."

"Why?"

"Rowland spent the last twenty years in this stupid contest over the strip mall…when he should have looked behind him."

"What?"

She gave me a canny little smile. "You know what that land, and the big Taylor plot next to it, back up against?"

"No clue."

"Walpole U."

My jaw dropped. "Walpole? Wow."

"They've been eyeing surrounding property for years. And now that they have that money from the chicken-sandwich guy, well, you know it's going to happen. But my pal over in Cheshire says their council probably won't okay much more expansion."

"And the school has to go somewhere."

"Yep. Old Rowland was sitting on a gold mine; he just didn't know which one.

"No kidding." Now for my question. "What about the Taylor trust land? Is that anywhere in the area?"

"It's right next to it. But I don't think Walpole should get too excited about it. I know Amy Taylor's been looking at the open space preservation process."

"It would make sense for her," I said. "She's a big supporter of the Historical Society, so it fits."

"Yep. But it's a lot different if a college is looking at the land than if it's a strip mall," Bethany said. "Much different use, and some things would still be preserved."

"True." I nodded. "Has Walpole started anything official here?"

"Nope…but I'd guess it's just a matter of time." She glanced down at the pattern. "This is so pretty. I'm so excited to have a girl on the way."

"After being a boy mom." I smiled. "I know that one."

"My two were two years apart. Love everything about 'em…but I can't wait to dress this little girlie."

"Nice." I'd often thought it would have been nice to have a girl, too. But I'd been older than the average first-time mom, and the early tests had suggested trouble. Henry, of course, turned out to be just fine, but Frank and I decided not to roll the dice a second time.

And then, I was really glad to not be a single mother of two.

But I wasn't above hoping for a granddaughter one day.

Bethany took the pattern, and ran a finger over the flowers, then gave a rueful sigh. "Bet she's a tomboy, and it won't last."

"It'll be at least a couple years before she can assert herself."

"Good point. I'll make the best of the time while I can." She beamed.

Behind me, a harried-looking woman slipped in the door. I recognized her as the assistant from Sally Birdwell's real estate office. Better get out of the way.

"See you later," I said. "I want to see the finished dress."

"Absolutely."

As I walked back to the Society, I thought about Walpole University.

School expansions were nothing new around here. Yale had a big chunk of New Haven, and by now, Hamden was essentially a wholly owned subsidiary of Quinnipiac. Walpole wasn't as grand as those; a small religious school, it had been off in that corner near the town line for decades. A couple years ago, though, the owner of a big sandwich chain had left his fortune to Walpole, and we'd started to hear more about them. Community events, sports teams moving up a division, that sort of thing.

A major expansion would make sense.

If Bethany was right and there was nowhere to go but back, the land was suddenly important.

Really important. I knew enough about land and zoning to know the road access from the strip mall was a big deal. And the Taylor land? More space, at least…and a creek ran through it, so maybe water rights. Or something related to the way it fits into the landscape and the other parcels. There might be a survey or other study on record to give some kind of hint.

Whatever it was, Jensen and Linley were both in this up to their eyeballs.

From different sides, I had to believe. Linley wanted to push ahead on the strip mall…and Jensen was a member of the group fighting it.

And both might have some stake in the Taylor land, though that was still in Amy's control…right?

I texted Joe as I crossed the Green. More information to share.

If I got a chance to share it with him over some nice wine later, that was my business.

Chapter Twenty-Five: Hearth and Hounded

Of course, Jensen was still at the Society when I returned.

She startled when I walked into the 1806 bedroom, and I immediately understood why: she was filming the whole thing with her phone.

"Hi." I stood in the doorway, arms crossed. One of the advantages of my size is that I'm a little intimidating, whether I want to be or not. Just then, I wanted to be.

"Um, hi." She had the grace to look slightly guilty. "I'm just getting some video…"

"I'm assuming that's for your own private use. If it's not, I'll have to clear it with the Society board, and—"

"Oh, yeah. Just for me, to get some ideas."

"Fine." I smiled. Keep it friendly as long as I could. "Then do whatever you need to do. I'll be in the pantry working on a fall exhibit if you need me."

"Thanks, Christian."

"Sure."

Like it or not, fall was coming up fast, at least in museum time, and I really needed to lay some groundwork. I slipped into the pantry off the kitchen, where we kept the old cookware and other accoutrements, and started looking at the big pieces, hoping for inspiration for the fall kitchen exhibit.

We are extremely lucky to have a huge eighteenth-century hearth, complete with an oven built into the brick of the wall. It's mostly intact, because the family that owned the house built a big new mansion a few streets over and kept the older building for poor relations and servants, none of whom merited a kitchen makeover.

Most of them would have eaten at the new house, anyway.

So, unlike almost every other surviving house, from the late Colonial period, we have a virtually intact kitchen. It's a showpiece, and I like to celebrate it with displays demonstrating how it was used.

This is also one of the places where I really get that strong resonance of the people who lived here and used the space. I freely admit this sounds more than a little paranormal, but I always feel like the kitchen is welcoming me when I work here. I try to set it up to provide the same warmth to our visitors.

Fall exhibits are always special, and a little touchy. It would be lazy, not to mention inaccurate and more than slightly colonialist, to go with some kind of easy Thanksgiving theme. That's not fair to the place, or the people who come to visit.

We'd done a winter holiday feast last year, with background on Indigenous solstice celebrations and the Puritan distaste for Christmas festivities. This year, I was thinking along the lines of a family supper on a cold night. Maybe a big pot for stew, and an exhibit on breadmaking with a kneading board. Could use one of the big pie pans, too, because in the Colonial-period, sweet pies weren't dessert, but breakfast, or maybe even a main dish, depending on the family and the day.

I enjoy fun facts, and our visitors do too.

School groups, especially. I have a whole presentation on Victorian bathroom habits that's a real winner…with a little careful editing to avoid calls from irate parents.

Pie should be pretty safe.

Even as I started making notes on my legal pad about the display, I knew my luck was running out; no way Jensen would leave me alone long enough for me to finish the preliminary points. And I wasn't sure I should give her free rein anyway.

So, I was a little extra careful about my handwriting. More than once, I've scrawled some key point on a tablet, only to find it completely unintelligible hours later...and to discover I had a disaster on my hands because of whatever I'd left out.

The pantry is a public area, and pieces not featured in current displays are stored there if they're older, or just look interesting. But we have a lot of stuff packed in there. It sometimes takes a bit of doing to find things.

Which is how I ended up crawling into a low shelf to find the metal pie pan I wanted, carefully moving pieces around as I heard various footsteps. I didn't pay much attention to a light set of treads until they stopped near me, and a wry little chuckle erupted.

"Hi, Christian. What are you looking for?"

Jensen.

Standing over me, as I crawled around with my country girl backside sticking out. Jensen, of course, being a suburban WASP and a devotee of whatever particular form of fitness torture was fashionable at the moment, had no visible backside.

These are the days that try women's souls.

"Hi, Jensen." I took a breath and slowly extricated myself and my pie pan. "Just working on an exhibit."

From my spot on the floor, I was once again reminded that she was, as always, perfectly turned out, in a white tee and pink gingham skirt, with espadrilles in exactly the right shade of pink. I wondered if she had someone to pick out these getups for her or if she kept a spreadsheet.

"What's the exhibit? That stuff looks really old."

"Oh, it is. Some of the oldest stuff we have."

Her eyes gleamed. "Regency old?"

"Even older." I held up the pie plate. "I bet you know what this is used for."

"Pie?"

"Sure is."

"Squirrels or birds or something...or apple?"

"Could be anything. Even four-and-twenty-blackbirds." I waited for

Jensen to get the joke. When she didn't, I went on: "Well, probably not that many blackbirds, but you get the idea."

She nodded. "Look, even after all morning in the bedroom, I'm having trouble getting the vision."

"How so?" This was obviously some Yale MFA kind of existential angst. Getting the vision wasn't an issue for me. Getting the work done was. But I might be able to help her, anyhow. As I returned some of the other pieces to their shelves, I stopped at a wooden box. "Here. Carry this into the kitchen for me, and we'll talk."

"It's okay to—"

"Sure. It's survived this long. You're not going to do anything terrible to it."

Her face relaxed a little. "Thanks."

"C'mon. Just hold that late Renaissance spice box for a minute and walk back here with me." As her fingers tightened on the box, her face changed. It gave me an idea. Let's try a test. If the box doesn't at least give her some kind of pull toward the past, she's wasting her time, and so am I.

Okay, see how we go.

Fortunately, the kitchen was a bit cluttered with the things I'd brought out to consider the previous day, and Jensen had to stand holding the box for a moment while I cleared a space on the table for it and the pie pan.

By the time I had the pan in place, and I reached for the box, she'd taken on the same slightly awed expression I'd seen on dozens of blasé tweens, overexcited fourth graders, and know-it-all volunteers.

Good. I guessed right. The piece got to her.

I never had any doubt about the power of the past, of course. What was in question was whether Jensen felt it. And her reaction suggested there was at least a little hope.

"Now, do you want to give me that so I can put it down here?"

"Um, can I hold it for another minute or so?"

"Of course." I smiled, "Feeling something?"

"Wait. You feel it, too?"

"I couldn't do this if I didn't," I assured her. "But I'm not a fiction writer. I don't process things the way you do. Is it giving you ideas or a sense of the time and people?"

"Not exactly. I'm just feeling sort of—warm and welcome here. Almost like when you walk into a room, and people look up and see you."

"This kitchen has that effect on a lot of folks."

"Weird. I've never noticed it before."

"Maybe you weren't open to it," I said. "The box probably helps."

"Yeah?"

"Yeah." I didn't really want to give her this, but I was in now. "I get kind of a resonance from certain objects, which is why I gave you the spice box. It's one of the pieces we can prove was brought over from England by one of the early families."

"The Taylors?"

"No, sorry. The Winfields, the people who built this house. They left it and the contents to the Society in the late 1800s, and that box was found in the pantry. It took a few more years for people to figure out it was as old as it is."

"How old?"

"It's late Renaissance, hard to say for sure. We know it must be at least 17th century.

"Sixteen-hundreds?"

"Yes. Possibly late fifteen-hundreds. The carved designs don't seem to match any of the known families, or any of the obvious aristocratic and royal possibilities, so we think it was a gift, but we don't know from—or to—whom. It would have been from someone of high status to someone of perhaps slightly lower status, and that's where our knowledge ends."

Jensen looked down at the box. A small coffer of beautifully inlaid and carved hardwood, it was designed to hold a nutmeg and its grater, wrapped sticks of cinnamon bark, or cloves. Spices were a bit more common, but nearly as precious, in the late Renaissance as they'd been in the medieval period, and almost everyone but royals hoarded and cherished their supply.

The box had a loop for a lock, long lost with the nutmeg grater, and the inlay featured the sort of swirling design you often see in brocade, with fanciful flowers and objects in the swirl. Each had some heraldic significance, but none of it added up to an answer for where it came from. We kept a few nutmegs and cinnamon sticks in it, wrapped in a bit of unbleached cotton fabric, just as they would have been at the time.

"It's been around that long?"

"At least." I chuckled, as much at myself as her. "We Americans are always a little floored by things of great age because we don't see too many."

"I suppose." She took a breath. "I'm still stuck on this box being brought across the ocean into an uncertain world all those years ago and the lives that must have happened around it. And it's still here."

"It is. One of the interesting things about studying household objects as opposed to, say, court records. Not that court records aren't important."

"But they're not personal in the same way."

"Well, they can get plenty personal. When this box was brought here, there were plenty of convictions for fornication."

"Forni—no."

"Yes. But only if the couple didn't 'do the right thing' and get married, allowing a child to be born out of wedlock and therefore without protection. Of course, it's sexist and retrograde, but it was the seventeenth century."

"What happened to them?"

"The women?"

"Yeah." Jensen nodded.

"Some kept the child and later married. A marriageable woman was such a valuable commodity in those early days that even an out-of-wedlock child was not a complete reputation destroyer. Close, but-"

"Say that again."

"Reputation—"

"No. The part about a woman."

"A marriageable woman was an extremely valuable commodity."

"That. Why?"

I heard footsteps in the front room. And Lewis faintly "Can I help you?"

"You know, Jensen, we'd better take this up later. Call me this afternoon if you want."

She handed me the box. "Please, just finish the thought about marriageable women. I'm getting a story idea."

"Okay. This is before most people were born here. Most of the folks who emigrated were males, or families. A single woman of childbearing age would only come over if there were a very good reason. Something she wanted to get away from…or something she was coming to."

"And so scarcity means value?"

"Exactly."

"And a woman who, say, was trying to get away from something bad could do that in a new world."

"She surely could. And many did."

"Hm." Jensen nodded. "You know, there might be a book in here somewhere. Thanks, Christian."

"Sure."

"Look what I found at the thrift store!" Faith was practically bouncing with excitement, her arms full of yellowing cotton. "It's broomstick lace and has to be a hundred years old!"

Jensen looked at me, eyes wide and desperate. Clearly, she was slipping out of her zone.

"You can get right out this way," I said. Just don't go through the front room and bother Lewis, okay?"

"Right. Thanks."

I saw Jensen out, and turned back to the front room, where Lewis was walking through with a legal pad, making notes.

"What are you thinking?"

"Well, you know how we have all those old ads and posters in the ephemera collection?"

"Sure."

"And some of them are kind of…" He broke off, shrugged. "Things we wouldn't really display now."

"Right."

"Well, what if we did an exhibition of old stereotypes as a look at how we see each other?"

"Wow." I nodded. "What a great idea."

"Yeah? Some folks might be offended that we're showing them."

"That's the point of taking a critical look. This is the very reason we save things."

"Will people get it?"

I grinned. "This is Connecticut. New England. We have open minds here, remember?"

"There's that."

"And Dina, Tiffany, and I will beat them senseless if they don't."

He laughed. "What's open-minded about that?"

"Open your mind, or I'll open your head, buddy." I said it in my best Bronx accent, picked up from Frank. "Old New York saying."

"Works for me. I'll go help Faith lay out the broomstick lace, and then start blocking out the exhibit space."

Problems solved for the moment, I holed up in my office with the paperwork and the kitchen notes. Maybe an hour later, I was deep in my groove when I heard footsteps — and a tense clearing of throat.

"She's watching me."

Lewis was standing in the doorway, looking frazzled.

"Who?"

"Mrs. Stark."

"When did she get here?"

"Maybe twenty minutes ago. I'm trying to figure out how much space I have for posters before I go downstairs and get all excited about what I have."

"Good idea."

"I think so. Easier without an audience, though." He shook his head. "I know she's grieving, but it's getting a little weird. She's just sitting in the front room. Watching me take notes like I'm the floor show."

"Ugh." I put down the notebook and patted Lewis's arm. "I'll talk to her."

"Thanks, Doc."

"Don't mention it. Literally." I sighed. Part of the fun of running the joint. Keep telling myself that.

"Better you than me, Lewis said. "Would you hate me if I went to grab an iced tea?"

"I'd hate you if you didn't."

He walked off, fast enough that I wondered if he was afraid someone might try to stop him. I wished someone would stop me.

I wasn't a Linley Stark fan on a good day.

But if 'twere done, best done quickly.

She was indeed, as advertised, snooping in the front room, pulling a book out of the shelves Lewis and I had painstakingly arranged for an earlier exhibit. I might have to kill her.

"Hi, Linley."

At the sound of her name, she jumped a little. "Oh, hello, Christian. Just enjoying the serenity here."

The Society is many things, but in the middle of exhibit planning, serene was not one.

Maybe our particular brand of crazy was a break for her.

She looked scrawny and tired, in a navy dress and cardigan. It could have been mourning, but she could just as easily have not felt like wearing her usual summer brights. I'd worn the same two blazers and three sweaters, all black and gray, for weeks because color felt like too much.

So, no judgment here.

But her eyes had a hectic glow now. Stress? Maybe just not sleeping.

"How are you doing?" I asked. The question was, of course, inane, but I hoped the sincerity of the ask put it over.

Her eyes narrowed for an instant, and then she just shook her head wearily. "About as horrid as expected. Rowland's calling hours are this evening, and I'm trying to stay busy."

"Ah." I nodded. "That one. I started writing thank-you notes and ended up sitting and staring into space."

"You have no idea."

Actually, I had a very good idea, but she was the sort of woman who needed her experience to be unique and special. I tried for diplomacy. "Probably so. It's a tough time and different for everyone."

"Sing that, sister."

For a second, I wondered if shed been drinking — I would not have blamed her! — and then I realized she was trying to be friendly. Maybe. "You know, I just made coffee. Would you like a cup?"

"Um…yes. That might help. At least it can't hurt."

"Nope."

I guided her into my office, sharing a brow flick with Lewis, who was just coming back from the minimart.

Linley sniffed as she walked into my office, clearly uncomfortable with the necessary clutter that goes with a well-used workspace. (That's my story, and I'm sticking to it!) But she didn't say anything as she sat down in the side chair, just arranged herself and smoothed her skirt with a little wince and waited for me to serve her.

I'm pretty sure there's never been a moment in my life when I just sat and waited for someone to serve me. Not in the training for a girl from Mars.

I filled my **We are in Fact Amused** mug, with its picture of a smiling Queen Victoria, and handed it to her. She looked at it for a second. "Who's that?"

Uh-oh.

"Never mind. Historians inside joke."

"Oh. Okay." She sniffed the coffee as if I might be offering her something poisonous—or substandard. Blinked in surprise and took a sip. "Well, that's quite good."

"I have a cousin in the coffee biz." I shrugged and topped up my own mug. "Do you have anyone helping you through all of this?"

"Yeah. I'm fine. I've got the accountant and the undertaker and the lawyer, so everything will be handled just perfectly. Morgan is on a summer study in Provence, and I ordered her not to come home."

She ordered her daughter not to come home?

Yikes.

Admittedly, Henry was smaller and sweeter, but I couldn't survive more than a few minutes without hugging or patting him for a while after Frank died. School was tough for the first couple weeks, and I embarrassed him incessantly with big hugs on the portico.

The crazy part was that Henry allowed—and probably even appreciated— it.

Who tells their kid to stay away and to grieve their father alone?

I pulled my face into carefully neutral lines and sat down at my desk. I didn't want to be too close to her, lest some of whatever made her that cold rub off on me. "Well, I'm glad you have everything under control. That's no small thing."

"It's as it should be. I'm really not some kind of cold fish, Christian. I'd love to hug the stuffings out of Morgan right now. But she's over there for this French immersion thing, and she's met a nice young man, and it's just not fair to ruin it." Linley managed a couple of elegant little tears.

Sure. Martyr mom.

Nobody's that good.

"I'm not judging," I said quickly. "We do what we need to do."

"Exactly."

I started organizing things on the desktop in hopes of giving her a hint. A couple of legal pads, a cookery book, a pot lid, a box of matches. "I really have to get organized."

"Don't we all."

I held up the matches. "These are a reminder to buy candles for Shabbat Friday…but I probably still won't remember."

"That's right, you're Jewish, Christian." A lame little chuckle.

I didn't engage, either on the joke, which was funny coming from Gerry Diamond, but not Linley, or the larger issue of my conversion. None of her damn business. "We light candles every week. This week, it'll be Friday night, since we're going to your great-aunt's Bat Mitzvah."

Linley smiled. "She's amazing, isn't she?"

"Yeah. I'm really looking forward to Saturday."

"I'm not sure I'm going."

"What?" I stared. "There's no reason you can't, even if you're in mourning. And a happy family event might help…"

I trailed off as she gave me a baleful look.

"I don't think so."

Yikes. Her tone and expression made it clear she considered her pain more important than Amy's happiness.

"Well, then," I said, because I had to say something.

"Well, maybe I should go," Linley said. "Maybe I should see if Morgan can get back here, at least to see me for a day or two."

"Might be good for you both." I stood, too. Try to be civil. "Or it may not. The one thing about grieving that's true for everyone is that it's different for everyone. Nobody gets to judge you and your choices."

Linley gazed at me for a moment, her blue eyes cold and, I realized, amused. "Oh, Christian honey, judging is the only thing most of us are good at."

Chapter Twenty-Six: Everything's Better with Italian Ice

The silver sedan pulled up at the camp pickup corner.

It would have made me nervous, except that by now I knew the car, and the TRUBILL tag.

"Hey. Can I interest you two in some Italian ice?"

"We don't take rides from people who just come up to us in the street, AlysDad." Henry gave him a teasing grin. "And definitely not treats."

"Well, I'm not just anyone."

"I know. Does the truck have no sugar-added?"

"As day follows night, good sir."

Henry's brow furrowed a little. Too poetic for him. "Is that a fancy way of saying, 'does a bear poo in the woods?'"

"Henry!" I chided.

"Exactly." Joe laughed but nodded to me. "Language around ladies, huh?"

"Yeah, fine, AlysDad. Kinda old-fashioned, isn't it?" he asked.

"Nothing wrong with a little old-school," I said. "Respect never goes out of style."

Joe shot me a smile over Henry's head, and I returned it. I do love a smart, respectful man.

"The truck's down at the Little League park. Let's go find out."

I climbed into the front, and both of us buckled up. The rules don't change.

"Do you mind if I have a word with your mom about a few things while we drive?"

"Not if she gives me her phone."

"Fair deal." I handed over the device to a very happy Henry. "You can play Demon Race mobile."

Joe turned off Main Street and onto the side street that led to the park. "So Dr. Alexandre called me today because of an unusual finding."

"Something else from Rowland Stark?"

"No." He shook his head. "The bones from the strip mall site."

"Why…"

"She knows I have a friend who knows artifacts." His ears turned a little pink. "It came up in conversation…and I probably sang your praises a little."

"Nice." I kept my tone as neutral as possible, even though my inner sixteen-year-old was thrilled he was talking me up.

"Well, you, Rabbi Aaron, and Lewis did have a look at the stuff from the site."

"We did."

"So it made sense that she'd reach out to me."

"Sure. What did she find?"

"The bones were lacquered. And had numbers painted on them." Joe's tone was so horrified that Henry looked up from the backseat.

"Specimens."

"What?"

Fortunately, he'd pulled into a parking space, so Joe was able to look at me.

"It's not some sort of weird serial killer—probably, anyway—they were most likely medical specimens. Victorian scientists used to number and catalogue their pieces. We have a couple specimen skeletons in the basement at the Society. And a box of assorted bones, too."

Joe laughed in relief. "Of course."

"It would definitely look weird to anyone who's used to dealing with seriously sick stuff, but that's probably all it is."

"Makes sense." He shook his head. "Now that I think about it, I think that's probably what Dr. Alexandre suspected. She wasn't nearly as troubled by the whole thing as I was."

"Uh-huh." I patted his arm. "But she went through med school. You didn't. A specimen skeleton would never occur to you."

"I guess." He turned to Henry. "C'mon, let's go get that Italian ice."

Once we were all happily supplied with our treats of choice—Henry with no-sugar cherry, Joe lemon—and me with the vile but fun blue—we sat at a picnic table and returned to the conversation.

"If they're specimens, it means we were right," I said. "Somebody did salt the site. Not once but twice."

Joe licked his ice cream and contemplated. "Can you trace the specimens? Since they have numbers and everything."

"Probably. I'll take a look at ours tomorrow. I think there's some documentation tucked in with them."

"Do you just keep them in the basement?" Joe looked concerned.

"If I thought about it, I'd be creeped out a little, but yeah." I shrugged. "They were a donation, and there's no really good way to get rid of them. I tried to palm them off on Yale Medical School, but they've got enough of their own."

"Heads up!" Henry called, tossing his crumpled-up ice cup at Joe.

Joe put one hand up and easily made the catch. "Good throw."

"He throws right, and bats left, you know," I said. Garrett had figured it out during a game of catch earlier in the summer, and it made all the difference in Henry's pickup games.

"Maybe toss the ball around when we get back to the house," Joe offered.

"Cool," Henry grinned. "You done with yours, Ma?"

"Yep." I handed over the empty cup.

Henry crumpled it and made a neat basket in the trash. "Two points!"

"Nothing like mixing your sports metaphors." Joe laughed. "So you'll check your skeletons tomorrow?"

"Yeah. And please, they're the Society's, not mine." I shook my head as Joe crumpled his cup.

"Fair enough." He tossed the cup to Henry, who made a smooth catch, then tossed it in the trash.

As we started walking toward the car, Joe's hand on my back, Henry skipped ahead, happily blowing on a dandelion. Lovely summer moment.

"The specimens weird us out, but they're probably not all that unusual. A fair number of doctors and museums had them."

"Where did they…" Joe asked.

"I'd guess mostly executed convicts or indigents," I started. As I said it, another possibility clicked. "And you know, it's also possible that even though they're specimens, they could still be Indigenous."

"Well, doesn't that add to the unpleasantness," he said. "Will we even be able to figure it out?"

"I had a forensic anthropologist look at ours a few years ago. They were pretty sure both were white males. One had a clearly visible hangman's fracture."

"Ugh."

"Yeah. Let's just leave it there." I knew more than I wanted to about the grisly details of old-fashioned executions.

Joe took my hand. "I suspect we can find something better to talk about on the way home."

"I'd guess. Want to hear how Garrett found out that Henry bats left?"

"That'll do."

Chapter Twenty-Seven: Boot on the Other Foot

Next morning, Ed and Norm arrived at the Green just in time to wave at the bus and exchange a quick hello with the ladies.

I suspected, considering his walking schedule, that the timing was no accident, and very quickly realized I was right. Ed's the strong, silent type, as you'd expect from a retired Statie, but, every once in a while, he needs to talk things out, and he's learned he can trust me.

By now, I recognized the tension in his posture and the little trace of a scowl on his normally happy face. Not to mention the way he kept his eyes on Norm while we started walking to the Society.

Totally fine by me. I'd do just about anything to avoid thinking about what I had to do when I got to work. Skeletons in the basement, yay.

Not that I had any intention of mentioning it to Ed.

"Did you hear the storm at about three a.m.?" I asked. "Had a heck of a time getting back to sleep."

"Heard it." He shrugged. "I was already up."

"Oh?"

"Not sleeping great lately."

I took a guess. "Since the explosion?"

Ed kept his eyes on Norm, who was happily scouting for squirrels. "Yep. Kinda weird, you know."

"Weird, how?"

"Done a lot of scenes. Disasters, fires, worse, you know."

"Yeah." I did know. Ed had been at just about every seriously bad crime or mishap in the state during his thirty years on the job. Some really horrible things.

"Part of the deal. Not my job to have feelings about it. My job to get some justice—or answers."

"Right."

"Been in a few hairy situations here and there too."

I nodded. "But you came through. And we all came through on the Fourth."

"Yeah. And I'm grateful. You know I don't go in for any of that churchy stuff, but I made sure to send some thanks to Whoever might be listening."

"So did I." Even though I've made my choice in religious practice, I don't think there's One Way. I think Whoever is listening, even if we talk to She/He/It/Them in different ways.

"But this damn thing bugs me."

"Bugs you as in criminality?"

"Well, that's practically a given."

"It is?"

"Come on, Christian. I'm not a big fan of these big boys playing dress-up, but they've been firing that thing twice a year for the last half a century or so without incident. Until now." He met my gaze, waited.

"So something changed." I love to logic things out with Ed. His mind works entirely differently than Garrett's or mine, thanks to the cop training, and I always learn a lot.

"Exactly. What's different this year? If you find out what's different now, and who benefits or loses out from it, then you'll be well on the way to finding out what happened."

"Could still be an accident."

"It could. If they changed powder makers, or some such thing. But it's more likely that someone did it or had it done."

"Had it done? You thinking the widow?"

"Spouse is always the first suspect," Ed agreed. "Even in something freaky like this."

"True. But there are a lot of suspects. Rowland Stark was not especially well-liked."

"Understatement of the year." He nodded. "Not a great guy."

"So why are you losing sleep over somebody blowing him up?"

"Shouldn't be. Except that somebody almost blew up my husband, and a good chunk of my family with that guy."

"Ah." I kept my gaze on Norm, as he did. "And it's probably the first time you're the one worried about someone in danger instead of the one on the line."

"Been thinking I put my wife through a lot back in the day."

"She signed on for it, I'm sure."

"She did. But I didn't understand until this week what it was really like."

"The fear?"

"Yeah. And I bet you know how we macho men react to fear."

"Been angry about everything, right?"

"Dumb fights. Just went round with Garrett over eggs for breakfast, if you can believe it." He let out an awkward bark that might have been an attempt at a laugh.

"Eggs?"

"Found myself yelling about cholesterol. Stupidest thing yet."

"Ya think?" I patted his arm. "You've never had the shoe on the other foot. And Garrett probably knows why you're being—angular."

"Angular?"

"Yeah. You know, like Cookie when he doesn't want to be held." I moved my hands around like I was trying to grab a slippery cat. "He turns into a ball of angles."

"You know, 'ball of angles' is a pretty good description of the way I've been feeling."

"Good name for a rock band, too."

A small but genuine chuckle. "Probably need to climb down a little."

"Teensy bit. Let the guy have his eggs, for heaven's sake."

"Think I'll make them for him, now that you mention it." He gave me a smile. "Thanks, Christian."

"You got there. I just listened while you did."

"You're pretty good at this stuff."

"Earned it the hard way. Had to do a lot of working and thinking the last few years."

"No kidding." He rested a hand on my arm. "Done good."

"Thanks."

"Okay, your turn. You serious about Joe?"

"It's moving that way." I couldn't stop a blush. "Getting kind of interesting."

Ed's eyes narrowed. "He's not pushing you…"

"Not even a little. Actually spent the time to carefully explain to me that he'll respect whatever my religious boundaries are."

"Oh, hell," he growled. "I suppose we'd better just start planning the damn wedding."

"We are not anywhere near there yet."

"Will you agree that I'm familiar with the way old-school men behave?"

"Sure."

"Well, when an old-school man, like your cute friend Joe, spends as much time with a lady as he does without making a hard move, while talking about respecting your religion, he's already made up his mind."

"Yeah?"

"Yeah." Ed sighed. "It's not a bad thing. I'm just going to warn you one more time that if you marry this fella, there will be a lot of nights at home alone."

"Done that before. The right man is worth it."

"And…"

"Jury's still out, but signs are pointing that way."

"Why do I think you've made up your mind, too?" Ed asked.

"You think I'm going to admit it yet?"

"Nah." A real laugh. "I'd be disappointed in you if you did. Gotta make that boy work for it."

"A little effort never hurt anyone," I said.

"Nope."

We were at the Society, and the Empress was sitting in the bay window, glaring at Norm. Time for me to move on to the next—much less pleasant—

thing. And if you think I was going to tell Ed, you're nuts.

"Well, thanks for the walk," I said. "I'd offer you coffee, but I think you have some eggs to cook."

"I do." Ed smiled. The little tense spot in his jaw had relaxed, even if he still looked a bit tired. "Thanks, Christian."

"Glad I can help once in a while. You guys have been so good to me and Henry, it's nice to give something back."

"Nah." He held my gaze, very seriously. "You two are a pleasure. Awfully nice having you so close. I wasn't the most involved dad, big surprise, so it's a treat being able to be around now."

"Let's just say we're both good for each other and leave it at that."

"Mutual admiration society." Ed turned. "Think I should make him a scramble with cheese?"

"Don't overdo it."

Chapter Twenty-Eight: Skeletons in the Basement

When I got inside, the Society was quiet. Too quiet. Lewis was starting the day at Yale, looking at some ideas for his front-room exhibit and double-checking sources for his dissertation. I probably should have waited for the docents to arrive, but I wanted to get it over with. The stairs are very steep, and we don't normally allow anyone to go down there alone, because there's no way we want to find an eighty-year-old in a heap on the basement floor.

I didn't want to end up in a heap, either. But I didn't want those damn skeletons hanging over my head.

So to speak.

We kept them in the far end of the root cellar. It was clean, whitewashed, and well-lit, but it was still a three-hundred-year-old hole in the ground. A chilly three-hundred-year-old hole in the ground. You'd have to be far less sensitive to vibes than me not to get a creepy feeling up the spine.

If 'twere done, 'twere best done quickly.

Shakespeare, of course, not the Reverend Donne, but good enough.

The far storeroom was kept closed but not locked like everything downstairs. We have a decent security system, and a small staff, and honestly, I'm not too worried about people running off with our sheet music and seamed stockings.

We do have several very old and valuable pieces, but they're upstairs and separately secured.

When I'd taken over, the downstairs looked like one of the less well-organized Ancient Egyptian tombs, with stuff haphazardly piled in wherever it might fit. Or not fit, as the case may be.

I'd spent every spare moment of my first two years organizing, and if it wasn't exactly in apple-pie order, it was certainly relatively neat, with a clean white plastic shelving and drawer set up on the walls, trunks, and other containers filling most of the middle of the room. I hadn't been here in a while, but I knew the space well, and it looked like someone else had been moving things around.

Probably Lewis, looking for pieces for his exhibit.

Except he was painfully organized.

Maybe I was imagining things because I was nerved-out.

The skeletons lived, er, were kept, on the bottom of a shelving unit near the far wall. They had large, purpose-built black leather-on-wood cases that looked a bit ominous but not coffin-like, and I'd stacked them one on top of the other, with the box of assorted bones at the foot. It was sort of a sample case of finger, toe, and other small bones, apparently for closer study. That was a guess. The whole setup had been a donation from a Yale medical school professor, which is why I tried and failed to give it back to the Ivy.

All right.

"Let's do this."

My voice bounced off the stone wall.

Creepy.

Okay. I reached for the first skeleton case. It was lighter than I remembered. But I'd been doing a lot of yoga lately, so all my muscles were smooth and tight, just in case somebody might see more of me.

It wasn't the yoga.

I flipped the burnished brass locks and took a breath, steeling myself for the entirely normal human reaction to the sight of bones. From the dust we came, and to the dust we shall return…but it's still pretty fraught.

Except the case was empty.

"Oh, holy hell." I pushed the first case aside and opened the second.

No one home here, either.

What about the small case?

Empty.

I sat down on a trunk.

Who steals skeletons?

I couldn't give the damn things away a few years ago.

Only a few people even knew we had them. It wasn't something we advertised, though some of the older docents liked to bring the young volunteers down and show them the bones to scare them. When I found out, I strongly discouraged them…but there's only so much you can do with septuagenarians.

And I'd have to be a lot dimmer than I am not to go to the obvious issue: were the skeletons at the site ours?

If they were, how did they get there? Probably didn't walk.

Plenty of new questions.

Chapter Twenty-Nine: (Regency) Love Overload

That afternoon, Garrett and Norm were at the Society door when I headed out for the camp bus.

By then, I'd texted Joe about the skeletons and sent along our records so Dr. Alexandre could review and possibly match them. Until the M.E. did her work, we couldn't go much further…and honestly, between Lewis's exhibit and a couple of minor crises involving the planning of fall talks, I'd pretty much sent the skeletons to the basement corner of my mind.

Besides, I was thrilled to see Garrett looking relaxed and happy for a change.

"Ed came home from Norm's morning walk and made me a lovely omelet," he said after hugs and pats were exchanged. "Do you happen to know anything about this?"

"I'm a barely adequate cook. You know that." I tried, and failed, to cultivate an innocent expression.

"Well, he definitely talked himself out of his funk, so if you're the one who listened while he did, thank you."

"Glad to. It makes sense that he'd have a hard time being the worried spouse instead of the spouse in danger. It's never happened to him before."

"As he pointed out, while grating Parmigiana on my fresh basil, spinach, and tomato omelet."

"Was it good, the omelet?"

"Very. You should try it. A nice sneaky way to get Henry to branch out on veggies."

"True." We walked a few hundred yards in companionable silence, with Norm sniffing for errant squirrels.

"So, did I tell you our skeletons are missing?"

Garrett blinked. "Who steals skeletons?"

"Someone who wants to salt the strip mall site, maybe."

"Maybe," Garrett said as he reined in Norm, "but you have bigger problems right now."

"Bigger than missing property?"

"Yes. This is about your name."

"My name?" I asked. I did not like his serious expression.

"Have you seen what your client is saying online?"

"I checked her feed a few days ago when that video from the explosion surfaced, just to make sure she wasn't sharing it. But nothing since."

"Well, you'd better." He scowled.

"Why? Her feed seems to be all about reality TV crap and occasionally a promo for her book."

"She's started talking up this *Regency Love* thing."

"But it's not sold, and it's pre-production, and…"

"And I bet she's hoping to develop a following to increase her chances of getting a deal."

"I guess that would make sense…wouldn't it?"

"Maybe. I'm not sure this is the way to go about it, though." He pulled his phone out of his pocket, swiped and tapped a couple times, and handed it to me. "Just hit Play. It's amazing what AI can do if you don't have much in the way of ethics or sense."

"AI?"

"I'm sure this is from one of those sites that uses AI to animate bits of stock video."

"There are…"

Garrett glared. "Yes. Here in the 21st century, we have many useful things, and some rather terrifying ones."

"Which is this?"

"Terrifying, if you support real-life actors, writers, and artists."

"Okay." I nodded. "Just wanted to be sure we were on the same page."

"Could a fella from Akron and a girl from Mars ever NOT support unionized workers?"

"Duly noted." I watched as Norm sniffed a dandelion, found it wanting, and kept walking. "So what is this video Jensen posted?"

"A trailer for *Regency Love*. Play it."

I tapped the button. It started with a closeup of the bodice of a high-waisted white dress—yes, an actual heaving bosom—and went on from there.

"Imagine taking Regency romance behind closed doors…" intoned a low, sultry female voice. I wondered if she was AI, too. "A dozen singles will come to the Regency Mansion"—stock picture of the Royal Crescent in Bath—"to learn the secrets of seduction."

A woman's hand lighting a generic silver candelabra dissolved to video of the 1806 Bedroom, zooming in on the bed. And then it got worse—a cut to a hand, a different woman's hand, running down the bare chest of a studly man. More cheesy music and a dissolve to a small candleholder.

"And when the Candle Ceremony comes, who will choose to share light—and the warmth?"

Cut back to the bed. Our—the Society's—bed.

"Coming soon: *Regency Love,* in which singles will find a whole new way to connect, without the distractions of modern life."

Then—the hand of yet a third woman put out the candle. Not with a pewter snuffer, which would have been period-appropriate, but with her fingers. A little flash in the background and then a final slide:

Historical advice from consultant Christian Shaw. Regency Love is a Jensen Brockway Production. For inquiries and more information, go to jensenbrockway.com.

"What the actual…" I gasped. "She used our room—and put my NAME on it!"

Garrett, blast him, let out a chuckle. "I told you that one has no respect for anyone, living or dead. Never mind history."

"She wouldn't know history if it bit her in the—"

"Corset." He grinned. He wasn't really enjoying my discomfort, just reveling in the absolute cheese of it all. "Cheer up. You've done your part, explaining to her what's going on and why it won't work."

"Yeah?" I shook my head. "She put my damn name on it."

"That's good, actually." The grin faded to a canny smile. "Now, you have a way out of this."

"I do?"

"You do." He beamed. "You can quit in a principled huff over the trailer and be shed of the whole mess."

"I don't think I've ever had a principled huff in my life."

"Now's a great time to start." He patted my arm. "You give Jensen formal notice. I'll write your statement. By tomorrow afternoon, you'll be up to your eyeballs in offers from serious people."

"You think?"

"Watch and learn, Young Grasshopper." A reassuring smile. "Do you really think I'd steer you wrong?"

"No, but you might have questionable judgment."

"You've seen the trailer."

"Yeah." I sighed. "It's the only questionable thing here. I don't think anyone will recognize the 1806 Bedroom, but it's sure not good."

"No, it is not."

We were almost to the Green, and the camp bus was within sight.

"All right. Let's pick up Henry, and then we'll get to work."

Within an hour, Henry was clean, fed, and hanging out on the couch with Cookie and his tablet. I'd sent Jensen an email formally telling her to cease and desist using the video of the 1806 Bedroom because she did not have the required approval of the Society. I also officially ended our contract because she'd used my name without my permission. The deal, worked up with the help of a friend of Garrett's who does some work on Civil War pieces, required credit on a finished work, but did not allow my name to be used for anything else without my permission.

Garrett's friend had been burned.

Now, apparently, so had I.

But unlike Garrett's friend—and directly thanks to his experience—I had a clause in the contract allowing me to break it and demand immediate payment to date in case of a violation. My email to Jensen did exactly that.

Once we sent the notice, Garrett logged into the Social Network account I keep for connections with distant relatives and former coworkers and wrote up a post. He scrounged up a pic of me placing a porcelain dish on the Society mantel from an article in the town weekly, and assembled the whole thing into a very nice little piece:

"For anyone who wishes to know: I am no longer consulting on the Regency Love project for Jensen Brockway Productions. The lack of commitment to historical accuracy made me uncomfortable, as did the clearly salacious intent of the project. The use of my name to give it some credibility was the final straw. As a professional historian, and equally importantly, a person with a sense of history, I can no longer be a part of this production. I wish Ms. Brockway well in her future endeavors."

I high-fived Garrett. "Wow. That'll do it."

"You like?"

"I love. Post it."

"Good." He hit the button. "Do you have a private Flutter account? Or PhotoThing?"

"No…"

"Well, you will when I'm done. We'll call you Professor Stuff."

"We will, huh?"

"We will. You have to fight back on the ground where the battle takes place. She put your name out on social media in connection with this mess, so you'll need to take it back." He patted my arm. "I'll monitor the accounts for you for now. And I'll pass on any offers. Which you'll be getting."

"I hope you're right. I feel kind of bad spiking her in public."

"She made it public. As you put it, she used your damn name."

"She did that."

"You didn't have a choice, Christian." He gave me a naughty little smile. "Unless you wanted people to think you're a part of this *Regency Love* mess."

"Good Lord, no."

"So you did the only thing you could. When she calls to yell at you—and she will—refer her to your lawyer."

"I don't have a lawyer."

"Sure you do. Don't tell me Joe wouldn't have fun with this. He gets to defend his woman and take a break from murders."

"I'm not his woman."

"Okay. Whatever you say." Garrett shrugged. "Anyway, you have legal counsel if you want it. I'm going to go home and make my husband his favorite dinner."

"Yeah?"

"Oh, yeah." Back to the grin. "I think he's earned it.

* * *

That evening, Joe's late-evening jog brought him to my door close to Henry's bedtime.

Early in his last trial, we'd maintained the fiction that it was just coincidence. These days, though, it's become a comfortable routine. He'd appear at my door, a little charged-up and glowy from a real jog, exchange a few gentlemanly pleasantries with Henry, and then join me in the living room for a glass of nice chianti.

Not the usual sports drink, but of course, the New Haven Italians are different.

Neither of us treated these little visits as dates—they were unofficial tryouts for something far more serious, and the casualness was a big part of the point. So he was in worn-in but not grubby navy joggers and a gray Yale Law tee, and I didn't worry about what he thought of my leggings, washed-out chambray work shirt, and ponytail.

"Just half a glass, okay? I have more stuff to plow through tonight."

"Fair enough." I poured the two small drinks and joined Joe on the couch. His jog wasn't long or intense enough to get him repulsively sweaty; he just had a healthy sheen, and his normally very pleasant cologne morphed into something warmer and muskier.

I'd forgotten how wonderful it was to just sit and be comfortable with a partner.

"No word from Dr. Alexandre on the skeletons just yet," said Joe after a sip. "But it's a pretty good bet they're yours."

"I won't be surprised." I drank a bit of my own wine. "I wish the skeletons were my only problem."

"Yeah?" He heard the concern in my voice. "What else?"

I gave him a quick outline of the online Jensen mess. He scowled as I explained what she'd done, but his expression relaxed as I explained how Garrett had pulled me through.

"Garrett is right," Joe said. "You had to cut off Jensen fast and hard. Once she dragged your name into it, you didn't have a choice."

"I guess. And I sent the letter the way my contract requires, so..."

"Are you worried about her suing you?" he asked.

"Maybe a little."

Joe cackled. A shocking sound that made me think of nothing so much as the Wicked Witch of the West.

"What?"

"Oh, I hope she tries. It would be so much fun to shut her down."

"Really?"

"Really. You followed your contract to the letter, so she'd just come at you because she screwed up, and you called her out. I could have a lot of fun with this."

"But you're..."

"I am indeed a duly appointed assistant state's attorney, so I can't really do it myself." Small shrug and canny smile. "But I have a friend or two at Magen and Renzulli who still owe me favors. And who like seeing the right thing happen. One in particular really enjoys smacking around Karens, which—with apologies to all women named Karen—Jensen seems to fit the profile."

"She does. And it is too bad a nice name has those connections."

"Anyhow, I'm going to be Mr. Macho Dude here for a second—but know it's because I have a couple of ferocious female pals of varying racial and ethnic backgrounds at the ready, okay?"

"Okay."

"Don't you worry your pretty little head about this, my dear."

"Nice."

"Oh, so not nice. If I have to unleash Vera Monroe on her, it will not be pretty. But Vera will have a great time. In fact, I'm kind of hoping she does jump ugly, so I don't have to buy Vera a Christmas present this year."

"Yeah?"

"Yeah. So find something else to worry about for a while."

"Okay."

The comfortable silence hung between us for a bit. It wasn't a bad thing. Then he took a breath. "So I'd like to ask you a favor."

"Sure. Whatever I can do."

"You might want to let me ask before you say yes," he said with a nervous chuckle, edging his tone.

"What?"

"Well, it's Aly."

"Aly?"

"Yeah. See, she's the tallest kid in her class, and she's having a little trouble with it. And—I thought maybe you could help her understand that it's a good thing to be a tall girl."

"I can talk to her," I said. "But it's kind of her mother's area, and I—"

"Her mother suggested it. Amber's tiny. She heard Aly mention how tall you are and thought maybe you could offer some encouragement."

"Oh." I'd never met Amber, but I imagined something like: 'Why don't you ask your giant girlfriend if she can help.'

"Seriously. I can tell Aly until I'm blue in the face that she's the most beautiful sight I've ever seen or ever will see, but it doesn't carry a lot coming from Dad."

"There's always the discount. They assume we think they're wonderful and don't hear praise. Cost of being a supportive parent."

"True." He laughed. "So, can you nudge her a bit in the direction of tall and terrific?"

"I like the way you put that." I took a breath. "Problem is, I didn't feel very terrific at her age. I grew into it later."

"Oh." He was clearly disappointed.

"But you know, now that you mention it, it would have been a lot easier to grow into it if there were a reasonably cool non-mom lady hanging around to tell me that it gets better…and that someday I'll be glad to be noticeable."

"Are you? Glad, I mean?"

"It's good for teaching, and I'm really glad I was able to pass my size on to Henry." I sighed. "And I've made my peace with being big."

"Tall and graceful."

"Oh. That's sweet, but I've always wanted to be small and portable."

"Portable?"

Oh, dear. I'd just been joking, honestly, but it played into almost every tall girl's deepest fantasy. "Well, no one ever sweeps a six-footer off her feet, you know."

"Hmm." Joe's voice turned from concerned dad to something else entirely. "Maybe we'll have to remedy that."

"Really?"

"You never know what might happen one of these nights."

"Ah. There's that."

"Hold that thought for now. You'll talk to Aly next time we're all in town?"

"Sure. Anything I can do. Maybe I'll let her prowl through my vintage oxfords and blazers and see that there are some fun things that little girls don't get to enjoy."

"Good idea. I've got to get back to those reports."

"I have to finish writing that corset article."

"I think you have a better deal."

Chapter Thirty: A Summer's Day

Wednesday, finally, we had an almost normal day.

My alarm went off at the right time, Henry didn't argue about clothes and only grumbled a little at the required morning coating of sunscreen and bug repellant, and everyone was in a cheerful and relaxed mood at the bus stop, chatting amiably about gardens and Kule's strawberry sorbet.

Even better, Joe turned up as the coffee was brewing, carrying a couple of big showy irises.

"Wow. To what do I owe this pleasure?"

"Saw them on my way out and thought of you. We have all those fancy plantings in the front, and I never do anything with them. These ones are really pretty and smell nice."

I took the flowers. They were beautiful: ruffly petals in shades of pinky-peach with a lit-from-within glow and a surprisingly lovely scent. "They are nice. I'll put them in water."

As I turned to kiss Joe on the cheek, he pulled me in.

"Wow," I said, a very pleasant moment later. "A very nice morning indeed."

"Yeah, well. This little coffee break is all the time I have today. I'm going to be at the office late tonight working on some pretrial motions."

"Sorry." I rummaged out a water bottle left over from the last board meeting, snapped it open, and placed the two stems in it. "The flowers are elegant enough for everything."

I moved the little box of matches to clear space, glad I'd made the online order for Sabbath candles with enough time to spare.

"Definitely." He walked over to the coffee maker. "Want me to pour?"

"Oh, thanks."

"Sure." Joe smiled as he handed me my mug. "I make a nice breakfast, too."

"Bet you do."

He didn't go for the obvious follow-up because this was clearly just a little light slap-and-tickle to brighten our busy days.

After a cup's worth of cheerful and inconsequential conversation, he went on his way, exchanging a handshake with Lewis at the door and striding out to the silver sedan. Lewis shot me a grin as he headed for the front room.

The rest of the day was almost routine—or would have been if Linley hadn't arrived as I was walking to the door for camp bus pickup.

"I'm trying to stay busy," she announced. "Is there anything I can do?"

Since I'd seen an item about Rowland's funeral on the news website, I guessed we were her new distraction.

"Um, maybe…" Lewis and Faith had the broomstick lace spread on the worktable, and they were carefully looking over it. "Hi, you two—would you like an extra pair of eyes?"

From their expressions, it was clear they would not have minded the extra eyes…if they hadn't been in Linley Stark's face.

I gave Faith and Lewis an *I owe you* look and turned to Linley. "They're looking over this new piece…maybe you can pitch in."

"Sure!" She beamed and clapped her hands. "Let me help."

Faith and Lewis glared over her head.

"I'll be back with Henry in a few minutes," I promised, patting my pocket to be sure I had a packet of the peanut butter crackers he likes for getting his numbers back up at the end of the camp day.

I wasn't sure if it was Faith or Lewis who growled in response, and it didn't really matter. I knew I had to get back pronto. As I stepped onto the porch, my phone buzzed with a text from Tiffany. She had a late call and wondered if I could get Ava.

"Glad to," I texted back. "You two still alone tonight? Want to do bachelorette dinner at my place?"

By the time the bus pulled up, Tiffany and I had made our plans—and

Garrett had texted me, asking if we had anything in mind for the evening. We aren't all on some kind of cosmic party line…but it sure seems that way sometimes.

Anyhow, at least I had a good evening to look forward to as Henry, Ava, and I walked into the Society, ready to rescue Lewis and Faith from Linley. And then get the kids back to my place to dust off. Thankfully, it was a dry day, so they weren't muddy. Just grubby. They couldn't do much harm in the entry hall.

I opened the door, and the kids bounced in. Henry's numbers were back where they belonged, thanks to most of the packet of crackers. Worked out well having Ava along—I didn't have to worry about him overcompensating because he shared the extras with her.

The Empress was in the foyer, and she took one glance—and sniff—toward the two dusty kids, sneezed loudly, and scampered off.

I couldn't argue.

"Stay here, okay? Play a little Demon Race," I said, handing Henry my phone. "We'll get over to the house as soon as I take care of one thing." Ava was already helping him load the mobile version of the game, so they'd be fine for a few minutes.

And it better be just a few minutes, I realized, as I walked into the workroom. Lewis and Faith were at the far corner of the table. He had the notebook, and she had the little plastic knitting markers she uses to flag spots that need work. Both had the quietly tense face polite people get when they're trying desperately to avoid being rude.

No wonder.

Linley was on the other end of the table, with a magnifying glass, combing over the bedspread. She had the officious expression of someone who has no idea what they're doing but is determined to make sure everyone knows how important they are while doing it.

Uh-oh.

"Hi, folks!" I called brightly as I walked through the door. "Linley, I'm sorry. I just realized I didn't finish the documentation on this piece, and we can't work on it until the paperwork is in order."

"Oh." She stood up with a face that matched the pouty syllable. "Are you—"

"Yes," I said quickly, cutting my eyes to Lewis and Faith. "It's really important to get a few shots of the untouched piece before we get down to restoration."

"Well, then." Linley sniffed and put down the magnifier. "I have other things to do anyway."

"I'm sure," I said. "Why don't I walk you out?"

As I guided her toward the hall, Faith and Lewis rolled their eyes in unison.

In the foyer, Henry and Ava looked up from Demon Race as Linley passed. Henry stared at her.

She stared back. "What are you looking at?"

"Um, nothing, ma'am," Henry said, in his usual polite tone.

Ava mumbled something polite, too. Tiffany and I are both sticklers for the formalities.

As I opened the door for Linley, I allowed myself a maternal humble brag. "Henry has a photographic memory."

"He what?" Linley's face suddenly looked sharp and pale.

"He has a photographic memory. It's usually a gift—he does really well in spelling and such at school. But he sees the world a little differently."

"Um, okay." Linley nodded.

"Thank you for helping Faith and Lewis today," I said firmly.

"It was really nice to get out for a while."

"Well, there's always something to do here," I assured her. "It may not always be as pretty as the broomstick lace, but there's always something interesting."

"Good to know," Linley said. She glanced back at Henry and Ava and then turned for the porch stairs. "I'll be around."

I wasn't sure whether to take it as an offer or a threat.

Lewis and Faith were in the hall chatting with the kids by the time I turned back inside.

"Thank you," Faith said. "I was just about ready to throw her and that magnifying glass out the window."

"And I was ready to help her." Lewis, normally one of the calmest and gentlest people I know, had a combative set to his jaw. "She was really snotty with Faith."

"And you, too," Faith replied and turned to me. "Tell me she's not coming back."

"Probably, but I'll make sure she's not near you," I promised. "There's a lot of sheet music that needs to be filed downstairs."

Both smiled.

"Much better." Faith nodded. "Woman gives volunteers a bad name."

"No kidding," Lewis agreed.

I nodded to the kids. "Well, I'll finish the paperwork on that piece from home."

"Yeah." Faith chuckled. "Looks like somebody needs to be hosed down."

"Probably just dusted off, but yeah."

Lewis, a Harmony Hill alum, grinned. "It's not a good camp day if you don't come home dirty."

"Got that."

As we walked out, Henry grabbed my arm. "Ma, that lady."

"Mrs. Stark. She's pretty messed up because of her husband."

"Yeah. The guy who got blown up."

"Ick," Ava contributed.

"She was there."

"Well, yes, Henry," I said. "Everyone in town was."

"I guess." His tone suggested more, and he had the expression he got when he was reviewing something he'd seen. He had described it to me as a video running in his head—and at least as far as I knew, it was as accurate. "She was right near him, right up front."

"Okay."

"She gave him a kiss and hug. I didn't see anything else…but it was right before it happened."

I didn't think a pre-firing embrace was part of the annual protocol, but fortunately, the head of the Second Fifes, and a trained observer, not to mention a key responder to the scene, would soon be eating dinner at my house.

Might be more to talk about than zucchini tonight.

Chapter Thirty-One: Zucchini-Free Zone

Ed and Garrett were bringing tomatoes, and the lettuce I'd bought at the farmstand yesterday was now-or-never, so dinner was easy: air-fry up some chicken tenders, whip out some assorted chickpeas, pickles, candied nuts, and dried fruit, plus a couple bottles of dressing, and set up a quick salad bar on the kitchen counter. The "everything bagel" flatbread I'd picked up at the grocery on Saturday (high in taste and low in carbs), and a big bowl of Henry's bittersweet chocolate squares rounded out a nice meal even before Tiffany walked in with two pints of Kule's sorbet, one strawberry, one no-sugar-added chocolate.

She was the first to arrive, an hour or so after I'd herded the kids home, supervised a quick neatening-up with the change of clothes Tiffany keeps at our house, and gotten them settled with games while I finished that paperwork.

I met her at the door. "Wine or seltzer?"

"Seltzer's fine." Wry smile. "It wasn't a wine day. At least not yet. Pretty routine. The late one was just a transport for a lot of stitches—guy didn't make sure the weedwhacker was off when he tried to change the string."

"Ow." I winced.

"Yeah. It's ugly and messy, but it won't kill him. Though he probably wishes it would right about now."

"Got any ideas for scaring away the bunnies?"

We turned to see Ed and Garrett on the walk, of course with Norm. And a basket of tomatoes in various colors. Thankfully no zucchini.

"Not the bunnies!" Tiffany exclaimed.

"Did they get into the tomatoes?"

"Ate all of my Yellow Gems," Garrett said, shaking his head. Every year, he grew the tiny little gold tomatoes…and every year, they never made it to the table.

"I say we need to get one of those big inflatable owl things," Ed cut in. "One of my girls has one in her garden, and it really works."

"Jana doesn't have bunnies." Garrett's exasperated tone suggested they'd been discussing this for a while. "She's got sparrows. They're scared of owls…bunnies don't care."

"Small animals always care about a big animal glaring down at them from the sky," Ed said.

Tiffany shot me a glance. This was clearly their current—currant tomato? — donnybrook, and we'd do well to stay out of it as best we could.

"Well," I said, "why don't we get inside and slice up these gorgeous tomatoes, and maybe we'll be able to come up with some ideas later."

The process of greeting the kids and catching up on the day, plus settling down to our meal, carried its own weight as it always does, and no one missed the Yellow Gems. Or the zucchini.

Once dessert was done, and the kids returned to their racing game, the grownups moved on to more adult matters.

"Kids sounded like they had a good time at the Society this afternoon," Garrett said.

"They got a good laugh out of the Empress," I agreed. "She sniffed, sneezed, and ran off."

Tiffany laughed. "Her Majesty wouldn't last long in a real house with kids."

"Nope." I nodded. "She's right where she belongs at the Society."

"What was that about Linley Stark?" Ed asked. "Henry made some odd comment about seeing her."

"She was there," I said. "The weird part wasn't him seeing her today. The weird part is he remembers seeing her on the Fourth."

"Everybody was there." Tiffany shrugged.

"Yeah," I said, "but he remembers seeing her very close to Rowland and giving him a hug and kiss just before the cannon went off."

Ed's face tightened.

Garrett, though, actually chuckled. "Oh, that."

"What?" Ed asked.

"She did that every year. Until this year, it seemed like some silly, overwrought thing. You know: 'Oh, one last kiss before the battle.' Silly."

"But it wasn't this year." Tiffany looked at the last of the strawberry sorbet.

"Go ahead," Ed said. "It's fruit."

Tiffany took the container and scraped the last bits into her bowl.

"I really don't think it's anything," Garrett said. "I didn't notice anything off with them."

"You weren't that close," Ed reminded him.

"Close enough." Garrett glared at his husband. "We've got enough going on without borrowing trouble. Henry took a hard look at Linley because she reminded him of the trauma. That's all."

It made sense.

And I really wanted to *not* worry about anything Henry might have seen.

"Borrowing trouble?" Tiffany asked.

"Old Scottish expression," Garrett said. "Both Christian and I had Scots grandmas, and we picked it up from them."

"Damn Scots. They take all the fun out of it for us Irish," Ed said, with a teasing grin. If he was willing to drop the question of Henry and Linley, it must not be a big deal.

"Crazy gringos, all of you." Tiffany started the laugh, and we all joined in.

Nothing to dispel concerns like a good laugh.

"I'm more worried about those damn skeletons," Ed said finally, taking one of the chocolate squares.

"So am I," Garrett agreed as he nodded to the square.

Ed broke him off a piece.

"Now that we've gotten you clear of that fool, Jensen," Garrett continued after a nibble, "we can worry about your skeletons."

"Skeletons?" Tiffany asked. "Not those gross old specimens you have in the basement."

"The very ones. They're missing."

"So someone ran off with the bones." Ed took a thoughtful bite of his chocolate.

"Easier than you think," I reminded him. "They'd fit in a couple of bags if you didn't care too much about preservation."

"Or basic human respect," Tiffany said. "They did belong to actual people, after all."

"Who probably died horribly, not that we need to dwell on it," Garrett said. "The point is, your specimens are missing."

I nodded. "And amazingly enough, two skeletons and some assorted bones—all nicely varnished—turned up at the plaza site."

"Suggestive," Ed said.

"Jensen would be my guess," Garrett said.

"It's too easy, isn't it?" I asked. "Easy and obvious."

"Like that trash she writes?" Garrett replied.

"*Girl With a Dead Guy*, or whatever?" Ed asked.

"Good thrillers died with Hitchcock," pronounced Garrett.

"Not fair." Tiffany held up a finger. "Just because you don't like to read something doesn't mean it's bad."

"I will be the first person to buy a copy of a certain EMT's memoir," Garrett assured her. "But those thrillers with suburban housewives faking their disappearances or running away with international drug dealers or running a brothel in the basement are silly."

"And beloved by bored suburban housewives," Ed put in. "As long as you understand that it has nothing to do with real crime, it's fine."

"They're a harmless enough outlet for a lot of people," I said, squirming a little at being forced to defend thrillers. "And Jensen is a pretty good writer, stylistically. A lot less over-the-top and clunky than many of these."

"Being a good writer doesn't mean she's a good person," Garrett said.

"Ain't that the truth." Ed let out a wry chuckle. One of his last cases was a famous sportswriter who killed his wife.

"And there's nobody like those fancy Ivy League types for thinking they know the only true way," observed Garrett.

"Sanctimonious bastards, sorry girls," Ed said. "The question is, does spiking that mall project accomplish anything other than keeping the land open?"

"I don't know," I admitted. "Although Walpole University is rumored to be eyeing the area, so anything's possible."

"Walpole?" Garrett whistled. "They just got a boatload of money from the chicken sandwich guy."

"And a boatload of money changes everything." Ed reached toward the candy bowl and thought better of it. "What I don't know is if it has anything to do with the murder."

"Still way too many suspects." Garrett shook his head.

"A whole lot of the town wanted him dead," Tiffany agreed. "If it was business, it could be almost anybody."

"We can't rule out Jensen," I said. "Not just because she's a jerk, but because that sanctimony can lead to bad stuff."

"Sure can," Tiffany agreed.

"We also have to rule in Linley, though, because she's the wife." Ed reminded us.

Garrett sighed. "True. It probably isn't directly money with her, though. Remember, Rowland's money isn't her only source of cash. She comes from a serious fortune."

"The quarries." I nodded.

"She bored me stupid at one of your events," Ed said. "I have no idea why she thought I would care, but she spent a good ten minutes explaining how she used to watch them work in the family quarries. How they got the stone out, and so on. It was interesting, but kind of a weird conversation."

"She's kind of weird," I said.

"There's that."

"Anyhow, I think we can agree they're both good possibilities," Tiffany said.

"And that we're all going to be very careful around them," Ed added, with a paternal glare at her, and me.

"Of course." I nodded—without even crossing my fingers.

"Good." Garrett nodded calmly.

"Now, let's get to something really interesting," Tiffany said with a wicked little smile. "Why isn't Joe here tonight?"

"Working on motions for a pre-trial hearing in a different case tomorrow," I said. "He doesn't have to be here every night, you know."

"But he's keeping an eye on you, right?" Ed's expression was very serious.

"Of course."

Garrett gave Ed a little back-off glare.

"That's good." Ed nodded. He took a breath, clearly thinking about whether to say more.

Tiffany and I were carefully not looking at each other. The whiff of paternal testosterone in the air was so strong we would have collapsed in giggles.

"YES! GOT HIM!"

The cheer from the computer told us the kids had accomplished their goal for the evening…and not incidentally reminded us it was a camp night, and we'd better get moving.

Maybe two hours later, everyone had gone home without zucchini—an achievement in July—and Henry was asleep. I was in bed with a book, a reconsideration of the Victorian controversy over crinolines that I'd promised to review for a friend, when my phone rang.

Joe.

"Hi."

"Evening, *Dottore*. Just missing you a little."

"Missing you a little too." I put down the book and curled up around my pillow, like any girl wishing she was with her man. "Not a bad thing."

"Been thinking about the Stark homicide. I think I need to talk to that pal of yours again."

"Yeah?"

"Yeah. I've gone over the financials of every last one of the cannon guys, spent an entire morning at the diner drinking coffee with them and their pals, and looked under every rock."

"Thorough."

"Thoroughly useless. Some had motive, some just hated him, but none had a compelling reason to kill him now—or like that."

"No help there."

"Nope. So here I am without a good theory of the crime in a high-profile murder. Peachy."

"Sorry. We didn't get very far on who's salting the strip mall site tonight, either if it's any consolation."

"Dead ends all round." He took a breath. "I don't necessarily want to like the wife for Stark. But she's an awfully good choice."

"Still, she has her own money…I think."

"It's not just the money, *Dottore*. It's the bargain."

"The bargain?"

"He broke the bargain." Joe's voice was suddenly very soft.

"I'm sorry, I don't understand."

"I suppose we can call it the trophy wife bargain, for lack of a better term. His job was to bring in the money and prestige. Plenty of both."

"What was her job?" I knew, from his low, gravelly tone, that we were no longer just talking about Linley and Rowland.

"Be beautiful and suitable. Seen doing appropriate things, while looking great. She would have seen herself as an asset to his efforts."

"Okay. So it's just money and appearances?

"It could well have been. A lot of these women don't mind if the man cheats as long as it's quiet, because it's not about fidelity."

"It's about status and finances."

"Exactly. His job to hold up his end. Hers to spend his money, be his appropriate partner."

"What about love and support?" I asked.

A bitter little laugh. "Sorry, *cara*. That's usually not included in the bargain."

"Not worth much, then."

"I agree."

I let the silence linger for a moment, unsure what to say. "Well, what if he breaks the bargain?"

"All bets are off." Joe took a breath. Considered, and decided to go all the way. "It's why Amber left. When I stopped making a partner's share, she no longer felt bound to hold up her end."

"Really?"

"Really. I hadn't realized I made the bargain until I broke it."

"Wow."

Another breath. More thinking, and then careful, slow words: "I married a pretty, basically nice, woman I thought wanted to build a life and a family. She married an up-and-comer who would bring her a certain lifestyle."

"You weren't in the same marriage," I said, keeping my tone as gentle as I could.

"Well, I thought we were, until I came home with a job offer and a purpose after meeting with the State's Attorney."

"I'm sorry." I didn't know what else to say. He'd become a prosecutor after the drunk driver who nearly killed his brother walked because of bad lawyering.

"I'm not sorry."

"No?"

"No. We're okay. She's where she belongs, and I'm where I belong."

"That you are. I like having you around. And so does Henry."

"How is the little outdoorsman?" Joe's tone warmed, and I knew he was gladly seizing a subject change. We both did this sometimes. When we got too close to the bone, we'd back off to safer ground, often kid-related.

"He's been singing camp songs on the walk home for the last two days."

"Yeah?"

"If I have to hear 'On Top of Spaghetti' one more time…"

"All covered with cheese…" He chuckled. "Camp is fun. And Henry's a great fella."

"He is."

"Doing okay with numbers and everything at camp?"

"Yeah. I send extra snacks, and of course, I talked to the nurse before he went, but so far so good. They've had plenty of Type-1 kids before, so we're not reinventing the wheel."

"Nice. You know Aly's starting sleep-away band camp this weekend." He sighed. "I already miss her more than usual."

"I'm sure. I don't know how you do it."

"Some days, I don't know either." Sigh, comfortable silence. "This house is pretty awful without Aly."

"You've got Cannoli, at least. And that nice kitchen."

"How about I make you two dinner here some night?"

"I'd like that. Henry would probably like to watch space documentaries on your living room TV, too."

"Then he can stay there while we go in the kitchen…and season the pasta."

"Is that what they're calling it now?"

"I'm not sure what they're calling it now, but I'd like to work on the vocabulary with you."

"Nice."

"Naughty, *cara*. I am definitely not thinking nice little thoughts about puppies and daisies right now."

"Good."

Chuckle. "What are you wearing?"

"Old jammies."

"On you, it's probably hot."

"Hold that thought."

"Rather hold you."

"Yeah."

We were both silent for a long moment.

"Good night, *cara*."

"Good night."

Chapter Thirty-Two: The Internet is Forever

Next morning, Garrett met me after dropoff again, again with Norm and a concerned face.

"What's happening online now?" I asked.

"Nothing bad for you." He managed a wry, little smile. "You are a hero for telling Jensen where to stick *Regency Love*. You have at least five DMs and counting from producers who want someone with—quoting here—'your commitment to accuracy' to work their project."

"Okay, then what?"

"You know video and the internet are forever, right?"

"I was aware of this, yes. Something new from that guy in Massachusetts? Spring Break Sam?" It's awfully hard to get people to take you seriously as a U.S. Senate candidate when there's video of you drinking from a funnel while dressed only in an eyepatch. Not on your eye.

"No, this time it's not a Boys Gone Wild thing."

"Aw, shucks."

"Get your mind out of the gutter," he reproved. "Unfortunately, this is not fun."

"No?"

"Not even a little." We turned the corner, and he looked ahead to the Society, where a familiar silver sedan was waiting. Its owner was already on my porch, leaning in at the window and waggling his fingers. Probably at the Empress, who was known to hop up on the sill and bat at visitors.

"Good," said Garrett. "He needs to see this too."

I waved.

He saw me, and waved back, with a sheepish smile, embarrassed at having been caught playing with the cat.

"Hey," he said as we came into earshot. "Good to see you, Professor Kenney."

"Likewise, Counselor."

Joe stepped off the porch and shook hands with Garrett.

"So I've stumbled across something on the internet that you should see," Garrett said.

"And I've found some interesting new facts I'm hoping Dr. Shaw can help me with."

"Then I suggest I make us a nice pot of dark roast and we share our information.

"Works for me." Garrett nodded. "But can we drink it in the workroom? I don't think your office seats three."

I sighed. "Of course."

Ten minutes later, the coffee was brewed and poured, the Empress fed, watered—and given a treat and an ear-scratch by Joe—and we were all in an empty corner of the workroom table.

"All right, so what's going on?" I asked, looking at Joe.

"I can defer," began Joe, "if you'd—"

"Not at all." Garrett nodded to him. "Let's hear it."

"I spent last night going through bankruptcy records. And guess what I missed?"

"What?" I asked.

"Greg Collier, one of the cannon guys, was forced into bankruptcy by a failed deal with Rowland. The filing was in Middlesex County, so it didn't show up right away."

"Really," Garrett said.

"Hm." I took a sip of my coffee. "Business bankruptcy?"

"No. Personal. Plus, a foreclosure on a lake house in Kent."

"Kent? Pretty fancy territory," Garrett said. "Family place? Even most really well-off people couldn't afford one."

"Yep." Joe nodded. "Apparently, he mortgaged the place to the hilt and then finally lost it when the project with Rowland went under."

"What I don't understand is how people kept investing with this guy." I shook my head and drank a little more coffee.

"He made a crap-ton of money—uh, sorry, just talked to my daughter this morning-" Joe blushed as he continued, "an enormous amount of money on that waterfront hotel, retail, and housing complex in West Haven. People tried for twenty years to make those old factory redevelopment projects work, but only Rowland did it. So he had a reputation, and people just kept investing and lending him money."

"Everyone thought the strip mall in Unity would be like Sound Shores?" Garrett looked dubious.

"Well, part of the portfolio, for sure." Joe drank a bit of his coffee. "Remember, he was also involved in three or four other developments. At least one of them was doing well—the rehabbed truck stop in Wallingford was a license to print money, even if it wasn't elegant."

"And elegance was part of the game for him," Garrett said. "He never mentioned a word about the truck stop. He was always talking up the Unity Plaza, which is what he called it, never strip mall."

The three of us exchanged glances.

"P.T. Barnum was the first to raise promotion to an art form," Garrett said, "but far from the last."

"Are you suggesting our victim was a huckster?" Joe asked.

"I'm saying it flat out. That's how he got those poor stupid guys to invest in his projects."

"Guys plural?"

Garrett shot him a dirty look. "Remember, we told you Brad Majeskie lost money, too?"

"But he's a volunteer firefighter," Joe said. "Those guys are hardcore."

"Definitely. And we appreciate his service. But he also had means and opportunity—and probably motive."

"That's fair, but I think Collier is a much better suspect. He was in bankruptcy and foreclosure. I'm still nailing down the insurance coverage on the business, but there was definitely money from a key-person policy on Rowland. Which probably goes to the wife…so either of our cannon guys might be able to sue her and save themselves."

"Or just ask her to pay them back as she settles her husband's debts," I said. "Honorably."

Joe looked at me, cut his eyes to Garrett.

"Everyone doesn't have your sense of honor, Christian," Garrett said. He knew, but Joe had no reason to, that I'd paid off the last few hundred dollars of Frank's college loans after he died.

Joe caught something. Watched me for a moment.

"Anyhow," he said finally, "we have at least one extremely good suspect now, and a secondary one, as well."

"You still have a third suspect," Garrett said, reaching for his phone. "Same one as always."

"I know you like the wife," Joe began.

"Nobody actually likes Linley," I said.

"As a suspect," Garrett pronounced. "I can barely be in a room with the woman."

"Duly noted." Joe drank the last of his coffee and gave the cup a forlorn little glance.

"More?" I asked, moving to get up.

"Better not." He put a hand on my arm. "Don't need to be jangly."

"Anyhow," Garrett continued, tapping on his phone screen. "There's an online video that just might jumble the order of your suspects a little."

Joe and I waited as Garrett turned it and hit play.

"Welcome to Girls Can Do Anything!" chirped a female announcer as a blinding-pink late-1980s graphic burned the title into our retinas.

"Today, meet Linley Barnwell, who helps her dad blow up rocks in their family quarry."

I stared with what was left of my vision, as the camera cheerfully followed a teenage Linley and a spare older man as they tromped through gravel at the base of big stone walls.

"Watch this," Garrett said. "This was before people worried about terrorism, so they follow the process pretty closely."

"How old is she there?" Joe asked. "She looks fifteen, maybe?"

Like Aly.

"Probably. Maybe a little younger."

"Looks like one of those public service shows the Johnstown TV station ran when I was a kid," I said.

"They had girl power back there?" Garrett asked teasingly.

"Not really. I think ours was called 'Kids Can,'" and it was mostly about hoagie sales."

"Do I want to know what hoagies are?" Joe asked.

Garrett and I glared at him.

"I should know this?"

"Sandwiches," Garrett said.

"You know them as subs," I added.

"Okay. Maybe for lunch." Joe shook his head. "This video…"

"Makes it very clear that Linley knows her way around explosives." Garrett nodded and drank the last of his coffee.

"So the cannon guys are not my answer."

"They might be," I said.

"And they might not, too." Garrett put down his cup with a sharp click.

It's truly amazing how good Joe can look even when he's troubled.

* * *

Later that morning, Jensen granted Joe's wish and jumped ugly.

I was in the workroom when I heard a hiss and stomping footsteps.

I assumed the hiss came from the Empress.

"What the hell do you think you're doing?"

"I could ask you the same," I replied, keeping my voice calm and cool. "Using video from the Society and putting my name on your project without my permission."

"I paid you—"

"For my expertise. Not my endorsement. And absolutely not for images of the Society."

"Who the hell do you think you are?"

"Just your friendly neighborhood historian who doesn't like seeing the past pretzeled."

"You sanctimonious b—"

"Not to period, honey." I cut her off. "Middle- and upper-class women used very little profanity."

Her reply was more appropriate to Tony Soprano than the ton.

"Thanks for that. Get out."

"You'll be hearing from my lawyer."

"You'll be hearing from mine. Maybe from the cops, too."

Her face went pale. "What?"

"Well, those skeletons didn't walk over to the plaza site." It was a guess, but not a bad one. "I'm not sure how you did it, but you're an awfully good suspect."

"And you're going to whisper that in your State's Attorney's ear, aren't you?"

"I share information. No secret there."

"You think you're so smart." Jensen huffed. "You don't know anything about what's really happening."

"Care to enlighten me?"

Jensen glared.

"Didn't think so. Now leave. I have work to do."

"Better watch yourself, Christian. You might stumble into something dangerous."

"Goodbye, Jensen."

She turned and marched for the door, but not before the Empress took a swat at her ankle.

"Ow. I'll call Animal Control—"

"They brought her to us. Goodbye."

By camp pickup time, my fight-or-flight fury had calmed. By the time Joe sent a good night text after Henry was down and I was curled up in my bed with a new pop history book on Queen Victoria's children, the whole thing was funny.

Certainly not important enough to interrupt a mildly salacious exchange of Shakespeare and Donne.

Which, sorry, is none of your business.

Chapter Thirty-Three: Loose Talk

Anybody who doesn't think Joe Poli is brave might want to re-evaluate by the fact that he calmly walked up to Henry and me while we were waiting for the camp bus with the rest of the ladies—including his mother—Friday morning.

First, as any decently brought-up man (especially a New Haven Italian one!) did, he greeted his mom with a big hug and kisses on both cheeks. Then he turned to me.

"Hi there," he said, leaning for a very well-scrutinized kiss on the cheek. Even Sally looked a little envious. No wonder. I've seen Malcolm.

Lidia, of course, beamed. What's better than showing off her son, the lawyer, AND making Sally uncomfortable? Not much.

"Hey, AlysDad." Henry held out his hand for the friendly shake that was becoming their official greeting. "Just in time to say bye before camp."

"What are you guys doing out there?"

"My team is building a fort. It's HUGE."

"Love it."

"And we're winning the Gaga tournament so far."

Joe gave me a puzzled look.

"Israeli volleyball," I explained. "Very popular among the camp set."

"Aly hasn't mentioned it." He shrugged. "Maybe not her thing."

"Probably don't do it at music camp," Henry said. "One of my friends has a sister at band camp, and he says they just play their horns all day."

"Bet they do."

The bus pulled up, sparking the usual minute or two of absolute chaos as everyone checked bags, offered goodbye kisses and hugs that were summarily brushed off, and then waved like idiots. You would have thought we were sending them on an expedition to the Himalayas, not four miles up the road for the next seven hours.

"Walk you over?" Joe asked after the dust cleared.

"Sure. Got time for coffee?"

"Yes, please. No court today, so I can talk for a few."

"Nice."

As Joe lightly put an arm around me as we moved toward the path to the Society, I saw Lidia shooting me a wink. I grinned back.

All in good fun.

"I think your mom approves," I said.

"I know she does. 'Nice, smart lady, and pretty too.' That's a quote."

"Awww."

"All true. I might add pretty hot, but I'd never say that to Mama."

Naughty grin that raised the temperature a couple degrees. "Pretty hot yourself."

He was looking awfully sharp today, in a blue-check oxford and light gray suit pants. But he always looked good. Not flashy, not fancy. Just good.

We were the first people to arrive at the Society. Lewis had probably been up late studying, and the docents sometimes took their time on summer mornings. Why not?

Joe took a look at cookware and other things laid out in the workroom and petted the Empress while I made coffee.

"Really feels like a home, walking through the rooms like this," he said.

"That's the nicest thing you could say to me," I told him. "Exactly what we're trying for—a step back in time."

"Well, you're nailing it."

"Thanks."

The coffee beeped, and I poured his, then mine.

"You don't have to do that, you know," he said as he sat in the side chair.

"What?"

"Wait on me."

I laughed. "Honey, I'm a properly-brought-up country girl. I serve refreshments to any and all guests. Whether or not I'm dating them."

"Okay." He shrugged. "Just don't want you thinking you have to do some—I don't know. I just want you to know I do respect you as a professional and I don't think you're here to serve me."

"Wow." I smiled. "It's nice, but why are you putting so much on a simple polite gesture?"

"Held a door for one of the interns yesterday, and she chewed me out."

"Twentyish?"

"Yeah."

"Okay, here's the deal. When you're that young, you're fighting for every inch of credibility, and some people don't understand the difference between gestures of respect and politeness that we make to each other as fellow humans in the image of our Creator...and trying to make someone else feel small."

Joe smiled. "My turn to wow."

"Um, yeah. I ran with academic feminists for a while, remember? Decided I prefer people who understand that the world is better with a little grace and respect and that it's no insult to be treated like a lady."

"Can you even say that now?"

"In my own office, I sure can." I smiled. "I'll pour coffee for anyone I want to, and I'd suggest you keep holding doors. With that smile of yours."

"Nice."

"Though I'm not sure I want you giving everyone that look."

"Oh, the smile is for public consumption. The look is just for you."

"Good to know." I sipped my coffee. "Glad you had a few minutes."

"So am I. I do have a little business to do, though."

"Okay."

"Blake Talley called me again this morning—some thoughts about the cannon and the explosion."

"Saluting at dawn?" I asked.

"Must be."

A wicked little smile passed between us. Then mutual agreement to leave it there for the moment.

"What's his take?" I asked as innocently as I could.

"He agrees with us that the blast probably wasn't in the cannon, or close enough to the gunpowder to spark anything. So it probably happened in the few seconds when Rowland was approaching with the linstock. By then, everyone else has moved back."

"Which is why no one else was seriously hurt in the blast."

"Right. He thinks it's extremely unlikely to be an accident."

"Really."

"Says he's not even sure how it could happen, but he thinks somebody tampered with the linstock or the slow fuse to make it explode." He sipped his coffee. "So my question for you is, how would that happen—if it's even possible."

"I suppose somebody could put an explosive in the linstock or the fuse. But you'd have to know a good bit about explosives to do that. And you'd have to be pretty motivated."

"Anybody in the frame know enough about explosives to do that?"

I thought about it. "Sure. The cannon guys—including Greg, the guy who went bankrupt. Linley, of course, thanks to growing up in a quarry. And I think Jensen was in the army for a year or two. I don't know what unit."

"Jensen? Writer chick in uniform?"

"Well, remember, this was twenty years or so ago."

"Ah. Right after the Towers fell."

"Exactly. A lot of young people joined up at the time. I was just old enough to know it wasn't the way I could help."

Joe nodded. "I was in law school. A partner at the firm where I clerked died, but I never knew him."

A few seconds of silence. Different world. Different time.

"So," I continued, "Jensen just might have been around explosives in the military. I don't know."

"Easy to check."

"But Linley's a definite yes, after that video yesterday."

"I'd say."

"Right." I remembered what Ed had told me about that weird conversation with her. "Apparently, she bored Ed one time about being in the quarry with her dad. So she's got the background and clearly still thinks about it."

"Do you know any specifics about the explosives? Beyond the video?"

"I don't. I could see if Ed knows someone from the bomb squad."

"It's okay. I've got a few pals over with the Feds." Shrug. "I'm not going to put myself at Ed's mercy unless I have to."

"He likes you, you know."

"He doesn't trust me to do right by you and Henry yet, and he gives me the dad glare. I'm not going to him for a favor when I have my own connections."

This was clearly a thing among men, and equally clearly, I was going to get nowhere with it. "Okay. Whatever works."

"It does." His eyes took on a wicked gleam. "And Blake, by the way, once again sends his compliments."

"Nice of him."

Joe waited.

I waited.

We both started laughing.

"Okay," he said finally. "I'm not the least bit jealous, but I am curious about what you saw in a cannon guy."

I smiled. Blinked. Let it hit.

"Oh, all right. You win that round." He blushed, which, on him, was extremely appealing.

"Too easy," I said. "And you promised not to ask if I didn't ask about Anna Maria."

"True." He held up the coffee. "Drink to a truce?"

"Absolutely."

We sipped in companionable and friendly silence for a few moments.

Then his phone beeped. "Probably the e-mail from yet another bank dealing with Stark."

"Yeah?"

"Yeah." He sighed. "I'm still sorting all of that out, not that it probably has anything to do with anything. But I have to check and make sure there's not another potential financial motive lurking in there."

"Yep."

"I'd put my money on the wife. Except it's such a grisly way to go at it."

"Women don't usually blow up their husbands, you're right. Shoot or poison them, usually."

"Stabbings are also a favorite." He shook his head, remembering the recent murder trial. "Point is, this is an elaborate killing for a reason. If she just wanted to off him, she'd have put heart pills in his cornflakes or 'accidentally' shot him while cleaning a gun. She didn't have to concoct this elaborate mess."

"True. Though she's one of the few women who could, with her dad's stone business."

"Yeah," Joe said, unconvinced. "Everyone in town knows she's from that family. So if someone wanted to make it look like she was the killer..."

"This would be a very nice way to do it. Yeah."

"Exactly."

Joe drank the last of his coffee and studied me for a moment.

"Look, I hope I didn't give you the wrong idea."

"About what?"

"The split. She left because I wasn't pulling down the big bonuses anymore, but I'm not broke. Made enough before-"

"None of my business," I said quickly.

"It is if we're thinking big and serious. I don't bring a white-shoe partner's share to the table any longer, but you won't have to support my nasty habit of putting away bad guys."

"It's okay. Really. I do just fine for Henry and me between the Society and consulting."

"It's just...I don't want to miss any potential pitfalls. And money is a big one."

"No kidding." I held his gaze. "I grew up without much, and I'm pretty cautious."

"So am I."

"But not above the occasional splurge with found money, like the extra from consulting."

"That's fair." He smiled. "Another place we mesh."

"Uh-huh." I smacked his arm. "And we've just had The Money Talk."

"We did, didn't we? Pretty good." A grin. "Not many potential landmines left."

"True."

He put down the coffee mug and stood. "Look, just be a little careful, okay? There are a lot of pieces flying around here, and we have no idea where they're going to land. Or who's capable of violence."

"Okay."

His phone made another noise, a weird glittery twinkle, and he smiled. "Text from Aly. She set her ringtone. Just wait til Henry gets into that."

"I am so not ready." I shook my head. "Hopefully not for a while."

"Keep dreaming, *Dottore*."

"Yeah, well."

An angry noise from the phone.

"Gotta go. Email from my boss." Joe leaned in and kissed me on the cheek. "Love you, bye."

We both froze.

Sure, it was big and serious, and sure, we'd both been married, so we knew what that meant. But the words, especially just slipping out into the open like that…

Oh, my.

In it to win it. I took a breath.

"Love you, too."

For an instant, Joe's face lit up. But then, his jaw tightened, and he gave me a sharp glance. "You don't have to say it, *cara*. I understand it's tough for you after…"

"It is. But it's also a statement of fact."

"For me, too." He ran a hand down my arm, gingerly, almost shy. "So…"

"So we both have to get to work right now. And this will still be here."

"It will indeed."

For a moment, we just stood there like teenagers, smiling goofily at each other.

"*We gave each other a smile with a future in it,*" Joe said finally.

"Trust John Donne to have something for this."

I walked him to the door and watched him go. He turned back just before he got to the car. Gave me that amazing grin.

Totally eighth grade. And totally wonderful.

Gotta love love.

The rest of the day was pretty straightforward, with the usual minor Friday afternoon crises. Maybe ramped up a little because Lewis was starting to assemble ephemera and beginning to get nervous about his fall exhibit.

A few minutes before it was time to leave for pickup, my mother called, allegedly to make sure I was going to the Bat Mitzvah instead of coming over there for brunch…but really to tell me she was driving up to Gary's Seafood Shack in Branford with the Sarge and wanted to move brunch to Sunday.

I managed to keep my encouragement to a small cheer, and when she heard something in my voice, promised to give her all the deets on the ceremony and developments with Joe when we reconvened at Pokey's Sunday.

As I hung up, I took a deep breath. Good Lord, my mother is dating.

I don't think I'm ready for this.

With a little burst of nervous energy, I walked over to the kitchen to get a couple of cookbooks I wanted to review over the weekend.

When I got back, Linley was in my office.

"Hey," I said. "Isn't it a little late?"

"Thought I'd see if there was anything going on I could help with."

I felt bad for her. Sad and lonely.

There but for the grace of…

"Well, maybe you can help Lewis get the ephemera organized so it's safe til Monday." I turned to my bag and carefully placed one of the cookbooks inside. Considering the book was from the 1880s, it wasn't just tossing the thing in the bag. I had to slide it gently into the zippered compartment, smooth it down, and close it without damaging the cover.

From behind me, I heard Linley looking around the room.

"Nice flowers," she said.

Couldn't she just go find Lewis?

"A friend grows irises…brought me a couple." I didn't look, and hoped my tone was cool enough to get her to leave.

"Uh-huh."

I heard a scrabbling noise, like she was moving things around.

Linley was at my desk, looking a little off. No one so privileged would ever look guilty…but it was in the area.

I narrowed my eyes at her a little as I picked up my bag. Back her off.

"Did you drop these?" Linley asked, sounding almost friendly as she held out a box.

"Oh, my matches. Yeah. I remembered to order the Sabbath candles, but I probably need matches."

She watched as I put them in my bag. Just what I needed, another of these weird, stilted Linley conversations.

"Well," I said, "have a good evening. See you at the Bat Mitzvah tomorrow."

"Yeah, I might go after all. Could be fun."

"We get to celebrate Amy," I reminded her. "It's about as much fun as it gets."

Chapter Thirty-Four: Shabbat Sans Shalom

When Henry and I have some important service to attend on Saturdays, or we're tired after a tough week, we'll light Shabbat candles at home. When it's just us, we're not all that hung up on waiting for sunset or too much ceremony. We just say the blessings, light the candles, enjoy the moment—and then have a nice dinner.

I'd started the air fryer with the crispy chicken for our Caesar salads and put out the candles in the little silver holders Frank's grandmother had left him. Henry had been rolling around on the floor with Cookie, but when I brought the candles onto the side table, he came over.

"When do I get to light the candles, Ma?"

"When you're a little older." I'm not an overly cautious mom, but there are some safety things I have a hard time giving up. Plus, candlelighting is a traditionally female purview—usually the mother's privilege.

I handed him the box. Give him at least a little agency. "Get me a match."

"These don't look right, Ma."

"What?"

"The heads are too big," he said. "Do matches come in different colors, Ma?"

"Why?"

"These are kind of orange, not red like your usual ones."

I looked at the package.

Remembered Linley's father's quarry, and her stories about playing with explosives as a girl. Not playing anymore.

"Give me that." I took the box very carefully from his hand.

"Get Cookie's container."

Henry did as he was told, but not without staring at me.

While he was in the mudroom grabbing the carrier, I slowly placed the box on the sideboard. I didn't think it would just blow, but who knew?

"Ma?" Henry asked as I let out a long exhale.

"Let's just get outside, honey." I kept my tone as cool and reassuring as possible.

The cat protested as I scooped him up, but I managed to get him in on the first try.

"Outside. Now." I herded Henry to the door, as the cat let out a yowl and started bouncing in the carrier.

"What's wrong, Ma?"

I pulled my phone out of my blazer pocket. "I'm not sure, sweetie. But I'm not taking any chances."

Within ten minutes, Chief DiBiasi, Ed, and Garrett were in the yard. Ten more, and the State Police bomb squad joined them.

"I'm sorry, Dr. Shaw, but we're going to have to take your fingerprints and the little fella's for elimination," said a female trooper with kind eyes. Ed scowled but nodded in assent.

"That's fine," I said. "I want to make sure you get her."

"Her?"

"Her," I repeated. "Linley Stark, who handed me those matches at my office two hours ago."

"Oh, no!"

The shriek came from the sidewalk, as, insanely, Linley appeared. Still in her neat little navy dress and cardigan, but wild-eyed.

"Christian! Thank God you're safe. I just—"

For one hot second, everything went red.

All I could see was the woman who'd almost killed me in front of my son…and might have killed him, too. I didn't mean to go for her, but it was only when I felt Ed's hand on my arm and heard his sharp voice that I realized what I was doing.

"It's not worth it," he growled. "Don't get in trouble over her."

"C'mon, Christian." Garrett took my other arm. "Leave her to the cops."

"You think I—" Linley gasped.

"I know you did," I snapped. "You handed me that box of matches. And you—"

"I just saw the box sitting on your desk. I realized on my way home where I'd smelled that scent before. I came over here to warn you."

"The hell you did."

I said it, but Garrett and Ed were clearly thinking it.

"Mrs. Stark?" the trooper asked. "You'll need to come with us."

"But I didn't—"

"Get her out of here."

Joe.

He took the short walk in three brisk steps, his tone and demeanor straight cold command.

"Watch it, Joe," Ed cautioned as he blew past him.

"I'm sorry, Sergeant," Joe said quickly to the trooper. "Dr. Shaw and her son are—"

"No problem. We're taking Mrs. Stark down to New Haven for a little chat. You can stay here."

"I'll be down within the hour," Joe said. "We'll be bringing charges in this one."

"Charges?" Linley shrilled.

"Oh, give it up," I snapped. "You killed your husband, and you tried to kill me. The only thing I don't know is why you went after him now."

"You can't really think I would do such a thing. Me?"

So she was really going to try that one. A rich white lady couldn't possibly dirty her hands with murder.

Reminding myself I didn't need to smack her and get an assault charge, I stepped away from Garrett and Ed. "You did. Any number of people could have done the linstock, but you're the only one who could have done the matches."

"Those matches were sitting out on your desk. Anybody—"

"You're the only person who knows explosives, Linley." I took a breath and kept my voice deadly calm. "You tried to kill me in front of my kid."

"I want my lawyer." Linley's voice came out in a petulant wail, as she realized there was no way she could privilege her way out of this.

"Good idea." Joe's snarl was low and barely controlled.

"C'mon, Christian." Ed patted my arm. "It's going to be a while before they clear the house. We've got a new pitcher of iced tea and some of that nice no-sugar chocolate sorbet."

Henry perked up. "Sorbet?"

"That's right, buddy," Garrett said, shifting into jovial grandpa mode. "I think you've earned some chocolate tonight. Might even have some deli turkey in the fridge for the poor upset kitty."

The poor, upset kitty let out a wail.

Garrett and Ed turned, Henry between them, and started down their street.

"C'mon," Joe said. "I want to see you two safe with them before I go deal with her."

"But you can't handle the case."

"I can keep an eye on her until the next person on call gets there. You really think I'm not going to watch over this?"

I put a hand on his arm. "Don't blow the case."

"I won't." He nodded. "If her fingerprints come back on the matchbox, we've got enough to hold her until we can nail down the cannon and the financials."

"It's Friday night. They'll hold her through the weekend, right?"

"I'll make sure they do." Grim little smile. "And I'm calling my buddy at the U.S. Attorney's office to see if we can make a hate crime charge stick."

"Hate crime?"

"She tried to kill you with something she knew was going to be used in a religious observance. At least some of the elements of a bias crime are there. Worth a shot at adding a second level of prosecution." He took a long breath. "I'm going to throw everything I can reach at her."

"Maybe you should come wait at Garrett and Ed's."

"No. I need to tell the person who's handling what to look for. You two are safe, so I'll do my thing." The casual wording was sharply at odds with his tone.

"We are safe," I said firmly. "Nothing bad happened."

"But it sure could have." He took my hands, holding them between his. "She's not getting away with this."

Something in his tone scared me a little.

"Don't…"

"Don't worry. This is going to be totally by the book. This is why we have the rules." He pulled me in for a quick hug. "Go calm down Garrett and Ed."

"You're right. They're going to be nuts."

They were, sending out for enough Chinese takeout to feed an army and racking up sitcoms on the streaming service—all while crackling with barely concealed fury.

Once the bomb squad took the matches away, and DiBiasi gave us the all-clear to return to the house, Garrett and Ed walked us home, then stayed to tuck in Henry and Cookie and stand over me while I drank an inch of Frank's old Scotch.

"Scotch?" I asked.

"Scotch." Ed opened the bottle.

Garrett held out the glass. "Not negotiable."

Ed scowled. "Someone tries to blow you and your kid up, you get Scotch. If only so you can sleep tonight."

"I guess."

"Drink. We'll stay if you want."

"No. Let's try for normal. Linley's off the street, and we have the Bat Mitzvah tomorrow."

They weren't wild about the idea, but they grudgingly accepted it. Well, once Ed called DiBiasi to make sure he was sending a car past the house every hour.

I'd like to say the Scotch worked, but it didn't.

Every time I almost drifted off, I thought about how close I'd come to striking one of those matches.

As cool as he played, Henry was every bit as upset as I was. He wandered in sometime after midnight, Cookie trailing behind him, squawking. They joined me, Henry snuggling in, and Cookie nesting between our feet. Finally, deep in the night, lulled by the light snuffle of kitty and little boy snores, I fell into an uneasy sleep.

Chapter Thirty-Five: Today (and every other day) She is a Mensch

Henry and I were still in pajamas when Joe appeared, dressed for Amy's Bat Mitzvah in a spiffy light-gray suit and surprisingly fabulous floral tie, with a grocery bag and a determined smile.

"Couldn't sleep, so I thought I might as well wander over here and make breakfast."

Check on us, he meant.

Not that it was unwelcome.

"Italian dark roast coffee for the grownups," Joe said, reaching in the bag, "and I hear egg and cheese scramble is a favorite of the young mister."

"Yes, please." Henry grinned.

Ed and Garrett arrived while I was putting on my makeup, also stupidly early…and for the same reasons. I came out of the bedroom, carrying the cute cropped coral jacket that matched my long floral-print dress, to find all three fellas helping Henry tie his tie.

This crazy thing might actually work.

"Well," Garrett pronounced as I walked into the room, "you look ready for your speech."

"She looks lovely," Ed said, nodding to Joe.

"Like a sunrise," my man said. "That's not Reverend Donne. That's me."

Ed and Garrett exchanged smiles.

"Thank you kindly, gentlemen," I said, dropping a fake curtsy.

They all smiled.

"Well," Joe said, "you will be pleased to know that Mrs. Stark is being held on one count of murder and two of attempted murder, one of a person under eighteen."

"Serious stuff." Ed nodded.

"Entirely appropriate," agreed Garrett. "Dare we believe the worst is over?"

"Well," Joe said, "there's still the matter of salting the site and a few unanswered questions, but we can reasonably believe the only really dangerous person in the mix is in custody."

"That'll do for now," Ed said.

"Then we can all enjoy Amy's big day," I said, motioning to the door, "and tie up the rest of the loose ends later."

Rarely have I been so spectacularly wrong.

At first, though, we just gave in to the happiness of the day. We walked over to the *shul* together, and I left Henry with the guys while I went to check in with Dina and Amy.

Despite the importance of the event, both descended on me with great concern when I walked into Dina's office.

"I'm fine," I assured Dina, who'd called to check on me three times—one more than Tiffany. "Henry and I were fine when we talked last night, and we're fine now. And the guys are taking good care of us."

Dina, who'd taken careful note of Joe walking me to her office door, smiled at that, but left it—for now.

"Glad to hear it." Amy, who was looking radiant in a very stylish hot-pink dress, patted my arm. "This is just awful."

"We're really okay," I assured her.

"Linley was a horrid child, and she's grown into a horrid adult, Christian. I'm sorry that happened to you and Henry."

"It's not your fault."

"Well, I'm the most senior Taylor left, so it's my responsibility." Her face was tight. "I don't know how she ended up that way, but she obviously missed the lessons in decency and humanity."

"Clearly." Dina put a hand on my arm. "I'm just glad you two are okay. And so thankful for Henry's photographic memory."

"That's one special fella," Amy said. "I borrow Jensen's kids every once in a while."

"I suspect Christian would probably be willing to loan out Henry on occasion, too." Dina offered.

"I absolutely would," I assured her. "And you and Jensen will probably be all right once everything shakes out."

"I hope so."

"Well, you've backed her up through this whole *Regency Love* thing," I said. "And the preservation campaign, too."

"She was right there. Nobody wants that plaza."

"Nobody I've ever met," Dina agreed. "But Jensen shouldn't have put the skeletons at the site. Aside from the whole theft issue, it was disrespectful of the dead."

"I agree," Amy said. "All of that was wrong. Stalling it legally was the right way to go."

Then why did she give Jensen the Society entrance code? "You didn't know she was going to do that when you gave her the code, did you?"

Amy gave me a puzzled stare. "When I—what?"

"Someone had to give Jensen the code to get into the building at night and take out the skeletons. You're the only volunteer who…" I trailed off as I realized there was one other volunteer.

"Linley." Amy met my stunned gaze with her own.

"Are they working together?" Dina asked. "Why?"

"It would have to be worth a lot," Amy said. "They never really got along."

"They don't seem to have much in common," agreed Dina.

That's when it hit me. The one thing they did have in common: a grandfather. Amy's late brother-in-law. And through him, the two other shares in the Taylor land.

"It's got to be the Walpole University expansion," I said. "They must be thinking that if they combine Rowland's plaza site, with the Taylor land—both of which back right into Walpole's campus—they'll make a bundle."

"And they would." Dina shook her head. "I know the rabbi who runs the Hillel at Walpole. There's a lot of talk on campus about a big new project with the money from that chicken-sandwich guy."

"Not if I have anything to say about it." Amy scowled. "That's some of the last clean, open land in New Haven County."

Dina and I exchanged glances.

"So I'm all that's standing in the way of their big payoff." Amy's face hardened. Until this moment, she'd been a sweet little old lady in the middle of a big happy day. Now we saw some of the steel that had gotten her this far.

It was kind of scary, but not in a bad way.

"All right," she said. "I'm going to settle this."

"What—" Dina and I asked, almost in unison.

"Christian, make sure your fellas watch me. I'll stay close to Gerry, but if Ed, Garrett, and Joe want to ride shotgun during the party, I won't argue."

Then she turned to Dina.

"Rabbi, say a prayer. We're going to need it."

The service began in a normal and appropriate fashion. Dina welcomed us all, and Gerry, speaking for the synagogue board, welcomed Amy into the temple community. If his ears were a little pink, and the glance between them made me wonder for a second if there was glitter in the air, well that was entirely their business.

Then it was my turn. I happily started with thanking Amy for honoring me by asking me to speak at such a wonderful occasion, moved on to a few short sentences about Amy's work with the Society and my admiration for her, finishing with: "It's not often you get to celebrate such a joyful occasion with such an amazing person. Thank you, Amy, for including us in your day."

When it was time for Amy to read her Torah portion, she did it clearly, cleanly—and in absolutely enviable Hebrew. Mine is wretched, and one of the main reasons I've never gotten serious about conversion. Henry giggles and corrects me every Shabbat now that he's taking classes.

No corrections needed for Amy.

I wondered if she'd studied as a girl or if she had a good language program. I'd have to ask.

Lost in thought about Hebrew and learning apps, I whiplashed right back to the situation when I realized she was speaking English again.

"So now I have a few words for my loving family, friends, and community. First, I want to thank every one of you for being part of this day. As a little girl in Amsterdam, I never imagined this day would come—and come in this place. It feels like a miracle…and a joy to share with all of you.

"This community welcomed me almost eighty years ago as a war bride and has always been warm and safe. My late husband and I had a wonderful home and family here. And I've been able to rebuild my life in recent years. Now, I want to give something back to Unity and New Haven County in return. I'll be doing the paperwork Monday, but you're all the first to know that I will be giving the Taylor land on Route 70 to the Open Space Trust. It's something I can do to make sure this town stays as wonderful as it always has been to me."

I heard a gasp from further down the front row.

Jensen.

The message hit its mark.

Now, we wait to see what happens.

Chapter Thirty-Six: Pour One Out for the Bat Mitzvah Girl

Even as she held the room, Amy was watching me, and I nodded. Any casual observer would think I was encouraging her or approving of the donation. She knew I was letting her know Jensen got the message.

"Thank you all for coming today. I hope you'll join me for the celebration in the hall."

Dina moved to the *bima*, for a final blessing and some housekeeping matters.

Because I was a speaker, I was on the aisle, but next to me were Garrett and Ed, and further down the row, Henry and finally Joe.

Everyone rose for the final prayer, and as soon as it was over, I motioned to the gents.

"Look, I can't give you the details now, but you have to keep a really close eye on Amy."

"Why?" Ed's tone was pure cop suspicion.

"I think Jensen's going to take a run at her."

"Jensen?" Garrett shook his head. "What—"

"It would take too long to explain. Just stay close to her."

"Okay." Ed glared. "You're not doing anything stupid."

"Nope." I glared back. "She doesn't eat or drink anything you didn't personally hand to her…and Henry—watch everything around her. If anything looks out of place, tell someone immediately."

"Will do, Ma."

"What are you doing?" asked Joe, giving me almost the same glare as Ed. I was going to be in trouble if those two ever joined forces.

"I'm checking something. I'll be around."

"Checking what?" Now Ed.

Garrett cut his eyes to me, clearly holding back a laugh. He'd had the same thought I had.

"Key evidence if I'm right."

In the mass exodus to the hall, the guys made sure to attach themselves to Amy, with Ed managing to work his way between her and Jensen, carefully positioning himself so the younger woman would have to go through him to get to Amy, but without obviously telegraphing anything. Once a cop…

The hall was only a few steps away, down a walkway at the edge of the old churchyard. It was a 20th-century addition, but it was well done, with big French doors giving way to a patio area that faced the churchyard. If you weren't a New Englander, you might have thought it was a little weird to have a celebration space opening onto a graveyard. But the churchyard was so old it was no longer eerie—the newest grave was from the 1850s.

By Unity standards, that meant it qualified as an interesting place, not a scary one.

Because it was a pretty summer day, the French doors were open, and the head table was set up close to the patio to take best advantage of the room and the breeze. For those of you who keep score of such things, the linens were white, and the flowers a multicolored mix, piled into big vases tied with hot-pink ribbons, in almost the same shade as Amy's dress.

It was the one matchy note in an otherwise casual and unpretentious event. More power to her.

While everyone else staked out seats and got settled, I slipped into a corner and did a search on my phone. As we were setting up this trap for Jensen, I'd realized there was one more possible way to find evidence against her… which we would need if it came to a trial.

It was a shot in the dark, but if Yale's Peabody Museum was as good about digitizing their collections as the Met and the Jewish Museum were…

And they were.

Better, in fact, for my purposes.

I slipped the phone into my jacket pocket and started working my way back to Amy, who was now the center of an entire protection team of standup guys.

"The fellas seem to be doing their part," observed Dina, coming up behind me, punch cup in hand.

"Yep."

I let myself take one easy breath. And then saw something that chilled my blood. Jensen was approaching Amy's table with a bottle of champagne on a tray, surrounded by glasses.

This was it.

"Gotta go," I whispered to Dina.

"You don't think-"

I didn't hear her finish the sentence.

As I worked my way across the room, I was glad to see Ed keeping a close eye on Amy, and Garrett watching the bottle.

Henry was carefully absorbing the whole thing, as Jensen poured champagne into the four glasses on the tray and started by taking a quick sip from one.

Clever. A thriller writer would know how to do a good misdirect.

Ed, Garrett, and Joe exchanged glances. They got it, too.

I kept moving, now near the open French door, as I worked closer.

Henry, with all the seriousness of an eight-year-old who suddenly understands his gifts are important, watched her every move, and the glasses.

Our suspect had no idea what she was up against.

Jensen carefully handed a glass to Amy, who took it with a sunshiny smile that would have fooled almost anyone.

Henry studied the glass. I had to stare for a moment to realize it was slightly different in color and not as bubbly as the other champagne flutes. Not Henry. He recognized the difference immediately and nodded to me.

I met Amy's gaze.

She raised the glass to Jensen. Smiled.

"GOTCHA."

Jensen stared.

"We know what you did and why," Amy said. "How dare you?"

Joe, as the duly appointed officer of the court, reached over with a napkin covering his hand, and took the glass. Evidence.

For a second, Jensen froze.

I thought that was where it was going to end. Easy-peasy, wrapped up with a bow.

But nothing about this was easy.

Jensen took off.

I was the closest, and I grabbed for her, but missed. So I ran after her, out the French doors and into the old churchyard. I knew, but she apparently didn't, that the grass wasn't nearly as smooth as it looked because graves settle over time (you don't really want to think about why), and I moved just a bit more slowly and carefully, putting my faith in the founding folks of Unity.

Just as I was starting to worry Jensen would get away with it, she hit one of the uneven spots in the grass and almost fell.

The wobble, combined with my long reach, was enough.

I managed to grab the back of her cute little yellow sweater, a part of my mind registering the sheer buttery luxury of the summer-weight cashmere as I yanked her toward me. She wheeled on me, arms flailing, and got in a good whack to my nose.

Ow.

It felt like my face exploded. I'd taken a wiffle ball one time when I was playing with Henry, and this was ten times worse.

I hung on, though, and she kept fighting. We were both already off-balance and moving fast on the uneven ground, and it was no real surprise we went down. Rolled over a couple of times.

A thump on the side of my head told me we were close to a tombstone.

It wasn't enough to knock me out, just enough to make me really mad.

Jensen was still struggling, and I realized she was yelling. I couldn't make it all out, but what I could understand was horrible. The kind of words I'd never want Henry to hear, ever, never mind applied to his mother.

And then it got worse.

"She was supposed to kill you both. You and that nosy little brat of yours."

"What?"

"You should both be dead." Jensen managed an evil smile.

Enough.

Time to end this thing.

The thought that they came after my kid was more than enough.

I threw myself at her. I heard a thunk, and saw her head bounce, her eyes going from fury to unfocused for a moment.

It would do.

I pinned her down, looming over her on all fours, like some bizarre wrestling stunt. Sometimes, it's good to be the big girl.

"Stop it!" I snapped.

She started to call me one more name, but a gush of blood from above turned the word into a scream of revulsion.

Red splatter all over her face, with some splash on that sweet yellow twinset.

It was only when I heard Joe yell my name that I realized the blood must have come from me.

I remembered the nosebleed from the wiffle ball, messy and scary, but nothing serious.

"Keep Henry away!" I called to anyone who might listen.

"Don't move." Low, gravelly voice. "Don't even think it, Ms. Brockway."

It took most of the second sentence for me to figure out that the ice-cold cop voice was coming from Tony DiBiasi.

"Get a medic!" Ed.

"I've got you, *cara*." Joe. I felt his hands on my ribcage. "You can let go—she's covered."

"Henry." My voice came out as a thick whisper. "Keep Henry away."

"Garrett's got him inside." Joe pulled me up. "It's okay."

"Okay." I took a breath through my mouth. "I'm okay."

Everything looked a little weird, like I was underwater.

"I'm okay," I said again, even as more blood poured from my nose. If I just kept saying it maybe I could make it so.

"Dammit, Christian. I have to leave for Ava's recital in ten minutes."

Tiffany, tackle box in hand, looking up at me in furious concern. And annoyance. She'd taken the early shift so she could get to the recital, even though it meant missing the Bat Mitzvah. And now I'd ruined everything.

She nodded briskly to Joe. "Get her over to that bench."

Joe scooped me up, which had never happened to me before, and set me down on the bench a few feet away. It was so fast I only had time to register, not enjoy it.

Since I was not, however, dead, I made a mental note that I'd like to try it again sometime under more pleasant circumstances.

As he pulled back to let Tiffany work, I saw a huge spreading red stain on the shoulder of his shirt.

"I'm sorry," I said. "Get lemon juice and hot water on it right now..."

He glared. "*Shah.*"

My jaw dropped.

"Isn't that what Rabbi Aaron says when she wants to say shut up without being mean?"

"Stifle, both of you," Tiffany snapped. "That's a lot of blood, and I don't like the look of her eyes."

We stifled.

As Tiffany started assessing me, Jensen returned to howling abuse, demanding a medic and screaming at the cops. Didn't they know who she was? Her lawyer was going to have their jobs. She was going to sue. Plus some obscenities and a little ethnic invective. It was every bad "Karen" incident, ever.

"I feel bad for people named Karen," I said.

Tiffany started giggling as she looked at my face. "My mother almost named me Karen."

I heard a growl that might have been a reluctant laugh from above. Joe.

A blinding light in my eyes. "What!"

"I'm just checking your pupils, silly," Tiffany said. "You may have a mild concussion. I think you should get looked at. Maybe the urgent care, maybe the ER."

"But the Bat Mitzvah…"

"Is pretty well over, dear." A small shape at the edge of my vision resolved into Amy Taylor. "There's still the after-party at Malina's."

"After-party?"

"Yes. We'd planned to have dinner at around seven on the patio."

"Maybe we should all get together there and sort it out," Dina said.

When did she get here?

"Great idea," Ed pronounced. "We'll get Christian to the ER, the cops will finish their work, and Tiffany can go to Ava's recital."

"Then we'll see you all on the patio."

Amy's regal proclamation would have settled the matter even if she weren't the Bat Mitzvah girl.

Chapter Thirty-Seven: What about Regency Love?

Show me a person who enjoys a trip to the ER, and I'll show you a serious nut job.

But the good whack on a granite headstone and an impressive nosebleed were enough to get my ticket punched, if you'll excuse the wording.

As Ed bundled me to his car, I tried to argue for the urgent care, but Tiffany shut it down, saying the only way to be absolutely sure I didn't have a serious brain injury or a facial fracture was a CAT scan, which you can't get there. So I was done.

Done and none too happy, thanks.

And no happier when Joe appeared after Ed settled me in the passenger seat of his large domestic sedan (it's a retired cruiser, are you really surprised?), leaning in my window, and taking my hand.

"I can't go with you. I have to help the on-call assistant."

"She's fine, Joe." Ed's glare made it very clear what he thought of that. "You do what you have to do and meet us later."

"I'll be with you soon as I can." He bent down, probably thinking about a kiss on the cheek, and thought better of it.

I must have looked awful.

"Love you, *cara*," he said, loud enough for Ed to hear.

"Love you."

"Good," Ed snapped. "Now, go do your work so you can be with her."

Joe nodded and turned for the churchyard.

As Ed put the car in gear, a terrifying thought hit me. "Henry. Where's Henry?"

"Safe with Garrett, remember?" Ed patted my arm. "He stayed with him when we ran out."

"Okay."

"Want to buzz them? I've got a nice little hands-free in the dash."

"Please."

By the time I exchanged a few careful words with Henry and deliberately nonchalant reassurances with Garrett, Ed was pulling into the ER.

A Saturday afternoon in the summer is not exactly a slow time for a small community hospital emergency room. It wasn't really a surprise we had to wait. Ed managed to find us a relatively quiet corner, with a combination of the glare and cute older guy charm, and put in a word with the nursing supervisor about cop family, but minor injuries are still minor injuries.

A very young and very frazzled medical assistant brought me an ice pack and some tissues for my nose, and that was all I was going to get for a while unless I had the misfortune to collapse in a heap on the floor. Considering what had probably been on the floor, I wasn't interested.

It could still have been a lot worse, sitting there on a stiff naugahyde sofa, with a Red Sox game on the TV and the low hum of various sorts of human misery. But then it got interesting.

Not good interesting.

"Let go of me!" an all too familiar voice snapped.

One of Unity's three officers was pulling Jensen into the room.

"Ma'am," said the cop, a young Black woman, "there is no need to be rude. We are here to get you proper medical treatment."

"Oh, shut up."

I wondered if Jensen would have been so snappy with Tony DiBiasi. She did look pretty rough, though, with a fat lip, wild hair, the makings of an impressive bruise on her cheekbone — and a great big red stain from my nosebleed down the front of that buttercup sweater.

Good for her.

While the officer got her checked in, Ed and I watched from our space, protected by her self-absorption and the out-of-the-way spot.

"All right. Wait here," said the clerk. "We've got a cardiac event and a compound fracture, so—"

"YOU ___!"

The pronoun was followed by a noun that nice women never use to describe another female.

Jensen had clearly realized I was here, too.

Ed tensed beside me and made eye contact with the officer. "If you don't shut her up, I will."

"You heard Sergeant Kenney," the cop told her charge.

I gave the little potty mouth my best glare.

"Never mind." Jensen threw herself into a seat like an angry toddler and shot me a glance. "You know that whole *Regency Love* thing was a fake. Nobody gives a damn about history."

"What?" I said it, but at least two other people thought it. I wished Garrett were there to defend his field of study—he's been known to throw things.

"I made it all up so I could get into the Society and help Linley get the skeletons. Then I stayed to make sure you all were buying it."

"So why announce it?"

"Seemed like fun. And you never know what gets picked up from social media. If we'd gone viral, I might really have done it."

I just shook my head.

"Did you Mirandize her?" Ed asked the officer, whose nameplate read **Brady**.

"Yup." Brady smiled. "Lawyer's supposed to meet us here."

Ed nodded.

So, that admission was fair game. I wondered if I could do better.

"Looks like I got you pretty good," I said. Ed elbowed me.

"Looks like I got you," Jensen fired back.

"Only one of us is walking out of here to her family," I reminded her. "It's over for you two."

Even in my beat-up state, I'd never have taken that bait, but then, I wasn't crazy enough to blow up random relatives in hopes of a big real estate score.

"You should be dead. You and your damn kid. If he hadn't seen Linley on the Fourth—"

"Stop." The cool voice belonged to a large redheaded man standing in the ER doorway. Even in a slightly rumpled green polo and khakis, he held the room. "I'm Ms. Brockway's lawyer, Michael Adair. And this conversation is over."

"Fine by me," I said.

"Good luck, Mike." Ed grinned. "You're gonna need it."

"That's your opinion, Sergeant Kenney, and you have every right to it." Michael Adair walked over to the clerk and exchanged a few words with her.

A little blonde woman in scrubs came right out and walked over to me.

"Ma'am, why don't we find a place for you in here?" She put a careful hand on my arm. "We'll be with you soon, and you shouldn't have to deal with this."

Ed and I exchanged glances.

As we went through the security door, I saw Michael Adair shaking his head as his client pointed her finger at him.

"You know who that guy is?" Ed asked.

"Who?"

"Michael Adair's the lawyer you call when you're REALLY in trouble in New Haven County. Very good and very expensive."

"Good for her."

The blond woman motioned us to an improvised space with a couple of chairs in a corner. "We'll be with you as soon as we can."

From that point, things improved dramatically.

The CAT scan showed no sign of serious damage, and the ice pack brought the swelling down enough I could breathe through my nose, even if I didn't want to look at myself for a while.

Periodically, as I was being tended and tested and schlepped, I heard a howl from Jensen, and a cool, but tense male voice urging her to calm down. Whatever she was paying Michael Adair, it wasn't enough.

We'd been there for maybe three hours, and the doc finally was running down the release instructions when Joe arrived, walking in with a brisk, concerned air and the same bloody shirt.

"All right," the doc continued after Joe nodded to us, and to her, skipping the introductions to avoid interrupting. "so your wife has to take it slow for a week or so. Limit reading, screen time, all of that."

"Um, she's not my wife," Joe said. "Though we are—"

"It's fine, doc." Ed shook his head as he cut in. "So our girl is fine and just needs to take it easy."

"That's about it. Ice for the nose, aspirin for the headache, and, of course, no alcohol."

"Of course," I said gloomily. "I can still go have caprese on the patio at Malina's tonight, can't I?"

Ed and Joe glared.

Dr. A. Raguso, though, smiled. "Actually, caprese is therapeutic."

Chapter Thirty-Eight: Consequences
Caprese

By seven, I was cleaned up and ready for the said caprese, thanks to a quick stop at my house for fresh clothes and a bag for me and Henry. Because of the concussion, I had to stay with a responsible adult, and there was no way I'd be without Henry.

Joe stopped at his house to change his shirt, then picked up Ed and me, carefully settling me in the front and apologizing for leaving Ed to the back. Even Ed seemed to think the apology was unnecessary—the sedan was top of the line with a big backseat and buttery cream leather upholstery.

Any time of year, Malina's is wonderful. Most New Haven County folks have a local, a red-sauce place we go for any reason or none, where we gather with our families of blood, work, and choice to enjoy a good meal and chew over the events of the day. Malina's is ours.

On warm summer evenings, it's even better. They open up the patio, fire up the bug-snuffers, and pour out big pitchers of lemon basil water. Another of those magical New England summer traditions.

We were the last to arrive; Garrett, Henry, and Ben were talking baseball trash with Gerry Diamond while Dina and Amy admired Ava's tiara and butterfly wings, and Tiffany regaled them with the story of the recital. Apparently, the youngest Majeskie kid had a stage-fright meltdown.

"…and then she ran off the stage. Leaving a puddle. Poor thing," Tiffany said.

"Well, about time you got here." Garrett looked me over. "Nice shiner."

"At least the nosebleed stopped," I said, only a little defensively.

"She has a mild concussion," Ed cut in.

"And she's grounded for a couple days," Joe added.

Great. They're conspiring against me.

"Ow…that looks bad, Dr. Shaw." Brittani, the server, a former schoolmate of Aly's, handed me a menu. "Maybe caprese will help?"

"Doc seemed to think so." I managed a smile that only hurt a little. "Lemon soda to start?"

"Sure thing. You too, Mr. Poli?"

"Yep. Thanks."

"I'll be just fine with some of the wine," Ed said with a smile.

"I'm trying not to envy you." I scowled. It hurt.

"Envy all you like." Garrett handed Ed a glass he'd clearly had waiting. "There will be plenty of wine after your brain isn't scrambled."

Scrambled or not, I'd have had to be in a lot worse shape not to enjoy settling in for dinner on the patio. We followed our usual unspoken agreement to keep to light and pleasant topics during the main part of the meal, catching up on the recital (Ava was magnificent!) Bat Mitzvah (Amy ditto!) and baseball schedule (the Mets were not!).

Only when the table was cleared and the gelato distributed did we start chewing on the serious business of the day.

"All right," Amy said, after savoring a bite of creamy fior di latte. "So you've got two merry murderesses, Joe?"

Joe almost choked on his stracciatella at the description. "It's not *Chicago*, Mrs. Taylor."

"And those two are anything but fun." She nodded. "I know. Trying to maintain a little wry distance because…"

"If you don't laugh, you'll cry." Dina patted her arm. "Rotten thing to have in the middle of your Bat Mitzvah."

Gerry gently wrapped an arm around Amy. "Still a beautiful day."

"Absolutely." Her smile returned as she took another bite. "Let's focus on the good."

"And there's plenty of good," said Joe. "Christian and Henry are safe, and those two are going down hard."

"I sure hope so," Tiffany said.

"Well, Jensen knows she's in trouble," Ed said. "She's hired Michael Adair."

"Not for long." Joe let out a bitter little laugh. "He already dropped her. Almost never takes a case involving harm to kids. I think his son's a little younger than Henry."

"I could almost respect that guy," Garrett said.

"Almost." Ed didn't sound convinced. "It doesn't take a huge conscience to be unwilling to defend a person who tried to blow up a mother and little boy."

"Might if she has that kind of money," Tiffany said.

"And it was all about money," I said.

"The Walpole University expansion," Joe nodded. "They were in line for a huge score if they could combine those two parcels of land and sell them to the school."

"And if they joined forces," Dina said.

Amy shook her head. "I'm a bit surprised they managed to get along, even with such an incentive."

"Well," Joe admitted, "I'm a little worried about linking Jensen to the overall plot, honestly. We've got her for assault on Christian and conspiracy on the matches. But I'd like a little more evidence she was involved in salting the site."

"The more evidence, the better," agreed Ed. "It would be awfully nice to have something damning and directly linked to her."

Something pinged in the back of my battered brain. I remembered checking my phone just before all hell broke loose.

"I can help with that."

Everyone looked at me.

"It's on my phone. I checked the Peabody Museum site…"

"Peabody?" Garrett asked.

"Yale. Remember, Jensen got her MFA in drama there and knows the place pretty well."

"Oh, she's got a degree in drama, all right." Tiffany took a big, happy bite of her fresh berry twist.

"Remember, there was a fake African sculpture on the site…"

"And a reproduction kiddush cup," Dina added.

"Plus one more thing," I said. "A pewter plate."

"A pewter plate?" Amy asked.

"I took it for a lame attempt for evidence of settlement," I said, pulling out my phone. "But it was a little more than that."

"Okay." Joe ate a bit more gelato and waited while I brought up the last website I'd visited before all hell broke loose.

So did everyone else.

"It's the same as the ones they have at the Peabody. Which were, as it happens, donated by the Taylor family." I turned the phone to Amy. "Does this look familiar?"

"There were several of them," she said. "I donated the four I had to the Peabody. Jensen's side of the family had a few more."

"Were they insured?" Joe asked.

"Of course. Anything that old has to be."

"Tracked and recorded, too." Ed nodded.

"Probably a small, unobtrusive sticker or mark on it somewhere," I said. "There are a bunch of ways to do it."

"And we've got her." Ed smiled.

"Just as well Michael Adair dropped her. Be bad for his record." Joe grinned.

"So all's well that ends well," Amy said.

"All's well that ends with everyone safe, together, and eating good food," Gerry corrected Shakespeare. "Remember the old Jewish adage."

"They tried to kill us; they failed; let's eat!" Dina pronounced it with an impish smile.

"Not the worst way to wrap it up." Lewis nodded and turned to Amy. "Think the Peabody would be willing to lend us those plates for my fall exhibit?"

"I'll put in a word," Amy said, beaming at him.

A warm, happy moment. But then:

"What I don't understand is how they thought they could get away with it," Ben said.

"I don't, either." I nodded.

"You're concussed, so you've got an excuse." Tiffany's voice had a sharp edge. "But the rest of you…"

"Oh, I know exactly what it was." Dina met her gaze. "Privilege."

"Exactly." Tiffany raised her lemon soda to the rabbi. "I despise the term 'Karen,' but the principle fits here. Those two are a perfect example of well-off white women who think they can get away with anything…and usually do."

"And who sees everyone else as less important than their needs, whatever they are," Dina added. "I don't know if either of them ever saw anyone around them as human beings created in the Image…but they sure don't now."

"Got that one right," Joe said. "It takes a particularly cold soul to blow up your spouse of twenty years."

"And an even colder one to try to blow up an innocent mother and her boy." Garrett shook his head, his glance giving away the concern he'd never voice.

"Yep." Ed's jaw was tight. "You're gonna throw the book at 'em both, right, Joe?"

"Talked to my colleague while I was driving to the ER. They're throwing the whole damn library, sorry, Sergeant."

"Appropriate."

Brittani dropped off the check, and we settled up, with a large tip.

Then Gerry stood. "I think it's time I see the Bat Mitzvah girl home."

"Sounds good to me." Amy took his arm with a smile.

As we watched them go, Dina, Tiffany, and I exchanged grins. Joe looked at me.

"Nah."

"Never know."

"None of your darn business, kiddies," Garrett said.

"Well, there's that," I said, picking up my purse.

"You taking them home with you?" Ed asked Joe.

"You know she can't be alone tonight," Garrett added.

I knew, even if Joe didn't, what it meant that they just assumed Joe would watch over us, rather than bundling Henry and me off to their place.

"So?" Joe turned to me.

"I'd like that."

"Cookie will hate it," Henry said.

"Probably." Joe shrugged. "But he's got treats. And taking care of your mom wins all ties."

Henry nodded solemnly. "And maybe Cannoli will sleep with me."

"I bet he'd be willing to sack out in the guest room for a change. Fun for everyone."

"Don't forget," Ed said. "Gotta check on her every hour or so. Concussions are—"

Garrett elbowed him.

Half an hour or so later, we were at Joe's house, Henry happily tucked into bed in a very beige guest room, with Cannoli doing his best to give the duvet a proper coating of dog hair.

Joe took my hand. "Let's sit in the living room for a while."

"Would you like—"

"I'd like you to sit down," Joe said. "Stop being a hero for five minutes, huh?"

"Okay. Only if you do, too."

"You win."

We went to the hot cocoa living room and sat down on one of the marshmallow couches.

"I think this is the happy ending," I said, trying to ignore the seriously off vibe.

"Look," Joe said, wrapping an arm around me, "I respect that you're smart and strong and fight your own battles."

"Thanks." I tried to burrow into his embrace, but he tensed. Something really *was* wrong.

"That said, don't ever go off like that again."

"I didn't—"

"You were reckless." He pulled away a little so he could make eye contact. Steely eye contact. "I'm not telling Henry or your mother, never mind Ed, that you aren't coming home because I screwed up."

"You didn't screw up."

"Yeah, I did, because I should have seen that you were in danger and protected you. So I want your word. No more freelancing."

After this day—and with that scary expression of his — I was happy to agree. "Okay. But you don't get to take stupid risks either."

"Fair." He gave a sheepish little shrug and gently toyed with a loose curl. "I love you, Christian Shaw, from your curly red hair to that freaky green toe polish even my daughter wouldn't wear. I love you, and I'm not going to lose you. Not if I can possibly avoid it."

"I love you." I planted a light kiss on his cheek. Looked into those wonderful, deep brown eyes. "Is this the part where we make up in the bedroom?"

He pulled back and took my hands. "Nope. Not while you're concussed— and not til those bruises heal."

"What…"

"I still think you are a beautiful, sexy woman, okay? I still have every intention of demonstrating my affection in the most concrete way possible— as often as possible." Joe twined his fingers with mine. Sighed. "But the black eye is a dealbreaker. Totally kills the moment."

"I understand." I did. "Everything you've seen."

"Just how I'm wired. Nothing hot about a battered woman. Even if she got beat up catching a killer, and even if she's my woman."

"Frustrating but overall a good thing." And then I processed what he'd just said. "Your woman?"

"Well, if you're okay with that. You can consider me your man if it helps."

"My man. I think that works."

"For now." He pulled my hands up and kissed the back of one. "About all that's safe right now."

"It'll do."

"Our two souls, therefore, which are one."

"Ah, I should have known the Reverend Donne had something for this."

Shy smile. "He has plenty, but I'm too tired to do better."

"You're just fine. *We're* just fine."

"I think so." He pulled me closer. "So why don't you just snuggle in here and let me hold you for now. The other stuff will be there later."

"Yeah?"

"Oh, yeah. Trust me."

"I'll take it…and you."

Acknowledgements

Many thanks, as always, to my editor, Verena Rose, and agent, Mira Perrizo, for giving this series a chance.

Special thanks to my best beta reader, Julie Von Wettberg, and neighbor Liliana Felix for their insight on life as the mother of a son with Type-1 Diabetes.

To my ever-patient family—of blood, work, and affection—deep appreciation for your support and understanding.

And, reinforcing the dedication, to my Sisters in Crime Sibs and other writer friends, this doesn't happen without you.

With love, respect, and appreciation,

Kathleen Marple Kalb

About the Author

Kathleen Marple Kalb describes herself as an Author/Anchor/Mom…not in that order. An award-winning weekend anchor at New York's 1010 WINS Radio, she writes short stories and novels, including the Old Stuff and Ella Shane series, both from Level Best Books. Her stories, under her own name and as Nikki Knight, have been in *Alfred Hitchcock's Mystery Magazine, Black Cat Weekly, Mystery Magazine,* and others, and short-listed for Derringer and Black Orchid Novella Awards. Active in writer's groups, she's served as Vice President of the Short Mystery Fiction Society and Co-VP of the New York/Tri-State Sisters in Crime Chapter. She, her husband, and son live in a Connecticut house owned by their cat.

AUTHOR WEBSITE:
  https://kathleenmarplekalb.com/

SOCIAL MEDIA HANDLES:
  Facebook: https://www.facebook.com/Kathleen-Marple-Kalb-10 82949845220373/
  Instagram: https://www.instagram.com/kathleenmarplekalb/
  Threads: @kathleenmarplekalb

Also by Kathleen Marple Kalb

Old Stuff Mysteries:
The Stuff of Murder (2023)

Ella Shane Mysteries
A Fatal Finale (2020)
A Fatal First Night (2021)
A Fatal Overture (2022)
A Fatal Reception (2024)
A Fatal Honeymoon (novella, available free online, 2024)
A Fatal Waltz (forthcoming, 2025)

Vermont Radio Mysteries – As Nikki Knight
Live, Local and Dead (2022)
Live, Local, and LONG Dead (2024)

Grace the Hit Mom Mysteries – As Nikki Knight
Wrong Poison (2023)
Hound of the Bonnevilles (2025)

Short Stories in Magazines, Anthologies, and online, including:
"Boss Cat Rules," in forthcoming Malice Domestic Anthology, *Murder Most Humorous*, 2025

"Public Affairs Homicide," in *Devil's Snare*: Best New England Crime Stories, 2024

"Mow Way Out," an Old Stuff Mystery, *Black Cat Weekly*, September 2024

"Things Look Different Up Here," in New York/TriState Sisters in Crime Anthology, *New York State of Crime*, September 2024

"Sorry Not Sorry," an Old Stuff mystery, M2D4, Mysteries to Die For Podcast and Anthology, Summer 2024 season

"A Fatal Saint Patrick's Day" (Ella Shane Mystery) in *Luck of the Irish*

Anthology, March 2024

"No Angels Here," *Black Cat Weekly*, December 2023

"The New York Goodbye," *Black Cat Weekly*, September 2023

"The Telltale Request," *Mystery Magazine*, September 2023

"Second Chances are…Murder," *Malice, Matrimony, and Murder* Anthology, November 2023

"Pie a La Poison," in *The Perp Wore Pumpkin*, Misti Media, November 2023

"The Custodian of the Body," (Old Stuff Mystery), *Black Cat Weekly*, May 2023

"This Never Happened to Wolfman Jack," M2D4 Podcast August 2023, season anthology, November 2023

"Don't Mess with the Boss Cat," CatsCast Podcast by Escape Artists, June 2023

"The Annual Mud Season Homicide," *Alfred Hitchcock's Mystery Magazine*, May/June 2023

"Owl Be Damned," Mysteryrat's Maze Podcast, January 2023

"Blame it on the Blizzard," *Deadly Nightshade: Best New England Crime Stories 2022*